Praise for
The Little French Bistro

"George envelops the reader in the sights, sounds, and smells of the coastal town, heightening Marianne's new experiences with lush descriptions of Breton life. Fans of Elizabeth Gilbert and Isabel Allende will adore this courageous story of new beginnings, second chances, and the power of self-love."

—*Booklist*

"The author of *The Little Paris Bookshop* has done it again. The message of this beguiling, second-chance romance—a rich life is possible at any age—will charm readers with its ring of truth."

—*Library Journal* (starred)

"It's never too late to change your life. This is the resounding message in Nina George's charming new book *The Little French Bistro*. At a time when women are fighting to be heard, this heartfelt story is a reminder that female empowerment is a vital force to be reckoned with. . . . What readers will take away is the enchanting vibe of a romantic French town in Brittany and the hope that comes when women own up to their potential."

—*Woodbury Magazine*

Praise for
The Little Paris Bookshop

"If you're looking to be charmed right out of your own life for a few hours, sit down with this wise and winsome novel. . . . Everything happens just as you want it to . . . from poignant moments to crystalline insights in exactly the right measure."

—Oprah.com

"The settings are ideal for a summer-romance read. . . . Who can resist floating on a barge through France surrounded by books, wine, love, and great conversation?"

—*Christian Science Monitor*

"[A] bona fide international hit."

—*New York Times Book Review*

"A story that reflects all the romance and sweetness of Paris itself."

—*San Francisco Book Review*

"George's exquisite, multilayered love story enchanted Europe for more than a year, and the US publication of this flawless translation will allow gob-smacked book lovers here to struggle with the age-old dilemma: to race through each page to see what happens next or savor each deliciously enticing phrase. Do both; if ever a book was meant to be read over and over, this gem is it."

—*Library Journal* (starred review)

"Warmhearted . . . a charming novel that believes in the healing properties of fiction, romance, and a summer in the south of France."

—*Kirkus*

"A beautiful story of grief, companionship, forgiveness and building a life worth living. A vulnerable, relatable tale of great love and loss, missed opportunities and moving on, *The Little Paris Bookshop* is, like the books its main character recommends, medicine for the wounded soul."

—*Bookpage*

"Engaging ... [George's] sumptuous descriptions of both food and literature will leave readers unsure whether to run to the nearest library or the nearest bistro."

—*Publishers Weekly*

The
Little French
Bistro

ALSO BY NINA GEORGE

The Little Paris Bookshop

The
Little French
Bistro

A Novel

NINA GEORGE

TRANSLATED BY SIMON PARE

B\D\W\Y
BROADWAY
NEW YORK

Translation copyright © 2017 by Simon Pare

All rights reserved.
Published in the United States by Broadway Books, an imprint of the Crown Publishing Group, a division of Penguin Random House LLC, New York.
crownpublishing.com

Broadway Books and its logo, B\D\W\Y, are registered trademarks of Penguin Random House LLC.

Extra Libris and the accompanying colophon are trademarks of Penguin Random House LLC.

Originally published in Germany as *Die Mondspielerin* by Knaur Verlag, an imprint of Verlagsgruppe Droemer Knaur, Munich, Germany. Copyright © 2010 by Nina George. This translation originally published in Great Britain by Abacus, an imprint of Little, Brown Book Group, London, in 2017. Subsequently published in hardcover in the United States by Crown Publishers, an imprint of the Crown Publishing Group, a division of Penguin Random House LLC, New York, in 2017.

This book contains an excerpt from *The Little Paris Bookshop* by Nina George, translated by Simon Pare.

Library of Congress Cataloging-in-Publication Data has been applied for.

ISBN 978-0-451-49559-4
Ebook ISBN 978-0-451-49560-0

Printed in the United States of America

Book design by Lauren Dong
Cover design by Kimberly Glyder & Alane Gianetti
Cover photographs: (top) Anna Mutwil/Arcangel;
(bottom) David Tomlinson/Lonely Planet Images/Getty Images

10 9 8 7 6 5 4 3 2 1

First Paperback Edition

For Jens

The
Little French
Bistro

1

❧

IT WAS THE FIRST DECISION SHE HAD EVER MADE ON her own, the very first time she was able to determine the course of her life.

Marianne decided to die. Here and now, down below in the waters of the Seine, late on this gray day. On her trip to Paris. There was not a star in the sky, and the Eiffel Tower was but a dim silhouette in the hazy smog. Paris emitted a roar, with a constant rumble of scooters and cars and the murmur of Métro trains moving deep in the guts of the city.

The water was cool, black and silky. The Seine would carry her on a quiet bed of freedom to the sea. Tears ran down her cheeks; strings of salty tears. Marianne was smiling and weeping at the same time. Never before had she felt so light, so free, so happy. "It's up to me," she whispered. "This is up to me."

She took off the shoes she had bought fifteen years ago—the shoes she had needed to resole so many times. She had purchased them in secret and at full price. Lothar had told her off when he first found out, then gave her a dress to go with them. The dress was bought directly from a factory, and was reduced due to a weaving fault; a gray dress with gray flowers on it. She was wearing that too today.

Her final *today*. Time had seemed infinite when she still had many years and decades ahead of her. A book waiting to be written: as a girl, that was how she had seen her future life. Now she was sixty, and the pages were blank. Infinity had passed like one long continuous day.

She lined up the shoes neatly on the bench beside her, before having second thoughts and placing them on the ground. She didn't want to dirty the bench—a pretty woman might get a stain on her skirt and suffer embarrassment as a result. She tried to ease off her wedding ring but didn't succeed, so she stuck her finger in her mouth and eventually the ring came off. There was a band of white skin where it had been.

A homeless man was sleeping on a bench on the other side of the street that ran across the Pont Neuf. He was wearing a striped top, and Marianne was grateful that his back was turned.

She laid the ring beside her shoes. Someone was bound to find it and live for a few days from the proceeds of pawning it. They could buy a baguette, a bottle of pastis, some salami; something fresh, not food from the bin for once. Maybe a newspaper to keep themselves warm.

"No more food past its sell-by date," she said. Lothar used to put crosses next to the special offers in the weekly newspaper inserts, the way other people ticked the TV programs they wanted to watch. Saturday—*Who Wants to Be a Millionaire?* Sunday—*True Detective.* For Lothar it was: Monday—Angel Delight past its best-before date. They ate the items he marked.

Marianne closed her eyes. Lothar Messmann, "Lotto" to his friends, was an artillery sergeant major who looked after his men. He and Marianne lived in a house in a cul-de-sac in Celle, Germany, with a lattice fence that ran along the side of the turning bay.

Lothar looked good for his age. He loved his job, loved his car and loved television. He would sit on the sofa with his dinner tray on the wooden coffee table in front of him, the remote control in his left hand, a fork in his right, and the volume turned up high, as an artillery officer needed it to be.

"No more, Lothar," whispered Marianne. She clapped her hands to her mouth. Might someone have overheard her?

She unbuttoned her coat. Maybe it would keep someone else warm, even if she had mended the lining so often that it had become a crazy multicolored patchwork. Lothar always brought home little hotel shampoo bottles and sewing kits from his business trips to Bonn and Berlin. The sewing kits contained black, white and red thread.

Who needs red thread? thought Marianne as she began to fold up the light-brown coat, edge to edge, the way she used to fold Lothar's handkerchiefs and the towels she ironed. Not once in her adult life had she worn red. "The color of whores," her mother had hissed. She had slapped Marianne when she was eleven for coming home in a red scarf she had picked up somewhere. It had smelled of floral perfume.

Earlier that evening, up in Montmartre, Marianne had seen a woman crouching down over the gutter. Her skirt had ridden up her legs, and she was wearing red shoes. When the woman stood up, Marianne saw that the makeup around her bloodshot eyes was badly smeared. "Just a drunken whore," someone in the tour party had remarked. Lothar had restrained Marianne when she made to go over to the woman. "Don't make a laughingstock of yourself, Annie."

Lothar had stopped her from helping the woman and tugged her into the restaurant where the coach tour organizers had booked them a table. Marianne had glanced back over her shoulder until the French tour guide said, with a shake of her head, *"Je connais la chanson*—the same old story, but she can only blame herself." Lothar had nodded, and Marianne had imagined *herself* crouching there in the gutter. A need for escape had been building in her for some time, but that was the last straw—and now she was standing here.

She had left even before the starter had arrived, because she could no longer bear to sit there and say nothing. Lothar hadn't noticed; he was caught up in the same conversation he had been having for the past twelve hours with a cheerful widow from Burgdorf. The woman kept squeaking, "That's amazing!" to whatever Lothar said. Her red bra was showing through her white blouse.

Marianne hadn't even been jealous, just weary. Many women had succumbed to Lothar's charms over the years. Marianne had left the restaurant and had drifted further and further until she found herself standing in the middle of the Pont Neuf.

Lothar. It would have been easy to blame him, but it wasn't that straightforward.

"You've only got yourself to blame, Annie," whispered Marianne.

SHE THOUGHT back to her wedding day in May forty-one years ago. Her father had watched, propped on his walking stick, as she had waited hour after hour in vain for her husband to ask her to dance. "You're resilient, my girl," he had said in a strained voice, weak from cancer. She had stood there freezing in her thin white dress, not daring to move a muscle. She hadn't wanted it all to turn out to be a dream and come grinding to a halt if she made a fuss.

"Promise me you'll be happy," her father had asked her, and Marianne had said yes. She was nineteen. Her father died two days after the wedding.

That promise had proved to be one big lie.

MARIANNE SHOOK the folded coat, flung it to the ground and trampled on it. "No more! It's all over! It's over!" She felt brave as she stamped on the coat one last time, but her exhilaration subsided as quickly as it had come. She picked up the coat and laid it on the arm of the bench.

Only herself to blame.

There was nothing more she could take off. She didn't own any jewelry or a hat. She had no possessions apart from her shabby handbag containing a Paris guidebook, a few sachets of salt and sugar, a hair clip, her identity card and her coin purse. She placed the bag next to the shoes and the ring. Then she began to clamber onto the parapet.

First she rolled onto her tummy and pulled her other leg up, but she nearly slid back down. Her heart was pounding, her pulse was racing and the rough sandstone scraped her knees. Her toes found a crack, and she pushed herself upward. She'd made it. She sat down and swung her feet over the other side.

Now she simply had to push off and let herself fall. She couldn't possibly mess this up.

Marianne thought of the mouth of the Seine near Honfleur, through which her body would sail after drifting past locks and riverbanks and then float out to sea. She imagined the waves spinning her around, as if she were dancing to a tune that only she and the sea could hear. Honfleur, Erik Satie's birthplace. She loved his music; she loved all kinds of music. Music was like a film that she watched on the back of her closed eyelids, and Satie's music conjured up images of the sea, even though she had never been to the seaside.

"I love you, Erik, I love you," she whispered. She had never spoken those words to any man other than Lothar. When had *he* last told *her* that he loved her? Had he ever told her?

Marianne waited for fear to come, but it didn't.

Death is not free. Its price is life.

What's my life worth?

Nothing.

A bad deal for the devil. He's only got himself to blame.

She hesitated as she braced her hands hard against the stone parapet and slid forward, suddenly thinking of an orchid she had found among the rubbish many months ago. She'd spent half a year tending and singing to it, but now she would never see it flower. Then she pushed off with both hands.

Her jump became a fall, and falling forced her arms above her head. As she fell into the wind, she thought of the life insurance policy and how it would not pay out for a suicide. A loss of 124,563 euros. Lothar would be beside himself.

A good deal after all.

With this in mind, she hit the ice-cold Seine with a sense of joyous abandon that faded into profound shame as she sank and her gray flowery dress enveloped her head. She tried desperately to pull down the hem so no one would see her bare legs, but then she gave up and spread her arms, opened her mouth wide and filled her lungs with water.

2

⚜

Dying was like floating. Marianne leaned back. It was so wonderful. The happiness didn't stop, and you could swallow it. She gulped it down.

See, Dad. A promise is a promise.

She saw an orchid, a purple bloom, and everything was music. When a shadow bent over her, she recognized death. It wore her own face at first, the face of a girl grown old—a girl with bright eyes and brown hair.

Death's mouth was warm. Then its beard scratched her, and its lips pressed repeatedly on hers. Marianne tasted onion soup and red wine, cigarettes and cinnamon. Death sucked at her. It licked her; it was hungry. She struggled to break free.

Two strong hands settled on her bosom. Feebly she tried to force open the cold fingers that, little by little, were cracking open her chest. A kiss. Cold seeped into her throat. Marianne opened her eyes wide, her mouth gaped and she spewed out dark, dirty water. She reared up with a long moan, and as she gasped for air, the pain hit her like a keen blade, slicing her lungs to shreds. And so loud! Everything was so loud!

Where was the music? Where was the girl? Where was the happiness? Had she spat it out?

Marianne slumped back onto the hard ground. Death hit her in the face. She stared up into two sky-blue eyes, coughed and fought for air. Feebly she raised her arm and gave death a limp slap.

Death talked to her insistently—asking a series of quick-fire questions as he pulled her into a sitting position. Marianne gave him another slap. He struck back immediately, but not so hard this time. No, in fact he caressed her cheek.

She raised her hands to her face. How had this come to be?

"How?" Her voice was a muffled croak.

It was so cold. And this roaring noise! Marianne looked left, then right, then at her hands, which had turned green from clutching the damp grass. The Pont Neuf was only a few yards away. She was lying beside a tent on the Rive Droite, and the hum of Paris filled the air. And she was not dead. Not. Dead. Her stomach hurt, as did her lungs. Everything hurt, even her hair, which dangled wet and heavy on her shoulders. Her heart, her head, her soul, her belly, her cheeks—everything ached.

"Not dead?" she spluttered in despair.

The man in the striped top smiled, but then his smile faded behind a cloud of anger. He pointed to the river, tapped his forehead with his finger and gestured at his bare feet.

"Why?" She wanted to scream at him, but her voice disintegrated into a hoarse whisper. "Why did you do it?"

He raised his arms above his head to illustrate a dive, and pointed to Marianne, the Seine and himself. He shrugged, as if to say, *What else could I do?*

"I had . . . a reason, many reasons! You had no right to steal my death from me. Are you God? No, you can't be or else I'd be dead!"

The man stared at her from under thick black eyebrows as if he understood. He pulled his wet top over his head and wrung it out.

His eyes settled on the birthmark on Marianne's left breast, which was visible through the buttons of her dress that had come undone. His eyebrows shot up in surprise. Panic-stricken, she pulled at her dress with one hand. For her whole life she had hidden the ugly birthmark—a rare pigment disorder, shaped like fiery flames—under tightly buttoned blouses and high necklines. She only ever went swimming at night, when no one could see her. Her mother had called the birthmark "a witch's mark," and Lothar had called it "a thing of the devil." He had never touched it and had always closed his eyes when they were intimate.

Then she noticed her bare legs. She tried desperately to tug down the wet hem of her dress and simultaneously do up the buttons to cover her chest. She knocked away the man's hand as he offered to help her to her feet, and stood up. She smoothed her dress, which clung heavily to her body. Her hair smelled of brackish water. She staggered uncertainly toward the wall of the embankment. Too low. Too low to throw herself off. She would hurt herself but wouldn't die.

"Madame!" the man begged in a firm voice, and reached out to her again. She rebuffed his hand once more and, eyes closed, swung wildly at his face and his arms, but her fists encountered only air. Then she kicked out, but he avoided her blows without retreating. Onlookers must have thought they were lovers performing a tragicomic dance.

"Mine!" she yelled with each kick. "My death was mine and no one else's. You had no right to steal it from me!"

"Madame!" he said again, encircling Marianne with both arms. He held her tight until she stopped kicking and finally leaned, exhausted, against his shoulder. He brushed the hair from her face with fingertips as rough as straw. He smelled of sleepless nights and the Seine, and of apples lying in the warm sun on a wooden shelf. He began to rock her in his arms. She had never been rocked so softly before. Marianne began to weep. She hid herself in the stranger's arms, and he continued to hold her as she wept for her life and for her death.

"*Mais non, non.*" The man pushed her away a little, lifted her chin and said, "Come with me."

He pulled her after him. Marianne felt unbelievably weak, and the rough stones hurt her bare feet. Refusing to let go of her hand, the man drew her up the slope to the Pont Neuf.

When they reached the bridge, the stranger shooed away a couple of tramps who were inspecting two pairs of shoes: Marianne's pumps and a mismatched pair of men's boots. One of the homeless men was clutching Marianne's coat to his chest, while the other one, who was wearing a woolly hat, pulled a face as he bit her wedding ring. The taller of the two took out a mobile phone, while the smaller one held out the ring to Marianne.

Now Marianne began to tremble. The shivers rose up from the depths of her body and swept through her veins. She knocked the ring out of the tramp's hand and attempted to climb onto the parapet again, but the three men jumped forward as one to restrain her. In their eyes Marianne saw pity, and a fear of being accused of something.

"Get your hands off me!" she shouted. None of them slackened his grip, and reluctantly she allowed them to guide her to the bench. The taller man laid his heavy coat around her shoulders, and the other scratched his hat and then knelt down to dry her feet with the sleeves of his jacket.

Her savior was making a phone call. The other homeless men sat down on the bench next to Marianne. They held her hands gently as she tried to bite her nails. One of them bent forward and placed her wedding ring in the empty nest formed by her palms.

She stared at the dull golden band. She had worn it for forty-one years. She had only ever removed it once—temporarily—on her fortieth wedding anniversary. That day she had ironed her gray flowery dress and copied a chignon from a three-month-old magazine she had pulled out of a recycling bin. She had dabbed on a little Chanel perfume, a sample from the same discarded magazine. The perfume had a floral fragrance, and she'd wished she had owned a red scarf. Then she opened a bottle of champagne and waited for her husband to come home.

"What do you think you're doing?" was Lothar's first question.

She gave him a twirl and handed him a glass. "To us," she said. "To forty years of marriage." He had taken a sip and then looked past her to the table where the open bottle stood. "That is an expensive bottle of champagne. Really?"

"It's our wedding anniversary."

"That's still no reason to splash out. You can't just spend my money like that."

She hadn't wept right then. She never wept in front of Lothar, only in the shower where he couldn't see.

His money. She would have loved to earn her own money. She'd worked hard, though; by God she'd worked hard. Recently she had volunteered at a hospice. Her first job had been on her mother's farm in Wendland, then as a midwife alongside her grandmother, and finally as a housekeeper, where she had actually earned a small salary, until Lothar had married her and barred her from running other people's households as she had to run his.

She'd been Lothar's cleaner, his cook, his gardener and his spouse. She'd nursed her own mother, who had lived with them for many years before the old lady had eventually died on Marianne's forty-second birthday. Until then, Marianne had almost only ever left the house to go shopping—on foot, because Lothar had banned her from taking the car. Her mother had a number of health issues—she often wet the bed—but she could still insult Marianne every day, and Lothar increasingly spent his evenings at the barracks or went out on his own. He wrote his wife postcards from his holidays and sent his love to his *mamushka*.

MARIANNE DROPPED the ring. At the same moment she heard a siren and shut her eyes until the shrill sound drew closer through the city's winding streets and stopped right in front of her. The homeless men retreated from the pulsing blue light, and when two paramedics and a small woman carrying a case rushed toward them, the man in the striped top stepped forward, pointed to Marianne, motioned to the Seine and tapped his head again.

He thinks I'm mad, thought Marianne.

She tried to force the same smile she had been giving Lothar for decades. "You're much prettier when you smile," he had said after their first date. He was the first man ever to call her pretty, in spite of her birthmark and in spite of everything else.

She wasn't mad, no. And she wasn't dead.

She gazed over at the man who had pulled her out of the Seine without her consent. *He* was the madman. He was mad enough to assume that one only had to survive to thrive.

She let the paramedics strap her to the stretcher. As they lifted her up and rolled her toward the open doors of the ambulance, the stranger with the sky-blue eyes clasped Marianne's hand. His hand felt warm and familiar. Marianne caught a glimpse of herself reflected in his big dark pupils. She saw her pale eyes, which had always struck her as being too big; her nose, which was too small; her heart-shaped face, and her gray-brown hair. When she opened her hand, her wedding ring lay on her palm.

"I'm sorry for all the trouble," she said, but he shook his head. "*Excusez-moi,*" she added.

"*Il n'y a pas de quoi,*" he said earnestly, patting his chest with his palm. "*Vous avez compris?*" he asked.

Marianne smiled. Whatever he was saying, he must be right.

"*Je m'appelle Eric.*" He handed Marianne's bag to the para-medic.

I'm Marianne, she wanted to say, but thought better of it. It was enough that he could tell his friends that he'd fished a madwoman out of the water. What good was a name? Names meant nothing.

She reached for Eric's hand. "Please. Please keep it," she said. He stared at the ring as she returned it to him. The doors of the ambulance closed.

"I hate you, Eric," murmured Marianne, and it was as if she could still feel his rough but gentle fingers caressing her cheek.

Marianne lay on the stretcher; the straps cut into her skin during the drive. The paramedic prepared a syringe and pricked a vein in the crook of her arm. Then he took out a second needle and pushed it into the back of her hand before attaching it to an intravenous drip.

"I'm sorry they had to call you out for me," whispered Marianne, gazing into the paramedic's brown eyes. The man glanced quickly away. "*Je suis allemande,*" mumbled Mari-anne. I am German. "*Allemande.*" It sounded like "almond."

The paramedic laid a blanket over her and began to dictate a report, his words taken down by a young assistant with a beard. The strong tranquilizer began to take effect.

"I'm an almond," mumbled Marianne before falling asleep.

3

IN HER DREAM SHE WAS SITTING ON THE PONT NEUF.
She took off a wristwatch that wasn't even hers, smashed
the glass on the stone, tore the hands from the watch face and
threw them into the river. Time wouldn't be able to stop people
anymore. Time would stand still as soon as she jumped, and
nobody would stop Marianne from twirling toward the sea.

Yet when she jumped, she fell slowly, as if through liquid
resin. Bodies rose through the water, floating upward past her
as she fell. She recognized the faces, each and every one of
them. They were her dead, the people from the hospice where
she had volunteered after her mother died, the place no one
else would visit for fear of being contaminated by death. Marianne had held their hands when the time came, and guided by
her hand, they had passed into emptiness. Some had offered
resistance, whimpering desperately, others were ashamed of
dying, but all of them sought Marianne's gaze and clung to it
until their own eyes went dim.

In her dream they groped for Marianne's hands. Their
voices mourned every unfulfilled wish, every step they hadn't
taken and every unspoken word. What none of the death-

bound could forgive themselves for was what they had left un-done. On their deathbeds all had confessed this to Marianne: the things they hadn't done, the things they hadn't dared to do.

THE LIGHT was dazzling, and when she opened her eyes, Lothar was standing at the foot of the bed. His dark blue suit with gold buttons made him look as if he'd just stepped off a yacht. Next to him stood a woman in white. An angel?

It was awfully loud here too. Machines were beeping, people were talking, and from somewhere came the sound of a television. Marianne put her hands over her ears.

"Hello," she said after a while.

Lothar turned to look at her. She couldn't see herself in his eyes. He came nearer and bent over her, examining her more closely, as if he were unsure of what he was seeing.

"What's the big idea?" he eventually asked.

"The big idea?"

He shook his head as though completely bemused. "All this fuss."

"I wanted to kill myself."

"Why?"

Which lie should she tell first? "It's all right," when nothing was all right? Or "Don't worry," when he should?

"I . . . I . . ."

"I, I," growled Lothar. "Now there's a good reason: I."

Why didn't she tell him: I don't want to carry on, I can't carry on, I'd rather die than carry on living with you.

She tried again. "I . . . I want . . ." She faltered once more.

It was as if her mouth were choked with sandstone. "I wanted to do what I want."

Her husband stood up straight. "Do what you want! Aha. And where's that got you? Just look at yourself." He glanced at the nurse, who was still standing there observing the scene.

Marianne felt color rise into her cheeks. Lothar sat down on the edge of the bed and turned his back on her. "After the call came through, I left the restaurant immediately. I had to pay for your meal, of course. The chef couldn't care less if you'd killed yourself or not."

Marianne tried to pull up the bedsheet, but her husband was sitting on it and her efforts were in vain. She felt naked.

"The Métro only runs until one. And they call this a global city! I had to take a taxi and it cost as much as the return coach journey to Paris. Do you realize?" Lothar exhaled loudly, as if he were about to start screaming. "Do you have any idea what you've done to me? Do you want us to grow apart? Do you want me to have to leave the light on every night to keep an eye on you?"

"I'm sorry," Marianne squeezed out.

"Sorry? Who do you think is most sorry? Do you realize how other people look at you when your wife tries to kill herself? It can ruin everything. Everything. You didn't consider that when you wanted to do what you want. As if you even know what you want."

Lothar glanced at his Rolex, then stood up. "The bus leaves at six on the dot. I've had enough."

"And . . . how do I get home?" Marianne heard the imploring tone in her voice and felt ashamed. She had nothing, not even her pride.

"The insurance will cover your trip back. A psychologist will be here tomorrow to travel home with you. My ticket's only valid if I leave today. You jumped off the bridge on your own, I travel home on my own; that way we both do what we want. Any objections?"

"Could I have a hug?" Marianne begged. Her husband walked out without looking back. As she turned her head, she met the eyes of the woman in the next bed, who was studying her.

"His hearing's not very good," explained Marianne. "He just didn't hear. Didn't hear, you see?" Then she pulled the sheet over her head.

4

An hour later, nurse Nicolette tore Marianne's bedsheet away and slammed a tray down on the bedside table.

Marianne didn't touch the food. It looked like roadkill. The butter was rock-hard and the soup was thin, containing only three cubes of carrot and a single slice of spring onion. She gave it to the woman in the next bed. Marianne flinched when the lady tried to stroke her arm in return.

Now she was pushing her IV drip along on its castors while holding the short hospital johnny shut because it kept flapping apart, showing her bottom. The soles of her bare feet squished every time she lifted them off the floor. She walked along the corridor until she reached another one that ran perpendicular to her block. Tucked away in the corner was the glass-walled nurses' room.

A small television set showed an excitable Nicolas Sarkozy venting his displeasure to the nation. A cigarette smouldered in an ashtray and the radio played as Nicolette leafed through a magazine and unwrapped a small *madeleine*.

Marianne moved closer. The music . . . Violins, an accordion, clarinets, bagpipes. She closed her eyes to watch her own private film. She saw men dancing with beautiful women. She saw a dining table, children and apple trees, the sun glinting on the sea at the horizon. She saw blue shutters on old sandstone houses with thatched roofs, and a small chapel. The men had their hats pushed back on their heads. She didn't know the song, but she would have loved to play it. The notes of the accordion pierced her heart.

She'd once played the accordion, first a small one, then, when her arms were long enough, a full-size instrument. Her father had given it to her for her fifteenth birthday. Her mother hated it and would say, "Learn to sew instead, it's not as noisy." Then one day Lothar had taken the accordion to the rubbish heap.

A red light pulsed beside a room number on the display board. Nicolette looked up in annoyance, caught sight of Marianne and turned away in a show of complete indifference. Marianne waited until Nicolette had disappeared before entering the nurses' room. She reached out hungrily for the bag of individually wrapped madeleines on the table, and as she did so she almost knocked a brightly colored square tile, which the nurses used as a place mat, onto the floor. Hearing a door slam, she dashed across the corridor and through a second door marked "Stairs," almost trapping the IV tube in the door as she pressed it shut.

She sat down on the bottom step and exhaled with relief. It was only then that she noticed that she was still holding the madeleine and that she was carrying the tile under her arm. She listened out for any sounds, but all was silent. She propped the tile against a window, and removed the cake from its wrapper.

So this is what it's like, thought Marianne. So this is what it's like to be in Paris.

She bit into the soft, sweet cake and studied the small hand-painted tile. Boats, a harbor, an infinite blaze of bright blue sky that looked freshly washed. The artist had created a magnificent scene in the tiny space. Marianne tried to read the names of the boats. *Marlin. Genever. Koakar.* And . . . *Mariann.*

The *Mariann* was a dainty red boat, bobbing half forgotten on the edge of the picture, her sails slack. *Mariann.* How beautiful it all was. The music on the radio seemed to belong to this place. So cheerful and gentle, so sunny and free.

By Marianne's second bite, she was sobbing so hard that she had to cough. The crumbs exploded from her mouth with a mixture of spit and tears. Things not done: that was what the dead had been trying to tell her. Unlived moments. Marianne's life consisted entirely of unlived moments.

She stared at the tube in her hand for a moment, then tore it out. It bled. That won't kill me either, she thought. Besides, I'm still wearing yesterday's knickers, and how's that going to look in the morgue?

She wiped away the tears with the back of her hand and blinked. She'd wept more in the past few hours than for decades. It had to stop; it wouldn't change anything.

She looked at the glazed tile again. She couldn't bear the sight of the *Mariann*'s slack sail. She flipped the tile onto its back. There was an inscription: *Port de Kerdruc, Fin.*

Marianne ate the remainder of the madeleine and still felt hungry. Kerdruc. She turned the tile over again and sniffed it. Didn't it smell . . . of the sea?

I've never been to such a beautiful place.

She tried to imagine what it might have been like if she and Lothar had been to such a place. But all she could see in her mind's eye was Lothar sitting at their living room table. She saw him arranging the neighbors' old magazines so that their edges ran parallel. She ought to have been grateful to him for the order he'd brought to her life. The house at the end of the cul-de-sac was her home.

She stroked the tile again. Would Lothar remember to water the orchid? She gave a little laugh. Of course he wouldn't.

Kerdruc. If it was a place by the sea, then . . .

She gave a start as the door opened behind her. It was Nicolette. She raged at Marianne and waved imperiously for her to come back up the stairs. Marianne couldn't look the nurse in the eye as she pressed past her into the bright corridor and let herself be guided back to her room without the slightest resistance.

With a practiced hand Nicolette inserted a fresh drip and slid two pink tablets between Marianne's lips. Marianne feigned obedience and pretended to wash down the pills with some of the stale water on the bedside table. Her neighbor whimpered in her sleep like a bleating lamb. When Nicolette had turned out the light and closed the door behind her, Marianne spat out the pills and took the tile she'd been clasping to her chest out from under her johnny.

Kerdruc. She stroked the picture. It was absurd, but she could almost feel the mellow air under her fingertips, and she quivered. She got up and walked slowly over to the window. The wind howled at her. Thunder drew closer, the clouds parted, and for a second a bolt of lightning lit the sky. It began to rain and the drops rattled against the windowpanes like beads from a broken necklace. The moonlight magnified the raindrops so that they looked as if they were dancing on the ground. She kneeled down. The thunder was so deafening that it sounded as if the storm were hovering directly over the hospital.

My little wifey who's scared of a storm, Lothar would have said.

She wasn't scared of storms. She'd pretended to be for his pleasure, so he could tease her and feel good about himself. Time after time she'd allowed herself to be drawn into playing such stupid games.

She looked out at the tattered sky and hesitantly cupped her full breasts with both hands. Lothar had been her first and only man. She had slipped from virginity into marriage without so much as a kiss. He had been her home ever since she had left her parents' house.

My husband neither touched my soul nor charmed my body. Why did I let that happen? Why?

She went over to the cupboards and found her clothes. They smelled brackish. She rinsed out her dress, dug out some deodorant and sprayed some on it. Now it smelled of roses and brackish water.

She stepped up to the washbasin, which was located in the center of the room. Didn't the architects realize how stupid it looked for a woman to have to wash herself while standing in the middle of the room? But she washed all the same. When she felt cleaner, she balanced on her tiptoes to look in the mirror.

No, there was nothing proud about this face. Nothing dignified.

I'm older now than my grandmother was when she died. I've always hoped that there'd be a wise old lady lurking inside me, waiting patiently for the outer layers to peel off. First her body, then her face.

Marianne lowered her eyes. There was no wise old lady looking at her now, just an old woman with the face of a wrinkled girl, a little wife, not much taller than she'd been at fourteen. And still just as chubby. She gave a bitter laugh.

Her grandmother Nane, a midwife, whom she had admired enormously, had died on a cold January night in 1961. She had slipped and fallen into a ditch on the way back from the Von Haags' estate, where she had just delivered a home birth. She hadn't had enough strength to crawl out again by herself, and it was Marianne who had found her grandmother's body. An expression of annoyance and astonishment at this freak occurrence was frozen on Nane's face. Marianne still felt a vague sense of guilt, for that evening she hadn't assisted her grandmother with the delivery as she usually did; she was caught up elsewhere.

She studied her own features. The longer she looked at herself, the harder she found it to breathe. Horror seeped into her, and she soaked it up with her whole being, as a garden does a devastating downpour.

What am I to do?

The woman in the mirror had no answer. She was as white as a ghost.

5

✤

MORNING CAME QUICKLY. THE PATIENTS WERE woken shortly after six, and when Marianne had dressed, she was led into an office on the first floor of the hospital. It looked as if it belonged to a doctor with two kids; it contained children's drawings, family photos and a map of France with little pins stuck in it.

Marianne got up from her chair and ran her finger along the coastline in search of Kerdruc. She could find no place by that name, but her finger stopped at an abbreviation: *Fin*. It stood for Finistère, an area of western France that bulged out into the Atlantic—Brittany.

She sat down again and stared at the tips of her shoes. After an hour, the psychologist turned up, a tall, slender Frenchman with wavy black hair who reeked of aftershave. Marianne thought he looked terribly nervous; he chewed his lower lip as he darted glances at her, avoiding her gaze. He flicked through the few sheets of paper on his clipboard, then removed his glasses and, perching on the edge of the desk, looked intently at Marianne for the first time.

"Suicide isn't an illness," he began in German.

"It isn't?" replied Marianne.

"No. It's simply the culmination of a pathological tendency. It's a sign of desperation. Deep desperation." His voice was soft, and he looked at her with his gray eyes as if his only purpose in life was to understand her.

Marianne felt a tingle in the back of her neck. This was strange. She was sitting here with a man who harbored the extravagant illusion that he might understand and help her merely by looking at her and talking to her as if he were the anointed one.

"And suicide is acceptable too. It has meaning for those who seek it. It isn't wrong to want to kill oneself."

"And that's scientifically proven?" she couldn't help herself asking.

The psychologist stared at her.

"Sorry."

"Why are you apologizing?" he asked.

"I . . . don't know."

"Did you know that seriously depressed people are easily hurt, yet they continually apologize, directing their aggression inward at themselves rather than at the person who provoked it?"

Marianne peered at the man. He must have been in his mid-forties, and she spotted a wedding ring on his finger. How she would have loved to believe that she could simply let herself go, pour it all out and allow him to console her, then read her life in his facial expressions. He would give her courage and medication, and she would be cured of her silly desire.

Suicide isn't an illness. Nice.

"Did you know that most church bells have clappers that

are too big?" she answered. "Most bell ringers pull too hard, and within a few years the bells sound like empty salad bowls clanging together. They're worn out."

"Do you feel like one of those bells?"

"A bell?"

I feel as though I was never here.

"You no longer wanted to live as you'd been living. Why did you choose Paris of all places to kill yourself?"

The way he says that. Like a reprimand. No one comes to Paris to die. Everyone wants to live and love here; I'm the only one who's dumb enough to think you might be able to die here.

"It seemed appropriate," she eventually answered. She'd done it: she had finally faced up to her urgent desire to speak the truth.

"Fine." He got to his feet. "I'd like to do a few tests with you before you go home. Come with me." He held the door open for her.

Marianne stared at her gray shoes as one foot came down in front of the other. Out of the room, across the corridor, through a swing door, into the next corridor, and so on.

Her father had been a bell tuner before he fell from the roof timbers of a church and broke almost every bone in his body. Marianne's mother had resented him for that accident for the rest of his life. It wasn't manly to land a woman in such trouble in those days.

Her father had explained the nature of church bells thus: "The clapper has to kiss the bell, very softly, and entice it to ring, never force it." His character had been like such a bell. If someone tried to force her father to react, he would grin and grit it out in silence until they left him alone.

After her grandmother's death, he had moved out of their shared house and from then on had slept in the work shed. Until Marianne married Lothar, she had been her parents' go-between, carrying her father's food out to the workshop, where he spent his time building miniature glockenspiels. Marianne often felt his affection for her as she sat beside him at his workbench. His daughter's affection touched him, as did her whispered confessions about the life of her dreams. One moment she wanted to be an archaeologist, the next a music teacher. She also wanted to build children's bicycles and live in a house by the sea. Both father and daughter were dreamers.

"You take too much after your father," Marianne's mother had said.

For decades Marianne had been unable to think of her father. She missed him. That was perhaps one of her secrets.

"Please excuse me for a moment," said the psychologist and waved to another doctor—Marianne recognized him from the previous night at the hospital. They spoke to each other in French and kept glancing over at their patient. Marianne walked to the window, turning away from them both so that she could slip the small tile from her handbag and admire it.

Kerdruc. Touching the picture, she felt such a tug in her breast that she could barely breathe.

Suicide is meaningful. She looked at the floor again. *I really don't like these shoes.*

Then she just upped and left. She pushed open the nearest swing door, found a flight of stairs, scampered down it and turned right at the bottom. She hurried along a corridor where patients were lounging on benches, and at the end of

the corridor she saw a wide-open door that led outside. Fresh
air at last! The thunderstorm had rinsed the dirt out of the
day, and the air was mild and balmy. Marianne ignored the
arthritic pains in her knee and began to run.

Her heart was in her mouth as she raced across the cobbled
street into an alleyway, dived through a gateway and dashed
across a courtyard and out the other side. She ran without
thinking, veering from one side of the street to the other. She
didn't know how long she would need to keep this up, but
when the stitch in her side became unbearable, she slumped
down by a small fountain. She let the water run over her wrists
and stared at her reflection in the pool.

Didn't they say that beauty was a state of soul? And if her
soul was loved, a woman would be transformed into a wondrous creature, however ordinary her looks. Love changed a
woman's soul, and she became beautiful, for a few minutes or
forever.

I would have loved to be beautiful, thought Marianne. Just
for five minutes. I wish someone I love had loved me. She
dipped a finger in the water and made circling motions. How
I would have loved to sleep with another man than Lothar.
How I would have loved to wear something red. I wish I had
fought.

She got up. It wasn't too late: she could still do what she
wanted, and she wanted to do it in Kerdruc.

6

MARIANNE SAT DOWN ON A BENCH NEXT TO THE newspaper kiosk on the concourse of the Gare de Montparnasse and stared at the departures board, which showed the 10.05 TGV Atlantique 8715 for Quimper. She was trembling with joy and apprehension. When the letters began to spin on the board and her train was announced on Platform 7, she stood up. Her knee was hurting again.

She had put down most of her cash on the ticket counter and studied the painting on the tile. Her money would only take her as far as Auray. She would somehow have to make her way to Pont-Aven and Kerdruc under her own steam.

She looked around as she walked alongside the snaking high-speed train. With every step she had the impression that something was taking over her body, as if a foreign creature were determined to enter, fill her and shape her anew. A sense of irritation stopped her in her tracks. What was it?

She caught hold of the handrail and tried to pull herself up the steep steps into the carriage. She could still climb back down, look for a telephone and call Lothar to ask him to come and fetch her, to prevent her from putting her plan into action. *But wherever I go, I'm already dead.*

She hauled herself doggedly up onto the next step and searched for her seat, which was by the window. She sank into it, closed her eyes and waited for the train to roll out of the station at last. No one took the seat next to hers.

When she glanced up, her eyes met a smiling face. This woman could bounce back from failure, that much was clear; her big bright eyes sparkled. Their gazes met, and Marianne snapped her eyelids shut again. She couldn't understand why the woman was staring at her like this. But she also wanted to store it away in her memory—the faint glimmer in her eye, the mauve cheeks, the sun playing in her hair.

WHEN MARIANNE got off the train three hours later in Auray, she took a deep, long breath. The air was smoother and clearer here than in Paris, less oppressive. She decided to buy a map and a bottle of water and then hitchhike. She would make it to Kerdruc somehow, even if she had to walk the whole way.

As she emerged from the other side of the station building, she spied a nun on the only bench in the shade. The woman was sitting in a curiously lopsided position with her head thrown back. It looked as if she'd left the world for a better place. Marianne glanced around, but no one was taking any notice of the woman. Very slowly she walked over to her.

"Bonjour?"

The nun said nothing. Marianne tapped her lightly on the shoulder. The nun gave a loud snore, and spit trickled from her open mouth onto her habit. Marianne sat down next to her, took out a tissue and gently patted the nun's chin with it.

"So now we've got to know each other, what do we do next?"

The nun let out a quiet groan.

"What a delightful conversation," murmured Marianne.

The nun's eyelids fluttered and she woke up. Her head twisted mechanically from left to right, and her eyes eventually settled on Marianne.

"You know," lied Marianne, "this occasionally happens to me too. I often sleep better away from home. Do you sometimes come to the station to enjoy a nap?"

The nun slumped to one side with a faint sigh, leaned her head on Marianne's shoulder and dozed off again. Marianne didn't dare to move for fear of waking the nun, who blew warm air into her ear every time she breathed out. The shadows shifted in time with the sun's progress across the sky. Marianne closed her eyes too. It was nice simply to sit there and let life and the shadows pass her by.

Some time later, a minibus screeched to a halt outside the station, startling Marianne from her torpor. A man in a cassock got out, followed by one, two, three, four . . . four nuns. They all gawped at Marianne and the sister, still slumbering on Marianne's shoulder.

"*Mon Dieu!*" called the father. They surrounded Marianne and helped the two women to their feet.

The nun looked well rested now, Marianne noticed. The man in the white-and-green cassock turned to her. She listened to him politely without understanding a word. She gathered her breath and said, "*Je suis allemande. Pardon. Au revoir.*"

"*Allemande?*" the priest repeated, before grinning to reveal teeth that were as crooked as the headstones in an abandoned forest graveyard. "Ah! *Allemagne! Le football! Ballack! Tu connais Ballack? Et Schweinsteiger!*" He held up his hands as if he were clutching a ball.

"Ballack!" he said again, and pretended to kick something.

"Yes, Ballack," Marianne repeated with some irritation, but she raised a clenched fist as he had and gave a halfhearted smile. The priest beamed back, and the nuns began to lead Marianne and their still slightly disorientated sister toward the minibus.

"No, no, no," said Marianne hastily. "Our ways part here. You go with God, I'll go . . . Oh, forget it. *Au revoir, au revoir.*" She waved one last time and made to leave.

A young nun tugged at her sleeve. "They call me Clara. My grandmother was German. Do you understand me?"

Marianne nodded.

"We wanted to thank you," explained the nun. "Please come with us to the convent."

Marianne noticed how the other nuns were stealing glances at her and giggling.

"But . . . I have to keep traveling. I want to reach Kerdruc today," said Marianne. She pulled out the map and tapped on the hamlet at the mouth of the river Aven.

"*Pas de problème!* Lots of tourists visit the convent, and their buses take them to many other places, including here," said Clara, pointing to the town of Pont-Aven to the north of Kerdruc. "Paul Gauguin lived there. Many painters."

The other nuns were already sitting in the minibus. Marianne hesitated for a second, but maybe it would be better to travel with the nuns than stand on the side of the road. She got in.

Inside the minibus, the old nun leaned forward from one of the tattered leather-upholstered seats. "*Merci*," she said, squeezing Marianne's arm. Clara turned around in her seat to look at Marianne. "Dominique is . . . ill. She disappeared from the convent yesterday and she can't get by on her own. She has no idea who she is, where she is or how to get home. *Vous avez compris*, madame? Thanks to your help, all good now, yes?"

Marianne guessed that Dominique might have Alzheimer's.

Clara turned around again. "What is your name?"

"My name is—"

"*Je m'appelle . . .*" the nun corrected her gently.

"*Je m'appelle Marianne.*"

"*Marie-Anne?! Nous sommes du couvent de Sainte-Anne-d'Auray!* Oh, the Lord moves in mysterious ways!" The nun crossed herself.

"What's wrong?" Marianne asked in fright, but the nun cheerfully announced, "Your name is the same as our convent's! Marie and Anne. We pray to St. Anne, the mother of the Virgin Mary. We are the Filles du Saint-Esprit Ker Anna, and for us Anna is the source of all female holiness. You were sent by heaven, Marie-Anne!"

And I'm going back there, my dear, thought Marianne. Oh no, I'm going to the other place.

"*Voilà!*" the priest called from the front. "Sainte-Anne-d'Auray!"

There was no need for him to add anything: the sight spoke for itself. Stretching out in front of them was a wide square, flanked by towering hedges, bushes and hydrangeas in full bloom. A magnificent cathedral stood sharply outlined against the deep-blue sky. The red leaves of the trees swayed, and Marianne saw fountains and caught a glimpse of a stepped bridge, which reminded her of some pictures of the Rialto Bridge in Venice that her neighbor Grete Köster had sent her. Grete was one of the few women who had never succumbed to Lothar's charms.

"*La Santa Scala*," said Clara, pointing here and there. "*L'oratoire, le mémorial, la Chapelle de l'Immaculée.*"

The minibus drove through a gateway toward a plain three-storey building. The Ker Anna convent. Clara and Father Ballack, as Marianne had nicknamed the monk, took her to the parlor, had some peppermint tea brought for her and then hurried off to the *messe des pélerins*—the pilgrims' mass, as Clara hurriedly explained.

On her way into the convent's plain central courtyard, Marianne met a priest who appeared more dignified than Ballack. He opened his arms wide. "*Ich bin Pater Andreas. Willkommen.* I spent a term studying theology at Heidelberg," he added, noting Marianne's astonished reaction to his German. "I would like to thank you in the name of the whole convent for taking such devoted care of a member of our community. It was announced to me that your further travels are in peril due to a lapse in the service of the French transport company."

"Yes, you could put it like that," she said, slightly taken aback by his formal tone.

"May I enquire as to the destination and purpose of your travels?"

"Kerdruc. I wanted to . . . I have . . ."

"Are you visiting friends? Or do you live there?"

Marianne hadn't prepared an excuse for this kind of question. She was going to Kerdruc because it was the place in which she wanted to end it all.

"Do forgive me—how impolite. Your further travels are your affair, not mine. I would be delighted if you would stay overnight. The meals in the convent are delicious, and we also have accommodation for pilgrims and guests. You probably saved Sister Dominique's life, but it is not *my* gratitude you have earned, but that of the French Church."

You mean the Pope doesn't care?

"I'd like to continue my journey," said Marianne.

The priest considered this. "At the end of the convent driveway you will find the public car park. Present my greetings to one of the coach drivers there and ask him to give you a lift! *Au revoir*, madame." He blessed her with an outstretched hand and strode off toward St. Anne's Basilica.

"Thank you," mumbled Marianne.

She thought of her father as the bells struck eleven o'clock. All at once she realized clearly that her desire to stand by him had stopped her from rebelling against her mother's moral castigations. She hadn't wanted to undermine his meek acceptance with her protests.

She strolled across the convent courtyard, lost in reminiscences about her father. How much they had had in common, how similar they had been! They had both loved the natural world and music, and had often invented stories to tell each other.

She listened to the buzzing of a bee that had become

caught in the hydrangeas. She walked around the corner of the gray building, past the sandstone chapel, and caught her breath with joy and amazement. What a garden! Mighty pine trees, lilacs, bamboo groves, palm trees, roses. A secret flower-filled idyll. She came to a stone bench at the back of the high-walled garden. How beautiful it was here, and how peaceful. She breathed out, and for a moment she felt she might stay here forever.

Oh Lothar. The realization hit her like a train: it was the unsatisfied longing for something to share that had eaten away at her. She and her husband shared nothing, neither the same wishes nor the same dreams. All that mattered were *his* desires.

A delicate, barely visible cloud floated many miles above her head, a mere streak of white foam against the deep blue sky.

"Cumulus clouds are the dancers of the heavens," Marianne heard her father say, "and their brothers the stratocumuli are the elevators of the skies. Neither of them likes the nimbostratus, the big fat crusher. He barely moves and all he does is spread a bad mood." Her father had paused for thought and then said, "Like your mother!" Marianne had laughed, but she had felt terribly guilty afterward. The children in the hospice kindergarten had giggled at the comparisons and went outside with Marianne to scour the skies for elevators and dancing clouds.

The warmth made her knee feel better and the burning sensation was now subsiding. She slipped off her shoes and walked barefoot across the soft, damp grass.

An hour passed and she felt that she really might stay here and count clouds and stems of grass forever, but instead she sighed and put on her shoes again. She advanced into the depths of the lush scented garden until she came to a small graveyard enclosed by white walls. White grains of sand covered everything, the paths and the graves, like a glittering bedsheet, and the grave mounds looked like plumped-up eiderdowns. A fragrant red rosebush flowered on each and every white sandy bed. How lovingly the graveyard had been laid out. It was as if the nuns had put their sisters to bed. They were merely sleeping. They were dreaming, and their dreams were as sweet as rose petals.

Marianne sat down on a weathered stone bench.

Where would my place for dreaming have been? Which gap might have been mine, the one only I could have filled? All the children I didn't bear because I wasn't in the right place. All the missing love. All the absent laughter. There are too many things I haven't done, and now it's too late.

She looked up to find Clara standing at the cemetery gate. The young nun walked slowly toward her.

"May I?" she asked, waiting until Marianne nodded and signaled for her to sit down next to her on the bench. Clara folded her hands on her lap and, like Marianne, gazed at the white sandy graves.

"Your journey is hard." It wasn't a question; it was a statement. Marianne stared at her fingernails.

"Do you think death is the end of everything, Marie-Anne?"

"I hope so," whispered Marianne.

"Here on the Brittany coast we believe something different. Death is not something that is coming, but rather something that is all around us. Here." Clara pointed at the air. "There."

She gestured toward the trees. Then she bent forward and took a little white sand in her hands. "Death is like this." She let the sand trickle from her left hand into her right. "One life goes in and takes a break in death." Now she let the sand run out of her right hand onto the ground. "Another life comes out. It makes a journey, *oui*? Like flowing water. Water in a *moulin*. In a mill. Death is that short break."

"I remember being told a different story at church," Marianne remarked.

"Brittany is older than the Church. This is Armorica! This is where the land meets the sea; this is the end of the world, as old as death itself."

Marianne glanced up at the sky. "So there's no hell, and no heaven somewhere up there?"

"Here we have a lot of different names for fear, for living, for dying. Sometimes the same word. Sometimes heaven and earth are the same. Hell and heaven too. We read the land, and in it we see that everything is equal. Death. Life. We are merely on a journey between the two."

"And does the land tell you where the journey is heading? Like a guidebook?"

Clara didn't laugh. "*Tiens.* You have to listen when the land speaks to you. The stones tell of souls that wept as they passed, the grass whispers of the people who have walked on it, the wind brings you the voices of those you have loved. And the sea knows the name of every person who has ever died."

Marianne wondered whether the sand under her feet would one day say, "Marianne was here, and soon afterward she died."

"I'm scared of death," she whispered.

"Don't be scared," said Clara, her voice full of sympathy. "Don't be scared! *L'autre monde* . . . the other world, *oui*, is like this world. It is in the middle of our world and looks the same; it is just that we cannot see those who are walking in it. There are fairies in the beyond, and wizards. Gods, demons and *korrigans*—trolls. And the dead who are no longer with us. And yet they are . . . here, next to us on this bench perhaps. All our sisters . . ." said Clara, pointing to the graves. "All our sisters are here and can see us. But we cannot see them. Don't be scared. Please."

Marianne raised her eyes. No ghosts, only roses.

"I have to travel on. I must complete my journey," she gasped. She pulled her hand gently from Clara's and walked away, every step making a crunch on the gravel beneath her feet. She found a tiny gate leading out of the convent garden and squeezed through it.

7

MARIANNE CAUGHT A MOUTH-WATERING AROMA OF freshly baked pizza as she watched a group of tourists poke around in the religious souvenir shop next to the pizzeria. When the group had passed her, the tour guide turned to her and said, "*Allez, allez!* Hurry up. Don't lag too far behind, madame! *Salida!*" Marianne looked around, but the woman had indeed been talking to her. "We have to get a move on if we want to visit Pont-Aven in daylight!"

Pont-Aven! Marianne cleared her throat. "Of course! I'm coming," she said, and hid her face as she boarded the coach. Her heart was almost leaping out of her mouth: someone was bound to unmask her soon.

As the coach pulled out onto the main road, Marianne sat down quickly behind a couple wearing matching rustling red anoraks. She spied a brochure on the seat beside her and held it up in front of her face. *Dolmen et Dégustation*, translated into English as "Stones and Scones." The program included a tour of the Penven biscuit factory in Pont-Aven; before that they were to visit the Carnac stones and do some oyster tasting in Belon.

Marianne unfolded her map. Carnac was on the coast at least, and thus not completely in the wrong direction. She tried to make herself invisible. She felt like a fare dodger—which was precisely what she was.

After half an hour's drive, the burgundy-colored coach swung to a halt before a field of stones. "The Ménec alignments near Carnac," the woman in the seat in front read out from her guidebook. "Eight thousand years old, maybe more. In any case, the stones were already standing when the Celts arrived from the Dark Land. Legend has it that this was an enemy army, and the fairies of Armorica turned its warriors into stone."

Marianne stared at the strange noses of granite as if she'd been hypnotized. Some people looked like this under their skin, she thought. Brittany granite made man.

THE COACH drove on from the stone armies toward Lorient. It took the motorway and left it again at the Quimperlé exit, then headed toward Riec-sur-Belon. Marianne unfolded the map again. A tongue of land separated the river Belon from the river Aven. Kerdruc lay on the gradually widening Aven before the two rivers flowed into the Atlantic together at Port Manec'h.

She pulled the tile from her jacket. Please, she thought, please let it be even half as beautiful as this.

The coach was now driving along a meandering road under a roof of deep-green foliage hanging from ivy-clad trees. It wound its way ever deeper through rows of trees and fields, and here and there one saw a granite house with colorful shutters and pink and blue hydrangeas outside. The coach eventually stopped in a downward-sloping wood-bordered lane, at the end of which Marianne spotted the front of a manor house and beyond it water and boats.

"This is the Château de Belon, the most famous name in oysters since 1864!" the tour guide explained.

Marianne slipped to the back of the group. To her right, long wooden tables stood on a shady grass terrace that offered a magnificent view of a wooded bend in the river. And beyond the final bend she saw . . . the sea! It sparkled, tiny stars dancing on the waves. It was so gorgeous.

Two young blond men in aprons were waiting for the guests, and a third man stood alongside them. He had an earring and was wearing leather bracelets and biker boots. He stuck something like a giant tin-opener blade into a flat oyster and divided it into two halves with a twist of his wrist. He raised it to his lips and, turning to the men on either side of him, said, "*C'est bon.*" Then he began to select further oysters from a gray crate, tapping two together as if he were listening for something before tossing them into a woven chipboard basket lined with gleaming wet seaweed that looked like fresh young spinach leaves.

The tour guide gave a talk about oysters, but Marianne listened with only half an ear; the view out to sea over the river and its gently rocking boats was simply too enticing. She caught snatches of explanations about small larvae and underwater nurseries.

"*Des plates ou des creuses?*" said a voice behind her. It was the man in the biker boots. He chatted as he first opened one of the smooth, round oysters and then one of the long variety with a rough, barnacle-encrusted shell. It made a noise like a twig cracking. He held out the rounder, flatter oyster to Marianne. "*Calibre numéro un, madame!*"

Her hand trembled as she peered into the shell. She looked up at the young man again. Though he was attractive, he didn't seem too sure of it. Dark-blue eyes with a glint of tenderness and longing. His gaze spoke of many unfulfilled nights.

I don't dare. She'd never eaten an oyster in all her life. She caught the man's eye again and noticed a smile on his sensuous lips. *Go on*, he encouraged her with a nod.

Marianne copied the movements she had seen him make, raising the oyster to her mouth, throwing back her head, and slurping. She caught the subtle tang of seawater; she tasted a nutty flavor and something like shell, and her nose was full of the concentrated aroma of what she imagined when she saw the sea—spray, waves, surf, jellyfish, salt, coral and teeming fish, the wide horizon and infinity.

"Sea," she said wistfully. One could eat the sea!

"*Ya. Ar Mor*—the sea," he said with a throaty laugh. He scraped out the remaining gray muscle with the oyster knife and passed her the shell again.

Ar Mor. Every oyster was like the sea, thought the young man. The same sea, wide and free, wild or gentle, delicate blue or black, that each of us carried inside us. An oyster wasn't only a delicacy. It held the key to our deepest dreams of the sea. People with no desire to throw themselves into the sea's embrace, those who feared the breadth of its horizon and its depths, its passion and its unpredictability, would never like oysters. They would feel only disgust, just as they were disgusted by love, passion, life, death and everything the sea represented.

"*Merci,*" said Marianne. Their fingertips touched as his hand took the oyster shell from hers.

You should have been my son, Marianne thought suddenly. I would have loved to have a son like you. I'd have danced to opera with you. I would have given you love, so that you too could love.

As she sat there eating one oyster after another and drinking a glass of Muscadet under the beeches overlooking the bay, with the sea in the near distance, Marianne's thoughts turned to death. Was there really nothing absolute about it, as Clara had said? Was it like this side of the world, but with more fairies and demons?

A sparrow landed on her table and flew off with her butter.

8

THE CLOSER THE COACH GOT TO PONT-AVEN, THE
more Marianne wished for it to slow down. She was
afraid that she wouldn't be able to stop herself from running
to the nearest phone booth and begging Lothar to come and
pick her up. She wasn't sure if she trusted herself to remain
free.

When the bus pulled up outside the biscuit factory, she
slipped quietly away. She walked through Pont-Aven without fully taking in how charming it was; a village of galleries,
crêperies and houses that must have been built in the eigh-
teenth century. Here, the past was the foundation of the present. She followed the meandering river through the village
until she passed the Hôtel Les Mimosas and came to the forest on the edge of what she knew was the artists' haven—that
world depicted on the tile.

A small sign told her that it was four miles to Kerdruc. Another seven thousand yards. Perhaps twelve thousand paces.
That was nothing.

Marianne had walked a lot in her hometown of Celle.
She'd felt like a bird that was constantly on the wing, gleaning

something here, something there. Lothar never let her take the car. "Not enough driving practice," he'd said laconically, "and anyway, you wouldn't find a parking space."

He never went shopping, and he'd be lost in the aisles now, she thought—a sergeant major wandering among the tins, tampons and tea bags. Not for the first time, she instinctively clapped her hand to her mouth. What foul thoughts she was having.

The air smelled of silt and the warm forest floor. Her nose picked up the delicate scent of mushrooms. Maybe she would make it to the sea by sundown and could then go to bed in it with the sun? The only sounds were the hum of insects, the call of a finch, a furtive cracking and a rustling of leaves. Nothing. Her footsteps were the only human noise on the winding forest path along the river Aven, which had now shrunk to the width of a man's shoulders; it was like the lengthening hallway leading to an unknown room. Foxgloves were in bloom on all sides. Digitalis—the plant that could stop your heart.

Maybe she should simply chew some of that, thought Marianne, but then it occurred to her that local children might come here to play. No child should have to discover a dead body in the bushes.

She passed tall old trees that let only a little green-spangled misty daylight filter through onto the path. After a slight rise, she came to a narrow road that led over a straight stone bridge spanning a dry riverbed, in the middle of which stood a windowless house. A *moulin à marée*—a tidal mill.

It began to rain, even though the sun was still shining, and the water set the air glittering. She imagined that this golden shimmer was the veil separating the here from the beyond.

In the middle of the bridge, she raised her hand and pushed it through the veil. The rain was very soft and very warm. She imagined that fairies and giants were passing her on this bridge and laughing at how she had stretched one hand into the underworld.

She hadn't known that the world could be so bewitching and so wild. No tower blocks. No modern buildings. No motorways. Just birds building their nests in the palm trees, and wisterias, peonies and mimosas sprawling over the rocks. There was sky, stones and other worlds beyond the golden cloudbursts.

A land like this shapes people, thought Marianne, not the other way round. It must make them proud and stubborn, passionate yet restrained. It shapes them like stones and tree trunks.

She ran, and the deserted land tugged at her limbs. She seemed to hear a whispering from the depths of the wood; she thought of Clara and how she had said that this land would only tell its stories to those who were willing to listen. She pricked up her ears, but she couldn't understand what the wind and the grass, the trees and the granite had to say to her.

THE RAIN stopped as she emerged from the wood, and the footpath ended at a dirty glass-recycling container in the middle of a small graveled car park. She looked around her. A road with no center line. Golden fields. To her left, a village appeared.

She felt numb from all the fresh air and walking. A rising breeze carried the magnetic, dusty scent of an imminent thunderstorm. Marianne's knee was throbbing. She passed hydrangeas of all colors. She ignored them, as she did the *chaumières*, the Breton sandstone cottages with the brightly colored shutters, and their gardens with flowering fig trees, fragrant oleander and sedges whispering in the wind.

Her whole attention was concentrated on the narrow village lane.

At the top of a small hill, she curved left around a three-storey white house, and all of a sudden, on a still Sunday in June, she had arrived at Kerdruc harbor.

9

K ERDRUC HARBOR HAD A JETTY REACHING OUT INTO the Aven at a right angle to the quay that ran upstream along the riverbank. Rowing boats were snuggled up against each other on the quayside like bright spoons in a cutlery drawer. Thatched cottages nestled on the slopes leading down to the river like white flowers amid the luscious green of the pine trees and the meadows of sedge. Dozens of motorboats and yachts were moored to an anchor cable between red buoys, and swung in the mouth of the Aven like white moonstones on a handcrafted necklace, dancing on the salty tide as it mingled with the fresh water of the river. Where water and sky, blue and gold, placid woods and rugged cliffs met, the sea began.

The restaurant on the ground floor of the three-storey white house, named Ar Mor, boasted a wooden deck, a red-and-white awning and a blue wooden gate. The guesthouse next door, Auberge d'Ar Mor, was a romantic, weather-beaten granite building whose entrance was overgrown with creepers and surrounded by faded hydrangeas.

On the far bank of the Aven, the left bank, was another

tiny port with a short quay, squat fishing boats and a bar with a green awning.

There was no one in sight. The only sounds were the gurgling kisses of tide and current, the irregular slap of steel cables on masts, and a woman's quiet weeping. That woman was Marianne, and she was weeping, unable to avert her eyes, because the view of Kerdruc spread out before her was so unbearably beautiful. Every place she had visited in the previous sixty years suddenly paled in comparison.

The feeling of having come home grew ever stronger. She smelled salt and fresh water, the air was as clear as glass, and a gleaming carpet of gold-and-blue silk lay over the river. The radiance of this beautiful scene shed a cruel light on every past horror, every insult tolerated, every unspoken retort, every gesture of rejection. Marianne was grieving, and her boundless grief made her regret every moment of cowardice in her life.

A cat jumped out of a tree and sat down behind her. When the sobs shaking her body still did not abate, the cat got up, paced around, sat down opposite her and stared.

"What?" cried Marianne, wiping the tears from her face.

The cat took three steps toward her and butted her hand with its head. It rubbed itself vigorously against her palm and purred deeply and raspingly; Marianne tickled the cat under its chin.

The shadows of the trees and the houses grew longer, and the silky water glowed ever brighter as Kerdruc sank into darkness.

Marianne made a quick mental calculation of how much money she had left. It might be enough to take a taxi to the coast, or for a meal and a drink, but it was not enough for a room. She breathed out heavily; it had been a long day.

There was a sudden clap of thunder. The startled cat twisted out of her hands and bounded away. Soon the first needles of rain began to darken the black asphalt. The steel cables slapped louder and louder, and the water became gray and unsettled as rain speckled the waves with foam. The boats by the quayside huddled together like shivering sheep. A cabin door rattled and slammed in the wind.

Marianne ran to the harbormaster's office and tugged at the door. It was locked. She dashed over to the restaurant. Locked. She banged hard on it. The rain was now coming from below too; the raindrops were hitting the ground so hard that they rebounded from it. Water was running down the back of Marianne's neck and into her sleeves, and it was soaking her shoes. She held her coat over her head and raced back along the quayside.

The cat galloped toward the jetty. It looked as if it was about to jump into the river, and Marianne set off after it in a flash. "Don't do it!" she called in horror as it gathered itself to leap, and landed in the last boat moored to the jetty. Marianne managed to clamber after it over the rocking gunwale. She slipped on the wet floor, grabbed hold of the door and squeezed through into the cabin and down the steps, slamming the door behind her.

Immediately the sound of the rain was reduced to a trickle, and from beneath the hull came a groaning and a murmuring.

The cat was sitting on the bunk. Marianne began to peel off her sodden clothing. She washed her clothes in the cabin's tiny bathroom, which had both a shower and a toilet. Then she wrapped herself in a blanket beside the cat and drew the curtains. She curled up to get warm, and the cat crawled into the hollow between her arms and purred into her throat. The rocking and swaying of the boat, the patter of the rain and the darkened bunk calmed her nerves. I'll rest for a bit, thought Marianne. Just a bit.

SHE DREAMED of the Carnac stones of Brittany. Every stone bore Lothar's astonished features. Only Marianne could set him free, and she searched long and hard for the most beautiful Lothar stone before deciding that she would rather fly away in an oyster shell. The oyster was warm, and she sailed over the clouds. The sea below was green, and tiny lights flickered on the waves.

It was to light that Marianne awoke, and it took her a moment to figure out where she was. The bright daylight glittering through the porthole told her that she had slept for longer than she had intended. She wound the blanket tight around her naked body, cautiously opened the cabin door— and stepped into a dream.

She was alone on a small white boat, all around her only water.

10

A SUDDEN CRY STARTLED HER. ABOUT SIXTY FEET from the boat, a man was swimming in the waves—a man with white hair, a mustache and large black eyes.

Marianne waved her arms for a few seconds, desperately trying to keep her balance, but ended up toppling overboard with a gasp. She sank below the surface like a rock. As the first gulp of water ran down her throat, she opened her eyes wide.

No! No!

She kicked out, and the knotted blanket came loose from her body and floated away. With a final effort she thrust herself out of the water and sucked air deep into her lungs.

"Help," she whimpered as a salty wave choked her cry.

"Madame!" the man called. She struck out in panic toward him and caught him in a sensitive spot. He yelped and went under.

"Sorry," yapped Marianne, groping for the boat ladder. The man surfaced again beside her. Marianne clambered up the ladder, hiding her nakedness with both hands in shame, then ran into the cabin and locked herself inside.

SIMON COULDN'T work out what was going on. A woman on his boat? A naked woman? He continued to tread water.

"Hello," he said. "Are you still there? I'm going to count to ten before I come up. If you're still not decent by then . . . well, I'm almost seventy and I need glasses, so you've nothing to fear."

He decided that he must still be drunk. He'd taken his boat out this morning without checking the cabin. He was longing for some strong coffee with a shot of Calva in it. There was no better way to get over a hangover than to carry on the next morning with the drink you'd left off the previous evening. He thought of the mysterious woman. Her eyes could knock a man dead—bright eyes the color of the fresh green buds of an apple tree in spring. The girl wasn't exactly young, but somehow she was still a girl. That shocked look on her face!

The elderly fisherman let the swell carry him rather than trying to swim against it. The water was cold—fourteen or fifteen degrees Celsius—but he spread his limbs and allowed the coldness to flow through him.

Better. Much better.

He climbed resolutely up the ladder, quickly pulled on his trousers, slipped his faded blue shirt over his tanned torso and expertly weighed anchor.

MARIANNE WATCHED him through the porthole. She hadn't understood a word of what the white-haired man had shouted from the water. His speech was full of guttural sounds in a language she'd never heard before. It must have been Breton.

She felt the hum of the boat's engine beneath her feet. What would he do next? She was trembling as she put her clothes on. She picked up her bag with one hand and a bread knife with the other, and opened the cabin door.

"*Bonjour, monsieur*," she said with as much dignity as she could muster.

Simon ignored her until they were out of the channel where tankers plied to and fro. When his boat had reached the usual spot, which afforded a view of the whole Glénan archipelago, he throttled back the engine and studied the strange woman. He chuckled at the sight of the comical little knife as he unscrewed his thermos flask, poured coffee and Calvados into a cup and handed it to her.

"Thank you," said Marianne, bucking up as she took a long swig. She hadn't reckoned with the alcohol and began to splutter.

"*Petra zo ganeoc'h?*" Simon tried again. "What do you need?"

"I'm German," Marianne explained with a stutter and slight hiccups. "And . . . my name's Marianne."

He pressed her hand briefly. "I'm from Brittany. The name's Simon." He started the engine again.

Good thing they'd sorted that out, he thought with a sigh of relief. He was from Brittany, she was from Germany—*un point, c'est tout.*

Marianne gazed out over the choppy waters around the boat. Black and turquoise, light green and navy blue. Clara was right: if you screwed up your eyes, everything was the same. For Clara it was heaven and earth; for Marianne it was where the sky met the water at the horizon, and the land toward which they were heading at increasing speed.

Down there, she thought. That's where I wanted to be. Why didn't I do it? Was I not cowardly enough? Or not brave enough?

She was confused by herself. She glanced at Simon. Her face was a picture of anxiety and doubt.

The fisherman wondered what this woman was afraid of. She was on constant alert, as if she were expecting a blow, yet at the same time she was drinking in her wide surroundings with thirsty eyes. *It's all right, girl. No need to be scared of me.* Simon liked people who loved the sea as much as he did. He had often gone out on one of the Concarneau trawlers that went hunting for ray and cod in the North Atlantic around Iceland and Newfoundland. That took some coping with—nothing but water and sky for weeks on end.

He thought of Colette. She was one of the few attractions of dry land. He had stolen some flowers for the Pont-Aven gallery owner's birthday and would go to Ar Mor to present them to her later—after, that was, he had dropped this spirit off. Who knows, this woman who had turned up on his *Gwen II* might be a wandering soul on its way to Avalon. Women: they were so damned complicated. As unpredictable as the sea.

He remembered what his father had said when Simon complained about the wild, unruly sea: "Learn to love it, son. Learn to love what you do, whatever it is, and you won't have any problems. You'll suffer, but then you'll feel, and when you feel, you're alive. You need troubles to be alive—otherwise you're dead!"

The trouble in the dress before him was staring out at the water. Simon recognized the yearning in Marianne's ardent gaze, full of wanderlust. He beckoned to her. She hesitantly got to her feet, and he guided her to the wheel, stood behind her and gently helped her to steer. They had left the mouth of the river Aven behind, and Kerdruc harbor was heaving into view.

11

PAUL DROVE INTO KERDRUC. IT WAS ALWAYS BEST TO sober up and let the wind and the sun wring the night from his body. His old friend Simon had left coffee, milk and pancakes on the kitchen table that morning, along with a bottle of Père Magloire Calvados. One of the chickens had jumped up onto the table and was observing its egg. Despite a quick nap on Simon's couch, Paul felt as if he'd been dragged through a hedge backward. Maybe he could convince Simon to let him help out in the farm shop. After Simon had stopped going out to sea to work, he had converted his fisherman's cottage in Kerbuan into a mini-market and now lived with his chickens in the kitchen.

He sold all kinds of stuff to gullible tourists. Ice honey, for example: collected by frost-resistant bees from flowers that grew in glaciated valleys in the Pyrenees. Oh yes. The tourists didn't need to know that it was just tangy buckwheat honey. Then there was Simon's scam with the menhir seeds—a paper sachet, emblazoned with a drawing of the fields of megalith stones in Carnac, containing a few crumbs of granite that had trickled from a crack in the outside wall of his house. "Menhirs grow very slowly for the first few hundred years," Simon would explain to his deferential patrons. It would help if they used some good old Celtic soil from Brittany as fertilizer— which meant he could sell them a handful of dirt from his garden to go with the bits of stone.

But the best thing about Simon's little store was that there were so many women in summer, and they found everything "nice" and "sweet." They wore short dresses and dreamed of catching a Breton fisherman and having their very own *Lady Chatterley's Lover* moment. Simon didn't really like talking to all these tourists, especially the sophisticated Parisian women, and he wasn't keen on pretending to be a rustic hunk. But for Paul, the gathering of so many different women in one place was a delightful occurrence.

He pulled up alongside Simon's battered Citroën, whose hood was pointing toward Ar Mor's terrace. *"Bonjour, Monsieur Paul,"* called Laurine, the young waitress from Ar Mor, as the former legionnaire got out of his car.

Paul went over to stand next to her. "Hello, Laurine." He peered at the mouth of the Aven, but all he could see was the *Gwen II* making for the quayside.

"There!" cried Laurine. Her overexcitement made Paul feel slightly dizzy. Simon was standing on the *Gwen II*, as always. And next to him . . .

"There!" repeated Laurine. "Yoo-hoo!"

"A woman?" Paul gasped. How on earth had Simon managed to pick up a woman *and* take her on a boat trip before lunch? The traitor! Hadn't they sworn last night that women were to play no further part in their lives? No major part, at any rate.

SIMON PREFERRED to manage the final few yards on his own. He'd enjoyed the smell of Marianne's seawater-soaked hair. Someone should invent seawater shampoo and market it, he thought. He'd have a word with Paul later about how they could put the sea into one of those plastic bottles. He suddenly caught sight of Laurine on the quayside, and behind her, Paul, with a sour look on his face.

MARIANNE LEANED on the railing while Simon was busy docking. She drank in the sight of Kerdruc harbor once more. Her heart clenched at the scene, and she felt as if she were returning home after a long sea voyage.

Nonsense. Nonsense, stop thinking such nonsense!

"Morning, Monsieur Simon!" called Laurine. Simon thought that Laurine could have been a model. He'd once suggested that she move to Paris or Milan and get rich.

She had looked at him with astonishment and said, "Rich? What for?" and she'd meant it. The twenty-three-year-old had the body of a woman, but her mind was often that of a child— too unsophisticated to lie, and too naïve for distrust.

Simon gave Marianne an awkward helping hand out of the boat. "I'll never touch another drink," he informed Paul as he stepped off the *Gwen II* and wound the rope expertly around a bollard.

"Me neither," Paul lied, glancing at Marianne with a quizzical, charming smile.

"Paul, this is Marianne. She's German."

"*Allemande*, eh?" said Paul, and took her hand in his, pretending to plant a kiss on it. "*Zwei brezzelle, beete.*" She withdrew her hand, aghast.

Simon nudged him. "Leave her, she's shy."

Paul switched into Breton. "I thought we'd come to an agreement about women. Some mate you are. As soon as I turn my back, you—"

"Oh put a sock in it. I was just going for a dip when she came out of the cabin naked."

"Naked?!"

"With the cat."

"And then? Did you—"

"Almost drowned me."

"The cat?"

"Trying to rescue the girl. She fell into the water!"

"I don't understand."

"Then don't ask."

"Have you already had breakfast?" asked Paul.

"Let's have a game of backgammon and a coffee," Simon replied. "The loser has to mind the shop today."

Marianne stood beside the two men the whole time, lost, her feet close together, her handbag clutched tightly to her chest. She felt defenseless. She could sense that they were talking about her, so she affected her most carefree smile. The cat rubbed up against her legs, and she found its presence calming. She cleared her throat. "Excuse me, I . . ." Her mind was suddenly empty. White noise, but no words.

Laurine leaned forward to give her three kisses on the

cheeks. Left, right, left. "*Bonjour, madame.* I'm Laurine," she said with a smile.

"Marianne Lanz," Marianne answered self-consciously. She still felt like a bedraggled cat, and presumably smelled like one too.

"Marianne? What a pretty name! Lovely to see you here. Did your journey go well?"

Marianne didn't understand a word. Laurine took her by the hand, while Simon and Paul began to lay cushions on the wooden chairs on the terrace, moving with the characteristic slowness of old gentlemen.

"*Kenavo,*" Simon called after Marianne. That was Breton for "see you later."

Laurine was terribly agitated, and as always when she was agitated, she whispered. "I'm taking you to see the chef. His name's Jean-Rémy. He'll be delighted to meet you!"

Marianne lingered apprehensively in the doorway as Laurine preceded her into Ar Mor's kitchens. "I . . . I'm sorry, but . . ." Nobody was listening to her. Nobody.

It was only when the chef looked at her, pushed back his red bandanna and smiled that Marianne's embarrassment gave way to relief. It was him! The man with the oysters!

"What do you think you are—a budding Hell's Angel?" Madame Ecollier had asked Jean-Rémy two summers earlier when he dismounted from his motorbike for a trial session in the kitchen. Black jeans, red shirt, studded boots. He had earrings, and a tattoo under the dark curls at the back of his neck. A case containing his favorite knife dangled from his belt like a revolver in a holster. Each of his leather bracelets represented one of the kitchens he had worked in during the thirteen years since he'd started out as a chef at the age of sixteen.

Nevertheless, Madame Ecollier had taken a shine to his outfit. "I'd prefer it if you resembled Peter Sellers rather than Johnny Depp, but never mind. Just cook and keep your eyes off our female guests—and your hands off my staff. And stay away from the drink, unless you're pouring it into a saucepan. Keep it simmering, Mr. Perrig."

Marianne found him delightful. "*Bonjour*," she said almost inaudibly.

"*Bonjour, Madame*," said the man who had offered her the first oyster of her life, as he emerged from behind the stainless-steel kitchen island. "Nice to see you again. I hope you enjoyed the oysters."

"This is our new chef," Laurine whispered breathlessly. "Marianne Lance!"

"Are you sure?"

"Yes," gasped Laurine. "Monsieur Simon fished her out of the sea. We have no idea where she is from."

Marianne looked confused, and Jean-Rémy caught her eye. Out of the sea? He remembered the impression she'd made on him at the oyster farm the day before: lost, and yet determined to find something very specific. That impression still lingered in her eyes, despite her efforts to conceal it behind a fragile smile.

Now Jean-Rémy looked at Laurine. Laurine, my kitty-cat, he thought, what have you done to me? He had to tear his eyes away from her.

Marianne was hoping uneasily that someone would explain why she was waiting here. She stole a glance at Laurine and Jean-Rémy, who were gazing at each other as if each was expecting the other to speak first. Eventually Laurine turned away and headed outside.

Jean-Rémy stared straight ahead, then slammed his hand down on the table in fury at himself. Marianne gave a start as she saw the chef grab his bleeding hand. He'd slammed it down on the edge of a knife that was lying on the surface. Her handbag fell to the floor.

In the hospice kitchen, the first-aid box had hung in an obscure place behind the door where no one could see it because the door was always open. It was the same here. She took out a gauze bandage, a compress and an elastic plaster, gently cradled Jean-Rémy's hand in hers and examined the wound—a deep, clean cut just above the ball of his thumb. Jean-Rémy had closed his eyes. She pushed back the red bandanna, which had slid down over his forehead.

She placed her left hand on Jean-Rémy's palm. She could feel his pain in her own hand, in her arm.

"It's nothing serious," she murmured.

Jean-Rémy relaxed and started to breathe more deeply while she skilfully bandaged his wound. She ran her fingers softly over his head, as she would have done with a little boy, although this particular boy was a good foot taller than she was.

"*Merci beaucoup, Madame,*" the chef whispered.

Marianne turned the largest empty cooking pot upside down and motioned to him to sit on it. She lowered herself onto a smaller pot opposite him. She made an attempt to speak.

"I don't know why I'm here," she began, leaning against the cool tiled wall. "My name's Marianne Lanz. *Bonjour. Je suis allemande.*" She thought for a second, but no further French words came to her mind. "Well . . . *au revoir.*" She got to her feet again.

All of a sudden, the lid of the pot in which the court bouillon was simmering on the gas stove began to dance and the stock boiled over, causing the flames to spit and hiss. Without thinking, Marianne went to the pot, turned the heat down and lifted the lid.

"Vegetable stock?" She took a spoon, scooped up a little liquid and swirled it around her palate. "It's . . . I don't want to offend you, but . . ." She found the pot of Guérande salt, gave it a shake and said, "Too much. Dearie me."

"Dearie me, yes. Laurine. Dearie me," groaned Jean-Rémy. He felt dizzy.

"Laurine?"

He shook his head, patting his heart as he did so.

"Oh, the salt was because of Laurine . . ." A pining cook could bring a restaurant to its knees in no time.

Marianne glanced around. She found what she was looking for in the cooler. Raw potatoes. She quickly began to peel and dice ten of them before tossing them into the court bouillon. Jean-Rémy watched from his seat and waited to see the results. After five minutes, she spooned some stock into a tasting dish. He tried it and glanced up at her in surprise.

"Starch. It's just the starch in the potatoes," she mumbled awkwardly. "We'll take them out again in ten minutes, and if it's still too salty, we'll throw in five hard-boiled eggs as well. No more dearie me. Dearie me gone. And now me too."

"Well done, Madame Lance." An idea began to form in his mind.

"What's going on here?" Marianne heard the woman's booming voice before she saw her. Her upright bearing indicated that she was the boss, as erect as a statue, her face lined and weathered by sixty-five years of life.

"*Bonjour, Madame,*" said Marianne hurriedly. She was tempted to curtsey.

Geneviève Ecollier ignored her and stared at Jean-Rémy instead. He looked like a deer caught in the headlights. "Jean-Rémy!" Her voice rang out like a gunshot. The tasting dish in his hand began to tremble, spilling a little court bouillon. "Oh for heaven's sake, what have you done this time?"

She ordered him to ladle more of the stock into the dish. Some diners had complained the previous weekend, and even if Geneviève didn't take these Parisians seriously, she couldn't stand it when their grievances were legitimate. She had tried the tuna dish, *thon à la Concarnoise,* after clearing the table, and yes, the sauce was so salty it shivered her timbers.

Court bouillon, made with carrot, shallot, leek, garlic, celeriac, herbs, water and Muscadet, was the heart and soul of Breton cuisine. Langoustines blossomed in it, and crabs drowned in bliss; skinned duck or vegetables simmered in it to perfection. The stock grew stronger with each use and would keep for three days. It formed the base for sauces, and a shot glass of sieved court bouillon could turn a mediocre fish stew into a regular feast. Always assuming, that was, that you didn't over-salt the base itself, something Jean-Rémy had made an unfortunate habit of doing in recent weeks. Eight liters of court bouillon, good for nothing but tipping into the harbor to poison the fish!

Geneviève tasted the stock. *Mon Dieu*, praise be to all fairies! He'd kept a steady hand this time.

Jean-Rémy only just managed to catch the tasting dish that Madame Geneièvre threw back into his hands. Then he explained to her how Madame Lance had saved them from having nothing but *steak frites* to serve their guests that day.

"Are you the chef we're expecting for interview?" said Geneviève, turning to Marianne with a rather friendlier demeanor than before. Oh please let it be her, she thought, please.

When Jean-Rémy realized that Marianne hadn't understood a single word, he answered for her. "No, she isn't."

"She isn't? So who is she?"

Jean-Rémy smiled at Marianne. One part of her expression begged him to let her leave, but another part—one of which she might not even have been conscious—wanted to stay. "She came from the sea."

Madame Ecollier studied Marianne: her hands looked as if she was used to working. She seemed to be neither coquettish nor especially worried about dolling herself up. Nor did she avert her eyes when you looked at her, something to which Geneviève Ecollier took exception.

Marianne squirmed under the restaurant owner's gaze, wishing she could simply disappear.

"All right then," Geneviève said in a calmer tone of voice. "You seem to have hurt yourself, Jean-Rémy, and anyway, you could do with a helping hand, whether it comes from the sea, the sky or elsewhere. Give her a seasonal contract. Laurine can show her the Shell Room in the guesthouse. We'll see how things work out." Then, with a curt nod at Marianne, she said, "*Bienvenue.*"

"*Au revoir,*" Marianne answered politely.

Madame Geneviève barked at Jean-Rémy, "And teach her some French!"

With a satisfied grin, he turned to Marianne. "Have you eaten yet?"

12

❧

"I DIVIDE WOMEN INTO THREE TYPES," SAID PAUL, BRUSH-ing his hair out of his eyes, before draining his shot glass and banging it on the table. He moved the glass down beside the others on the backgammon board between himself and Simon.

"I know, you always say that." Simon pulled a face as the apple brandy burned his throat. "I may be a simple fisherman, but that's no reason for you to keep lecturing me." He gave a mere hint of a nod for more drinks when Laurine raised four fingers in query from the restaurant doorway.

Paul continued. "Well listen to this. The first type is the *femme fatale*. She's exciting, but she doesn't distinguish be-tween you, me and anyone else. She's dangerous. You should never fall in love with that kind, because she'll break your heart. Got that?"

"Hmm. You do realize I'm about to beat you?"

"The second type is the friendly ones you can marry. You'll get bored, but you'll never be in any danger. They mean well by you and they never look at anyone else. One day they get the blues and stop living, because they only ever look at you and you don't really notice them anymore."

"Aha. And what type is the woman from the sea? Marianne?"

Laurine brought them four more brandies.

"Hold your horses. And then there are the women you live for," said Paul in a low voice. "They're the ones for whom everything you've ever done or not done has significance. You love her, and she becomes the only important thing in your life. You wake up to love her, you go to bed to love her, you eat to love her, you live to love her, you die to love her. You forget where you wanted to go, the promises you've made and even the fact that you're married." He thought of Rozenn, whom he had loved so much that everything was pregnant with meaning. And he thought of the man she'd left him for. Boy, more like. Seventeen years younger than Paul. Seventeen!

"You're not married to Rozenn anymore, you know, Paul."

"It wasn't my decision."

No, it had been Rozenn's decision. A few weeks after becoming a grandmother to twins, she had chucked everything in and fallen in love with someone barely out of adolescence.

Simon thought of the sea. Going to sea had been his decision, and it always made him feel welcome. He could mold himself to the waves the way he would have done to a woman's warmth, and dive into the water as he would into the body of a lover.

"You two have been at it a while by the look of it, *n'est-ce pas?*" A deep, husky voice, preceded by the scent of cigarettes and Chanel No. 5, the click of approaching high heels, legs in genuine silk stockings and, panning up, an elegant black suit, yellow gloves and a black hat.

Colette Rohan.

She presented her finely sculpted cheeks for the traditional three *bises* and kissed the air next to Simon's face as he shut his eyes and touched his cheek softly to hers. Over far too quickly, as always, he thought. Paul stood up, pulled the eccentric gallery owner close and gave her three sound kisses in greeting, then sat down again, threw the dice and moved his empty glasses around the backgammon board.

Simon said nothing and looked at Colette. His mouth felt dry and he heard the roar of the sea inside his head.

"Madame?" asked Laurine, blowing her bangs aside.

"The same as always, *ma petite belle*," said Colette and lowered herself into the seat between Paul and Simon, gracefully crossing her legs and waiting for Laurine to bring her a glass of tap water and a Bellini cocktail.

"What day is it today, Laurine?" asked Paul.

"It's Monday, Monsieur Paul. You come here every Monday morning and evening, whereas on other days you only come in at lunchtime, which is how I know it's Monday."

"And it's Madame Colette's birthday," Paul added.

"Ooohh!" gasped Laurine.

Colette took another sip of her Bellini before asking Simon for a light. She could only smoke after a drink. It had always been that way—at sixteen, at thirty-six and now at sixty-six.

Sixty-six, Colette thought with a snort.

Simon coughed uncertainly and pulled something awkwardly from his old boat bag, eventually pushing a poorly wrapped parcel across the table to Colette.

"For me? Simon, *mon primitif*! A present!"

She tore excitedly at the wrapping paper. "Ouch!" she growled as something pricked her. Paul guffawed. "Thistles," Colette noted in her husky voice, and took a long drag on her cigarette holder.

"They made me think of you," stammered Simon.

"You're always so full of surprises. Only two weeks ago it was that highly original ashtray made out of . . . what was it again?"

"Half a crab."

"Then a week ago a dead blue dragonfly . . ."

"I thought a woman like you would be able to make use of it. A brooch perhaps."

". . . and now these soulful thistles."

"Globe thistles."

"Men have given me bouquets of flowers that made the wreaths at Princess Diana's funeral look like bunches of primroses. I have received diamond brooches, and one man even wanted to make me a gift of a top-floor flat in Saint-Germain, but I said no. Stupid of me; pride is so tiresome. But truly, Simon, no man has ever given me presents like yours."

"You're welcome," he said. "And many happy returns of the day."

Hearing Paul's laughter, Simon had the feeling that there was something not quite right about Colette's joy, even though the yellow vase he had put the thistles in was a perfect match for her gloves. He'd paid attention to detail. Colette loved yellow, a typical color of Brittany.

"*Mon petit primitif*, it's . . . I'm having trouble finding the right word," said Colette, removing her sunglasses. She had spent the previous night weeping over love letters from men she could no longer remember. But these people here were allowed to see the marks, because the gaze of friends was a balm for all the tears a woman shed over her lifetime—tears of passion, longing, happiness, emotion, rage, love or pain.

"You know, globe thistles . . . are rare," Simon stuttered. "Like you, Colette. There aren't many like you."

Colette took Simon's face in her hands. She studied the deep crow's-feet around his eyes before kissing him gently on the corners of his mouth, feeling the wiry bristles of his mustache. He smelled of sun and sea.

"Um, by the way," Paul began, "the Romanian woman's arrived."

"Which Romanian woman, dear?" Colette asked mildly.

"The new chef. Simon fished her out of the sea yesterday, but she actually comes from Germany."

"Oh, right," Colette said, completely bemused.

"Sidonie and Marie-Claude are on their way," said Simon.

"It's about time. I'd like to start getting seriously sozzled on my sixty-sixth," sighed Colette.

Sixty-six. How quickly one aged. Sidonie was her oldest friend. Since . . . um, since when, in fact? They'd known each other since Colette had come back from studying in Paris and met Sidonie with a group of young people from Kerdruc, Névez, Port Manec'h and the surrounding farms. Colette had observed with great interest the eighteen-year-old in her Breton folk costume complete with tall headdress. At twenty-five, she had felt old next to her.

Sidonie, a sculptress, had not married again after her husband Hervé's premature death, and had renovated their old stone cottage in Kerambail, just outside Kerdruc, on her own. Colette loved her friend's smile. She smiled when she worked, she smiled when she was silent; she smiled as she chiseled away at granite, basalt and sandstone. And when she laughed, she looked radiant.

Having settled down at the table with Simon, Paul and Colette, Sidonie was now laughing at a story that Marie-Claude, a hairdresser from Pont-Aven, was telling.

"Honestly, honestly, those mad people in the woods serve their cats and dogs the best cuts of meat—and on china plates to boot!" Marie-Claude's imitation of Madame Bouvet, the housekeeper for Emile and Pascale Goichon—two colorful characters from Kerdruc—was so perfect that Colette had to cackle into her Bellini.

"That Bouvet woman is a quintessential Catholic tight-arse," said Marie-Claude, tickling her lapdog Lupin.

"Did you say 'tight-arse'?" asked Colette.

"No, she said 'fright-arse,'" insisted Paul.

"Or maybe it was 'quite-a-sight-arse,'" said Simon.

"What in heaven's name are we talking about?" said Colette.

"Ask Paul," said Simon. "He knows about that kind of thing."

"Where's Yann? I bet he's painted a few arses in his time," said Paul, grinning.

"Don't talk like that about my favorite artist," Colette ordered him. She was planning a major exhibition for Yann Gamé in Paris. The only problem was that he knew nothing about it. He wouldn't hear of it, preferring to continue painting his tiles—it was enough to drive you mad! The man had to paint some big canvases, but he shrank from greatness. Or had he simply not found his motif? Did he need a muse? The sea, a woman, religion; some people required no more than a cake, a good example being Proust and his madeleines.

"You sound like teenagers!" complained Marie-Claude.

"And you sound like my dead grandmother," Colette interjected. "How's your daughter? Has she squeezed out your grandchild yet?" She tore the filter off a Gauloise and loaded the cigarette into her ivory holder.

"My God! Yesterday I felt the same age as my daughter Claudine; today I'm going to be a grandmother. Well, in two months' time."

"Did she tell you whose bun it is in the oven?" said Colette, blowing a smoke ring.

"I tried to find out from her diary, but I couldn't pick the lock," Marie-Claude said sulkily.

Simon observed Colette. Her mouth was a picture of sensuality and her forehead was a mosaic of doubt, while also proclaiming that she would never renege on a hard-won conviction. Each of her features played its part in her aristocratic demeanor. How beautiful she was!

"Anyway, *mon primitif*, you wouldn't happen to know of a little darling who could give Emile and Pascale a hand, would you? His Parkinson's isn't getting any better and her . . . what's it called? Dementia? That thing that causes you to forget everything? The two of them are getting more and more isolated out there in the woods," said Colette.

"How come? They've got all those millions of stray three-legged dogs and one-eared cats. They can't be lonely. And I'm sure they came with a horde of fleas, free of charge," chirped Marie-Claude, checking the state of her carefully set red curls.

"And lice," Paul added.

"Maybe Pascale and Emile Goichon were cursed," whispered Sidonie.

"By another tight-arse?" asked Simon.

"Oh you're not going to start that all over again," complained Marie-Claude.

"We're allowed to—we're old!" Colette quipped.

"I'm not old," the hairdresser corrected her sharply, adjusting her curls. "I've just lived a little longer than some people."

"You know the tragic thing about long life expectancy?" Paul asked, suddenly turning serious. Everybody looked at him with expectation. "You have more time to be unhappy."

13

✿

"LAURINE!" GENEVIÈVE ECOLLIER'S CHIN JUTTED OUT like a ship's prow. The mug Jean-Rémy had passed her was quivering in Marianne's hands as the waitress reported hurriedly to the kitchen counter.

"Don't stick your bust out like that, child. There'll be lots of strutting roosters in here today. One day you'll let one lead you on board his boat, and next year he won't spare you so much as a glance."

Laurine crossed her arms in front of her chest, and two delicate spots of pink appeared on her cheeks. One of the Parisian yacht owners kept asking her onto his boat for a glass of champagne. She didn't know how she was going to say no after his third invitation, because the man protested that her rejections made him so desperate that he would unfortunately have to go and eat in Rozbras to recover from his grief. And that would be bad for Madame Geneviève, because on the other bank of the Aven was her great rival for the appetites and wallets of the yachtsmen who moored their boats between the two small ports of Kerdruc and Rozbras without ever weighing anchor.

Laurine didn't know how to resolve her dilemma. If she went with them, she would quickly earn herself a reputation; if she didn't, Madame Geneviève and Ar Mor would soon have no customers, because they'd all be sitting in Alain Poitier's restaurant or the *bar tabac* eating mussels in cream sauce.

"Laurine! Stop daydreaming! Today's special is *cotriade*, Breton fish stew. Belon oysters, *moules marinières*, and *noix de Saint-Jacques Ar Mor au naturel*, scallops in a gratin or with cognac sauce. In short, despite his testosterone imbalance, our chef is back to top form. Write it down, girl, or you'll forget again."

Marianne liked Madame Ecollier's voice. It was as full and dark as the coffee Jean-Rémy had made to accompany her small breakfast—a delicious cheese omelet.

Laurine obediently took down her boss's words on her waiter's pad. "What's tes . . . treso . . . tostron imbalance?" she asked.

"A salt addiction," summed up Madame Geneviève, pointing her arrow-slit eyes at Jean-Rémy. "It would be good if you would finally dismiss that lady from your thoughts!"

"Which lady?" Jean-Rémy cautiously enquired.

"The one for whom you empty salt by the packet into the stock!"

"Jean-Rémy is oversalting because of a lady?" asked Laurine.

"He's in love, and when they're in love, cooks overdo it with the salt."

"How about unhappy cooks?"

"They overdo it with the brandy."

"So who is Jean-Rémy in love with?" asked Laurine.

"Now, if that isn't an irrelevant question! *Allez, allez*, get to work, Laurine! Show Madame Marianne the Shell Room in the guesthouse, please."

Geneviève Ecollier flashed Marianne a smile. Yes, maybe this woman who'd washed up here at the end of the world was everything she'd been praying for in recent months. Weren't coincidences sometimes gifts of fate?

Jean-Rémy pushed a white bundle and a sheet of paper toward Marianne, who stared at it. He pointed to a figure in the middle of the page—892 euros; the number next to it appeared to be her working hours, six hours per day excluding Tuesday and Wednesday. Lodgings were included. He explained in simple French that she was hired to work at Ar Mor. And that she was going to have to learn French and he would teach her. Marianne nodded.

She took a look at the bundle. Chef's whites, very similar to the ones she'd worn at housekeeping school. Jean-Rémy's expression was beseeching.

Marianne felt grubby and unkempt in her old clothes. The uniform smelled of soap, and she longed to scrub the past few days from her skin and slip into the fresh whites. That was the only reason she signed her name on the dotted line.

"Great," Jean-Rémy said with relief, and handed her a beret-shaped chef's hat.

Marianne wedged the bundle under her arm and followed Laurine across the small courtyard to the guesthouse. She didn't notice the ginger cat scamper out of the door after her.

JEAN-RÉMY ARRANGED his pickings from the Concarneau fish market and packed the rays, dabs and tunas into polystyrene crates filled with crushed ice. The crabs scrabbled with their little legs. Madame Geneviève checked the bills.

"What would you think if I opened the hotel again, chef?" she asked with deliberate nonchalance.

"Good idea," he replied, "but why are you asking now?"

Geneviève Ecollier let out a loud sigh, then answered quietly, "That woman from the sea, Marianne. You know whom she reminds me of? Of myself. Of me when I'm scared."

Jean-Rémy nodded. Sometimes he saw his own dreams and doubts reflected in the faces of strangers. He set down a plate in front of Geneviève. He had decorated the omelet with red basil in the shape of a heart.

"Golly, Jean-Rémy. Are you trying to tell me something?"

"Indeed I am. *Bon appétit!*"

She ate in silence and then carried the plate into the scullery. "Whatever you say. Just don't ruin my stock again, you hear?"

Stock, and life too: it was so easy to ruin everything.

The young chef tried not to think of Laurine, but it was as hard as if he'd decided not to breathe. Breathe in: Laurine. Breathe out: Laurine. Whenever she was nearby, he couldn't tell a spoon from a knife and completely lost his wits. He was never going to be able to bewitch her as he could other women, gradually enticing them into his bed with addictive little appetizers: a bite of crabmeat in a cream of asparagus sauce here, the world's best *foie gras* on toast there. For Jean-Rémy, a scallop served in its shell with a teaspoonful of velvety cognac and some exquisite whipped cream was more romantic than all the roses in the world. He knew why it was different with Laurine than it had been with every other woman he'd met: he had fallen in love, and his feelings were true and deep and pure. Well, not absolutely pure: of course he wanted to sleep with Laurine. But he mainly wanted to be with her, every day and every night.

It was a mystery to Jean-Rémy how he could have lived side by side with Laurine for two years without ever having kissed her.

14

⚜

LAURINE ESCORTED MARIANNE THROUGH THE GUEST-house. A red carpet wound up the staircase, the walls were covered with fine, light fabric and there was a sea view from every window.

Marianne observed Laurine's graceful movements and understood why some men were magically attracted to a suffering woman, especially when she was grieving over another man. Yes, there was virtually nothing more erotic for certain men than trying to cure a woman of a rival. It was a selfish, masochistic, sadistic enterprise, and it was blind to how lovesickness truly felt.

No man ever wanted to comfort me like that, she thought. On the one hand, that was a shame; on the other, Lothar hadn't even comforted Marianne when a lump had been detected in her breast and it had taken some time to determine whether it was benign or malign. Her fear had scared Lothar, and she wouldn't mention it so as not to worry him. "I want to live, do you understand?" he'd shouted at her. "But this is just dragging me down!"

Shortly afterward, Lothar's lover Sybille had woken her from the wonderful illusion that a marriage, a house at the end of a turning bay and an indoor fountain were all a woman needed.

Lothar had been determined to return to their normal daily routine as soon as possible after his affair with Sybille. "I've told you I'm sorry. What more am I supposed to do?" And with that the matter was closed.

After a few years, her pain had subsided. Time had brought solace to Marianne, as had Lothar's secrecy about his other affairs, at least until it became too hard for him to keep lying. He started to leave a trail of clues in the hope that Marianne would make a scene and deliver him, but she had refused to do him that favor.

THREE STEPS at the end of the third-floor passageway led up to a small landing, from which a door on the right opened into a large white-and-blue-tiled bathroom containing a bath-tub with lion-claw feet and a gold-framed mirror.

Then Laurine opened the last door, which was decorated with a scallop shell. As the door swung open, Marianne blinked in surprise: the June sun was shining directly into her eyes.

Laurine smiled as Marianne stepped into the room, her mouth wide: that was exactly how Laurine felt each time she saw the Shell Room, under the eaves. It was the smallest room in the hotel, but it was also the most beautiful. Polished ship's floorboards, soft, bright rugs, a stained wooden chest at the foot of a double bed, a large round mirror on one wall and a rustic wardrobe in a corner under a painted ceiling. A delicate screen concealed a mirrored dresser with a velvet-covered stool beside it. The cat slunk past the women and jumped onto the bed.

The most beguiling thing about the room, however, was the view stretching out to sea from the high casement window. Marianne had to sit down on the bed for a moment. *A whole room, all to myself?*

Laurine opened the window wide, allowing sunshine to stream in, and then went back downstairs.

Marianne let herself fall onto the bed. It was neither too soft nor too hard, and the sheets were white and cool against her skin. Lying there, she took the tile from her handbag. She placed it on the white-lacquered bedside cupboard so she could gaze back and forth between the painted Kerdruc on the tile and the unpainted, real-life version outside. The artist must have stood exactly here. She couldn't decide which Kerdruc was more charming and bewitching.

She felt as if she had been presented with a gift, though she didn't know why, or whether she should accept it. The cat snuggled into the crook of her arm. It was silent in the guesthouse, but not the morbid silence by which she had often felt threatened at home. This silence was alive.

She recalled the various women she had met up to this point, and how they had tried to explain life to her. They had said a lot when they weren't speaking; it was the silences between their words that had touched Marianne.

I know nothing about love, she thought. I don't know the

highest price one should be prepared to pay for it. Or what men actually think about it—about love or about communication. Lothar had categorically refused to engage in true communication.

She spied a cobweb above the mirrored dresser. She thought of her neighbor Grete Köster and her unrequited love for the local hairdresser. One hot August day twelve years ago, Grete had remarked to Marianne over a glass of sherry they'd allowed themselves in Grete's cellar: "How hypocritical life is! When we were young, we had to keep our legs shut so people didn't think we were 'that kind of girl.' Our husbands got suspicious if we enjoyed ourselves too much, and then all of a sudden, at barely forty, we were too old. Is there a right age for women and what they have down below? I don't want cobwebs to set in!"

Marianne hadn't known how to answer. She'd never looked between her legs and therefore couldn't say much about cobwebs. Lothar hadn't been particularly interested either. "Down below" was uncharted territory, as unexercised as her heart.

MARIANNE STOOD up and went into the bathroom to take a hot shower. Afterward she wound the soft bathrobe around her body, left the room under the eaves and strode barefoot across the guesthouse's dusty carpets.

She counted twenty-five rooms on the three floors, every one with sheets over the furniture. Many beds were four-posters with romantic canopies. Every room had a door leading onto the wooden balcony that ran around the outside of the building. It was a gorgeous hotel that seemed to have been designed for lovers.

A sign in several languages was hanging on the toilet door. "We kindly ask our guests not to throw cigarettes down the toilet."

A large door at the end of a wide hallway led into an old restaurant. Opening it, Marianne suddenly found herself standing across from a painting. The view included men and women on the beach: some of them leaning into the wind, others letting it push them along. She twirled on the spot to study the endless picture. A stout church directly by the sea, and several women harvesting seaweed. She had stepped back into a time before Marianne Lanz existed, a time when her grandmother would still have been a child and had as yet no idea that she would one day meet a man who would bequeath his speckled irises to Marianne; a man whose name her grandmother never revealed. All Marianne knew was that her father's father had borne the same birthmark she did—three flames interlinked to form a Catherine wheel over the heart.

As she was climbing the stairs again, she noticed a concealed door on an intermediate floor. She opened it and peered into a dark room. Only gradually did silhouettes emerge. Dresses: summer dresses, evening dresses, dresses a woman wore when she was going to meet a man. Each dress a memory of the evenings it had been worn—in love, in discord, in pleasure. Now they hung in an ebony chest. Marianne started as she sniffed the sleeve of a magnificent red dress. It was freshly washed.

She continued on her way upstairs and perched restlessly on the bed, gazing around the room. She wished she had been a woman who could live alone and console herself when the lumps in her life—and her breast—got the better of her. But she hadn't been such a woman. Kerdruc had lifted her spirits, but she knew it was temporary. Tomorrow she would continue with her plan. The impulse remained deep within her.

A *whole room to myself.* But just for one night, just one. For one night she would see what it was like to be a woman who had a room all to herself.

She put on the chef's uniform and hesitantly placed the white hat on her head. She was only a little anxious about cooking at Ar Mor. She and the kitchen were roughly the same age: they would get on well.

15

JEAN-RÉMY WAS STANDING AT THE STOVE IN AR MOR'S kitchens, his injured hand hooked into the waistband of his jeans. He passed Marianne a bowl of milky coffee and a croissant, and she followed his lead, dunking the pastry while bending over the bowl and paying no attention to any crumbs that fell into the coffee. The radio was playing songs that she had heard spilling from passing cars back in the seventies— "Born to Be Wild," "These Boots Are Made for Walking"— and Jean-Rémy was wiggling his hips as he washed vegetables at great speed despite his injured hand.

Marianne had never seen a man dance like this before. She hoped he wouldn't ask her to join in.

"I've thought of a trick to teach you vocabulary, Madame Marianne," Jean-Rémy announced as he shimmied back and forth. "You have to learn the French and Breton words for all the . . . *trucs*."

"*Troocks?*"

"*Oui, les trucs.* This is a *truc* and so is that," he said, indicating the table, the knife, a head of lettuce. Everything was a *troock*.

"A thing?"

Jean-Rémy nodded. "Yes." He pointed to an unused order pad and made a scribbling gesture. Marianne grabbed a pen and began to tear off the perforated sheets as she followed him around the kitchen.

Jean-Rémy called out words to her, and she wrote them down exactly as she heard them: *freego, fennetrr, table*. At the end of their tour, she stuck the notes on all the *troocks* until the whole kitchen was plastered with slips of orange paper. Then they dealt with the larder and the fish.

Jean-Rémy switched to Breton. He loved this guttural language, which sounded very similar to Gaelic. *Kig*—meat. *Piz bihan*—peas. *Brezel*—mackerel. *Konikl*—rabbit. *Triñschin*—sorrel. *Tomm-tomm*—careful, red-hot! Marianne wrote and wrote; Jean-Rémy smiled. His thoughts turned less often to Laurine now that he was so busy with Marianne.

She had a hunger inside her, he thought. Everything fell into her as if into a deep lake. She wanted to touch and smell everything. The way she'd touched the foodstuffs in the larder! She didn't maul them; she lifted them up like delicate flowers to catch their fragrance, and her fingers seemed to delve into their soul. When Jean-Rémy looked at Marianne and her heart-shaped face with its large eyes, he was flooded with light, driving out the emptiness that swamped him with despondency when he thought of his boundless admiration for the young waitress. A sense of optimism coursed through him, and he longed to start making plans.

He had lectured Marianne on the importance of food and its effects on the soul, even though he knew that she barely understood a word. He talked about how he loved to go shopping, and how true gastronomy began with hunting down the freshest, choicest produce. He spent his days off in low season visiting distilleries and mussel farms, or strolling along the Aven and Belon rivers or around the Bay of Morbihan to find patient retired anglers reeling in wild fish. These men still understood the rhythms of Brittany's coastline. They knew that they had to be there at the right time, according to the dictates of moon and tides. High and low tide arrived a little earlier every day—two to four minutes earlier—and so they needed to be as swift and stealthy as foxes to catch the best moment for the fish to bite.

As the first steak orders began to come in, Jean-Rémy beckoned Marianne to his side. "No sear marks in my kitchen! That's the kind of torture housewives and barbecuing husbands inflict on steak. It's barbaric! Watch me. An oval pan. A little *amann*—butter. Medium heat, not too much *tomm-tomm*. That way, the butter stays close to the steak instead of spreading out, messing around with the shallots and getting burnt. Do you understand?"

Marianne watched him with fascination. He didn't wear the meat out; he caressed it. Soon he lifted the steak out of the pan onto a hot plate and pushed it under a three-level grill set to eighty degrees. He left it there to cook a little longer and then gave it another minute on the warm plate before arranging the trimmings around it. "*Voilà!* Any other way of cooking and the steak curls up and dies. So if all you've ever done until now is toss meat onto the grill, forget it. Try it even once, and I'll kill you." He drew his hand across his throat like a blade. Marianne blushed.

He fetched a chopping board with squid tentacles on it and

set it down among the shadows near the doorway. Seconds later, the orange-white cat emerged from its hiding place near the herbs. It waggled its backside in the sun as it gnawed away at this little delicacy.

Next, Jean-Rémy tossed the eight kilos of mushrooms that Marianne had washed into a deep pan of boiling water. He planned to reduce them until all that remained was half a liter of concentrated stock. A teaspoonful of this in a sauce was one of the little secrets that gave his food so much more flavor than other chefs'.

By now, Madame Geneviève and Laurine were constantly rushing into the kitchen and slapping order slips down on the counter. The young chef barked one-syllable instructions— "*Non*," "*Ja*," "*Tomm-tomm!*"—and then pointed to an aquarium containing lobsters and crabs.

"Choose a crab, Marianne," he called, gesturing at the lobsters and crabs staring back with their long-stalked eyes. He pointed to one of the cooking pots and to the clock. "Put it in the fish stock, for fifteen minutes."

"Put the poor thing in boiling water? But—"

"*Allez*, get a move on!"

"I'd rather not."

Jean-Rémy impatiently grabbed a crab from the aquarium. As he was about to drop it into the seething water, the hot steam caused him to jerk his arm back.

Marianne said, "Jean-Rémy, please don't. Not like that." Her tone was beseeching. They stared each other in the eye, and he flinched first.

She took a deep breath, carefully picked up the crab and set it down on the polished steel table. It scrambled around a bit as she searched among the bottles on the sideboard before reaching for the cider vinegar and pouring a few drops into the creature's mouth. The clatter of its pincers on the steel surface grew fainter before suddenly ceasing altogether.

"This may sound odd, but you can kill animals humanely too," Marianne explained to Jean-Rémy, who was still standing in the center of the kitchen with raised hands and a disbelieving expression on his face. "Vinegar sends them to sleep, you know." She cupped her hands to her cheeks, cocked her head and closed her eyes, then lowered the crab into the boiling water. "It's bathtime. See, it doesn't hurt so much."

Jean-Rémy noticed that the crab didn't recoil from the hot steam as the others who had accomplished this final passage had done.

Under Jean-Rémy's guidance, Marianne cut up the crab and prepared a sauce of onions, garlic, butter, sour cream and herbs, which he then flambéed with a little Calvados and deglazed with a splash of Muscadet. He tried a bit of claw meat: something was different. A tiny difference. It tasted of the sea. Marianne's little vinegar ploy had returned the taste of the sea to the crab.

"Nice trick, savior of sea creatures!" said Jean-Rémy. "Right, now let's get on with everything else, or there'll be a riot out there."

After an hour, Marianne felt as if she'd spent her whole life moving around a Breton kitchen among hissing gas flames and bright, shiny pots and pans. When the rush was over, Jean-Rémy poured some Muscadet into a couple of water glasses, cut up a lobster and waved to Marianne to take a dinner break with him on the sun-bathed doorstep in the backyard. The sun was dancing with the leaves of the trees, and the air was thick with the scent of rosemary and lavender.

"You're a good cook," Jean-Rémy remarked and raised his glass. "*Yar-mat.*"

Marianne had hardly ever drunk wine in the daytime, let alone eaten lobster. She observed Jean-Rémy out of the corner of her eye, and when he unashamedly used his fingers, she followed his example. For one delicious moment, life felt better than ever before.

JEAN-RÉMY HAD given her an advance on her wages at the end of her shift. The restaurant was closed the next day. Marianne had gone upstairs to the Shell Room and taken a bath, enjoying the weariness that suffused her body. The cat had sat on the side of the bathtub and licked itself clean. Now Marianne was lying on her bed, gazing at the banknotes she'd propped up against the tile. Her very own money.

She turned over onto her back and realized that she was squashed up against the left-hand edge of the bed, as if Lothar's body still occupied most of the space. She inched over into the middle and slowly spread her arms.

The cat made a daring leap and settled down between her calves. He needs a name, thought Marianne as she stroked him gently. But . . . if she gave him a name today, nobody would call him by it after tomorrow. For tomorrow she planned to say goodbye.

She got up again. She wanted to get a glimpse of Kerdruc at dusk. She switched off the light and opened one side of the window. All she could hear was the gurgling of the river, the soft slapping of the steel cables against the ships' masts, and the chirping of the crickets. At first the colors appeared to intensify, as if they were blossoming once more in the bluish twilight, but then they began to fade and dissolve into countless shadows.

A silhouette was moving toward the breakwater, and Marianne stepped back from the window as if she'd been caught red-handed. She saw Madame Ecollier stop on the quayside and raise a glass of champagne. Her entire body radiated defiance—defiance and anger. It was like gazing into a living diary.

Madame Ecollier was toasting Rozbras on the other side of the river. It looked neater, more elegant and more expensive on the far bank, like a model village, thought Marianne, her gaze following that of the restaurant owner. Kerdruc was an untidy, weathered relic in comparison.

All of a sudden Marianne had a strong feeling that Madame Ecollier had hidden the dresses because she hated the memories woven into their fabric, yet she couldn't do without them. She watched as the other woman drained her champagne in three quick swigs before hurling the glass far out into the harbor.

Marianne returned to her bed in some confusion, wormed her way into the middle with a barely perceptible smile and fell into a syrupy-sweet sleep within seconds. Her last thought was so fleeting that it barely registered: *It has been a lovely day.*

16

M ARIANNE WOKE BEFORE SUNRISE. SHE COULDN'T
recall ever having enjoyed such a deep and replenish-
ing night's sleep. She had felt so safe and secure. Looking out
of the window, she could smell the sea.

As she pattered past the deserted reception desk, she im-
pulsively took one of the yellowed postcards of the guesthouse
from a stand. They were all postage paid.

She wrote the address of Grete, her friend and neighbor
in Celle, on the fine lines, then paused. She wanted to thank
Grete for having been there for her, for her laughter and feathery slippers and for having sent her postcards from all over
the world when she'd traveled to forget her love for the hairdresser. Marianne had loved being let in on her adventures.

The hairdresser was married and had returned home to his
wife every night of the twenty years he had slept with Grete.
When his wife died, he followed her two weeks later, leaving
Grete seriously put out. "He had such a guilty conscience that
he even snuck off into the grave after her!"

"Thank you for everything. And for being who you are,"
wrote Marianne, then slipped the card into her coat pocket.

She found the sign for the coastal path on the left a hundred yards along the village's main street. Next to the sign was a postbox into which she dropped the card. She was certain that this would be her last sign of life to her hometown.

Four miles to Port Manec'h, where the Belon and the Aven flowed together into the Atlantic; twelve thousand paces and it would all be over.

Marianne passed an old thatched granite cottage with stooping eaves, a house as old as hope, before the narrow footpath peeled away from Kerdruc and led off into the dim woods. Trees like cathedral buttresses and walls overgrown with grass and ivy arched over the slender path. The fragrance of the woods blended with the peculiar aroma of seaweed, salt and spray.

A wood that smells of the sea.

The path narrowed, and lichen and muddy puddles grappled with the tight bends. On the far side of a hollow, Marianne came upon the first branch of the Aven. A trickle divided the loamy riverbed in two, and the footpath wiggled its way up a rise past towering, lichen-covered rocks. It was like being in the rain forest, with only sky, trees, water, earth and the blaze of the rising sun above her head.

She breathed in, breathed out. She screamed. She seemed to have no control over how long her scream lasted. She screamed breathing out and breathing in. The cry pulverized her entire life into fragments, and she screamed and spat them all out. Her soul spewed up pain.

Walking on, she felt as if something had jumped off her back, something that had dug its sharp claws into her skin. It was fear. Fear had jumped off, an ugly, red-eyed beast that was now scuttling through the undergrowth to look for someone else's back to possess. She heard a rustling and a cracking in the depths behind the green wall.

I never even noticed that I am alive, she thought.

High tide was driving new, salty water into the side channels of the river, and the scent of the wood was changing.

Her movements split the passing time, and Marianne no longer felt like a stranger in this place: it was as if she had merged with it and dissolved the unruly borders between man and matter. Moisture had gathered in the small of her back. She could sense her body more than ever before, could feel her muscles twitching with the unfamiliar exertion and wanted more, wanted to move, to walk, to work. And then the fragrance hit her—that singular fragrance!

Far below, under the primeval white cliffs, the sea washed against the shore. Marianne could smell it and hear it. She tasted salt on her lips, and she fell helplessly in love with the sight of the sea with the light dancing on its surface.

She followed the ancient customs path north along the top of the cliffs. She hoped against hope that it would soon lead her down to the water's edge so that she might at last dip her hands into this endless, scented expanse.

MARIANNE SANG to the beat of the waves slapping against the shore behind her—a narrow, terraced white beach under cliffs hemmed with sedge grass, bilberries, wildflowers and broom. She walked toward the sea, singing "Hijo de la Luna" as she went, one of the most beautiful songs she knew, full of longing and pain. In it a young gypsy woman begs the moon for a husband, but the moon demands her firstborn in return. The woman finds her beloved and the child is born. Its skin is light and its eyes gray. The gypsy man believes it to be another man's and stabs his wife to death, then abandons the child on a mountaintop. As it wails, the moon wanes to a slim crescent that could serve the child as a cradle. People criticize the mother and the moon: a woman who gives up her unborn child to get a husband doesn't merit a child's love, and the moon has no right to be a mother, for what can it do with a creature of flesh and blood? *What did you want with the child, moon?* Yet no one criticizes the man who kills his wife out of vanity, fear and foolish pride.

And it's always the same story, thought Marianne, lifting the hem of her dress a little higher. No one accuses men of anything; it is the woman who bears the blame if he doesn't love her, if she's too weak to leave or if she has a child but no wedding ring. We are the sex that blames itself. Lothar killed love and life, and I never managed to accuse him of anything! What did you want with my love? Tell me! What did you want with it?

She was awash with feelings and thoughts that kept rising to her lips but no further. Why had she never been bold enough to be candid with her husband, to demand of him, "Know my body! Respect my heart!?"

She railed at her own cowardice then fell silent. She could hear nothing but the roar of the sea. She ventured another two steps into the water, which was now up to her thighs. She walked farther into the painful, cold waves until they washed about her stomach and splashed her face with brine. The sea was a living organism, its surf like boiling milk. Watery claws snatched at her.

"It's all over for me," she whispered.

Another step. The claws clutched harder. She felt her blood pounding, her breathing, the wind snagging in her hair and the sun warming her skin. She thought of the Shell Room, and of the cat between her calves; she thought of Jean-Rémy.

So today was to be the last day on which she would see and feel the sea, just as the sight of the endless horizon was inspiring an unfamiliar feeling of boundlessness within her. This was the last time she would hear her own voice, but it had to be done.

Who said so? Salty spray spattered her face. Yes, who said so? Was she not free to do or not do whatever she pleased? She could do it right now! She had the power to decide at any moment that it was over.

She spun around to take in the rugged beauty of the coastline.

Tomorrow.

She turned and waded back to the shore.

Tomorrow.

17

Y ANN GAMÉ LIKED WATCHING PASCALE GOICHON, probably because they were both artists who regarded their work not as work but as a passion. Pascale's hands had a way of shaping clay that was only bettered, if at all, by her gardening or her cooking. When she could remember a recipe, that was.

Pascale was a woman who lived her life to the full, and sometimes the painter could barely stand to watch his old friend losing her memory. Her husband Emile and Yann had known each other since the evening almost fifty years ago when Emile and Pascale had fallen in love.

Yann stroked Merline, the snow-white retriever. She'd been the first dog Pascale had taken into her home, followed by a growing number of stray dogs and cats, which now populated the plot of land. From his seat on the terrace, he watched Madame Pompadour chase a bumblebee. Pascale had named the dogs after royal mistresses, even the males. The cats all had names inspired by fruit and vegetables. Mirabelle and Petit Choux—Little Cabbage—had made themselves comfortable in the sun by his feet.

"My muse? You're asking me if Emile's my muse?" Pascale repeated. The freckles under her bangs—formerly ginger, now milky white—seemed to be mocking Yann. "I work with emotions."

Her sculptures often showed a couple reaching out to each other, but only rarely was their passion fulfilled in an embrace. Often only fractions of an inch separated the figures as they implored each other for a kiss, forever frozen in yearning.

"Are Emile and his leg in good working order?" asked Yann. It was mad: Emile, a bear of a man, whose brain was gradually divorcing from his body. First his foot had started to twitch, then his leg. The whole of his left side would tremble and obey its own rules if he forgot to take his medicine.

"Are your tiles in good order?" Pascale asked in return.

"Yeah, everything in good order," Yann lied. Everything in good order, everything as always. He gave painting lessons to less able artists, visited Pascale and Emile twice a week, ate at Ar Mor on Mondays, painted tiles and composed mosaics for the rest of the week and otherwise waited for summer to shade into autumn.

"Order will be the death of us," commented Pascale. "So, what's wrong?"

He should have known that he wouldn't get off so lightly. He removed his glasses so that he didn't have to look at Pascale. It was hard for him to admit what was making him more and more desperate with each passing day.

"Art has always been everything to me, Pascale. And now I'm sixty I've realized it's not enough. My life is empty. An empty canvas."

"Oh get down from your cross; we need the timber. And

what do you mean by art, Yann Gamé? Art is a muscle that needs exercise. It doesn't care if it paints tiles, forms funny little people"—Pascale pointed to the clay sculpture in front of her—"or reels off lines of words. Art just *is*."

She made a gesture that combined rolling her eyes, shrugging her shoulders and pointing out at the countryside and the world, all in one. "It *is*, that's it. The question is how you *feel*. Do you feel lonely? I'll tell you something, Yann Gamé: what's missing in your life is love. Can you remember love? The feeling that makes people do stupid things or become heroes? No art in the whole world will ever love you back. You put everything you've got into art, but it gives you nothing back. Nothing at all."

Yann loved Pascale for those thirty seconds, for that speech. It was possible that Pascale might tune out of the conversation at any moment and ask Yann who the hell he was. Then she would shuffle into the kitchen and recognize nothing—not the table as a table, the sugar as sugar, or her husband as her husband.

Art. Love. Yann didn't consider himself an artist. He was an artisan, a craftsman. The little bit of "art" in "artisan" was enough for him. But what about love? Love was like a giant canvas—he didn't know how to fill it; he had no picture of this feeling inside him. It was the missing element.

He thought of how Colette Rohan was always trying to persuade him to paint larger pictures. Or merely pictures, not just tiles. The gallery owner had compared him with Gauguin, Sérusier and Pierre de Belay, and eventually convinced him to paint women—naked women.

Naked women in Pont-Aven? God, this was the provinces, not Paris!

"Colette Rohan wants orgies," he said, sighing. "Big pictures with big naked women in them."

Pascale gave a snort. "It's Colette's business if she sees bigger things in you. But who knows, maybe one of your tiny tiles has made someone's life a big thing."

"You honestly believe that?"

"It's nice to imagine," she said, smiling dreamily at him. "Will you promise me something, Yann?"

"No," said the painter. "I don't like promises. Tell me what I can do for you, and a yes will have to suffice."

"Will you fall in love again?"

Merline, who had so far lain quietly by Yann's feet, yelped and jumped up. He had pinched the dog's ear.

"Yes or no?"

"I can't promise I'm going to fall in love!"

"Why not, you shortsighted Breton twit! Falling in love is the best thing that could happen to you. Food will taste better, the world will be more beautiful and you'll finish your paintings quicker. Don't be such a coward. Fall in love! Open your eyes, open your heart, stop being so damned shy and reclusive, and start behaving like an idiot!"

"Why should I be an idiot all of a sudden?"

"The more willing you are to act like an idiot, the sooner you'll fall in love. Do it! Otherwise you'll grow old on your own and die earlier than you'd like."

Yes, Pascale, queen of passion. Yann knew full well that she had driven dozens of men crazy in her youth. As an air stewardess she had met men from all over the world. Yann was happier for those men than he was for his friend Emile. They'd surely got to know one of the most exciting women of their lives, but Pascale loved only Emile. The ways of love were sometimes strange.

Love—a feeling that swells in the face of death. It finishes and you're cold turkey, amputated of your head and your heart.

Yann had spent until his thirtieth birthday getting over his first great love. Thinking of Renée hurt a little less each year, and it took him a long time until he could finally feel angry about her affairs, which for her were as natural and necessary as breathing. He then began to forgive himself for loving her.

But did that other love really exist—the everlasting, golden, everyday love? *Toujours l'amour* was the term used for red wines of which you didn't expect much. Damn, thought the painter, I miss love, being loved, a face looking at me and smiling simply because I'm there, a hand searching for mine in sleep. Someone with whom I am fully me. Someone whose face I'd like to be the last thing I see before I go to sleep forever. Someone who's my home.

"All right then," he said after a while. He put his glasses back on. Yann Gamé felt like painting something he hadn't yet seen—the face of a woman who loved him. He couldn't imagine what this woman might look like who was silly enough to fall in love with a shortsighted painter.

When he glanced up, Pascale was studying him anxiously, obviously confused. "Who the hell are you?" she asked.

"I'm painting you," he answered, trying to find some cheerful words to conceal the pain her confusion caused him.

"That's right, *mon coeur*, Monsieur Gamé is painting your portrait," said Emile. He had just got back from shopping, a task that exhausted him now that Monsieur Parkinson had moved in and the three of them lived with Madame Dementia under one roof.

Pascale began to weep. "Madame Bouvet the housekeeper keeps shouting at me because I get everything mixed up."

Emile brushed some strands of hair into place behind his wife's ear. She was over seventy, but she looked younger every day. Her face was that of a young girl and her eyes were clear, the color of water. One couldn't tell that those eyes sometimes saw the world differently from how it was in reality. Right now they were looking back to their sixth housekeeper, who had been utterly overwhelmed by Pascale's symptoms and mood swings. Tomorrow Madame Roche would arrive: number seven. Emile hoped she was made of sterner stuff.

"Do you like me?" Pascale asked her husband.

Emile sat down beside her, took her hand and nodded. "I love you."

Pascale looked at him with momentary surprise. "Oh! Does Papa know?"

Emile nodded again.

"I don't think much of women who shout," Pascale declared, and braced her hand on Emile's knee to lever herself into a standing position. When she entered the kitchen and caught sight of the baskets of shopping, her hand flew to her forehead like a startled bird.

"I must tidy up!" she said to the two men. She reached for the straw hat hanging next to the fridge, then walked over to the tap, held the hat under the running water and began to use it to wipe the stains from the windowpanes. Emile hobbled toward her and laid his hand on her bare arm.

"*Mon coeur,*" he whispered, lacking the strength to say anything else.

Pascale turned to face him. "Oh yes," she said, beaming, "how silly of me," and put the hat on her head. Water streamed down her temples and cheeks as she picked up the sponge and rubbed the window with it while humming the "Ode to Joy."

Yann glanced at Emile, who shrugged and joined in with Pascale's humming. The couple began to dance slowly around the kitchen.

Yes, it did exist, this everyday love, *toujours l'amour,* and it took the sting out of pain.

18

☙

HER DOOMSDAY DIDN'T COME THE NEXT DAY OR THE day after that. For the past eleven days Marianne had woken shortly before sunrise and set off through the misty woods to die in the sea. But each day she grew stronger, shedding her world-weariness. The sun began to tan her skin, and the sea made her eyes brighter. Her knee seldom hurt her now.

Every morning she walked barefoot into the foaming waves, but the urge to surrender to them was always washed away by a defiance she couldn't fathom. Once it was the pumpernickel she was desperate to bake for Jean-Rémy during one of their evening French lessons. Another time she had promised to go with him to the organic market in Trégunc. Then there was one of the weekly Wednesday concerts that Laurine wanted to take her to on their evening off. And if she was already there, she might as well take a look at the island off Raguenez, at the northern end of Tahiti Beach, which one could reach on foot at low tide. This was where the two lovers in Benoîte Groult's novel *Salt on our Skin* had first slept with each other.

"I need a word with you," Marianne said to Jean-Rémy on the twelfth day. He was tying up dough in linen bags, which

he tossed into the simmering *kig ha farz* casserole, a traditional dish whose ingredients were pancakes, oxtail, flank of
beef, cured pork, savoy cabbage and celeriac.

Marianne pushed the cauliflower florets to one side; the
kaolenn-fleur came from a field directly by the coast. She
started reading from the small order pad she used as an exercise book.

"This silliness. With you and Laurine. Stop it. Send her
flowers every day. Be a man, not a . . . *triñschin* . . . an, umm,
cabbage-head!"

"Not sorrel?!" Jean-Rémy said with irritation before spell-
ing out Marianne's tasks to her. "First, mix the pig's blood with
flour, sugar, raisins, salt, pepper and a little chocolate. Paul's
twins are celebrating their birthday tomorrow and they've ordered *silzig*—blood sausage."

Marianne collected herself. "Jean-Rémy. I was talking
about Laurine!"

"Second, clean the *morgazen*—the squid. Remove the skin,
the spikes, the beak and the suckers."

At a sign from Jean-Rémy Marianne passed him a bowl
filled with bottle corks, which he poured into the pot with the
washed calamari tubes. The corks were intended to neutralize
the proteins that made the calamari so chewy, and render the
white flesh exquisitely tender.

"How about flowers?" Marianne continued to beseech him.

"The potatoes need peeling too!"

"Write her a love letter, will you?"

Jean-Rémy fled into the cooler. "Madame, tomorrow is the
first day of the summer holidays, and the next day half of Paris
will have moved to Brittany. The sleepy villages suddenly be-

come frantic beehives, with tourists swarming in and out of this place, hungry for mussels and lobster. We won't have a day off until the end of August. When do you want me to write letters?"

"At night?" Marianne said, then more gently, "You little *triñschin*."

CATCHING MARIANNE'S words, Madame Geneviève smiled to herself behind the bar. She was making an inventory of bottles, polished cutlery, glasses and cruet sets. She thanked every god in Brittany for this woman. Marianne had cleaned the guesthouse and washed and ironed mountains of bedsheets, pillowcases, tablecloths and curtains. The German woman was bringing the guesthouse to life.

Geneviève checked the buttons of her black dress and pulled her hair back until her temples hurt. Fate had done her proud: this Marianne had a heart so big that a supertanker could do a U-turn inside it. The guesthouse owner wished she had that much room in her own heart.

Yes, there had been moments. There had been that one man, that love, laying existence bare in a way that made everything else pale into insignificance, swelling her heart to bursting point and making it big enough to hold the entire world. But then fate had unleashed its fury upon her.

Geneviève sighed and walked out of the restaurant and along the quayside. Gardeners were transplanting seedlings into pots on the terrace and removing the tangled weeds from around the front door of the guesthouse.

Laurine was sweeping Ar Mor's terrace with a broom. "*Mon*

amour, oh, mon amour," she whispered to the broomstick, "*je t'aime,* sleep with me, right here and now." She closed her eyes and began to waltz.

"Laurine!" The startled young woman dropped the broom, which clattered onto the polished planks. Her face went dark red under her bangs. "What's wrong with you? Are you daydreaming?"

"Yes, Madame. I was dreaming that this was my lover and we were naked and he—"

"Silence!" thundered Geneviève.

Laurine picked up the broom and pressed it to her bosom.

"Go home and dream!"

"But there's no one there."

"There's no one here either."

The girl dumbfounded Geneviève. Nature had created her to make legions of men unhappy, and what did she do? She made *herself* unhappy.

Just as Madame Geneviève grabbed the broom from Laurine's hand, an old Renault came coasting down the slope toward the harbor. Geneviève turned pale and clung to the broomstick.

A man got out of the Renault. Tall and wiry, wearing jeans, the sleeves of his white shirt rolled up. He must have been handsome as a young man, and that handsomeness had matured into an expressive, virile, vigorous demeanor.

"Isn't that . . . ?" Laurine blurted out, eyes widening.

"It is. Go into the kitchen. Immediately," Madame Geneviève ordered, and Laurine obeyed her.

"What do you want?" Geneviève Ecollier asked the man, who approached her as tentatively as a wild animal.

"To see where my guests will soon be heading," he said in a voice that thrummed like a D major chord. "It looks as if you're reopening the guesthouse soon."

"Well, now you've seen it. *Kenavo.*"

"Genoveva . . . please." His imploring gaze brought about no change in her impassive face.

Madame Geneviève pressed the broom to her chest and walked back into Ar Mor, her back ramrod-straight and her head held high.

"Genoveva," the man called after her, tenderly, beseechingly.

MARIANNE RETREATED from the corner by the back door. She hadn't intended to eavesdrop, and she hurried to bring the bunch of thyme from the vegetable patch to Jean-Rémy.

"Have you said something nice to Laurine today?" she asked casually. Jean-Rémy handed her a bucket of mussels and signaled to her to remove their beards.

"I told her she's beautiful."

"No you didn't, *triñschin.*"

Jean-Rémy mumbled something unintelligible as he stirred another pan of washed mussels that were bubbling away in a mixture of white wine, butter and shallots.

"There was a man outside. Do you know him?"

"Hmm," Jean-Rémy growled. "Alain Poitier. From the other side. Rozbras. He's our competitor." He tipped the mussels into a large dish, picked out the unopened ones, poured the liquid through a sieve into a smaller pot and dusted the sauce with flour. Marianne passed him the saffron, the cream and the sour cream, and he added them to the mussel stock before boiling it down.

She reflected on what she had just seen. *Nothing is colder than a heart that once blazed.*

Alain Poitier wasn't merely a competitor, she thought. He was also the man who had shaped Geneviève's experience in such a way that her face only betrayed emotion at night and never in front of anyone.

Marianne wondered what kind of expression she herself might have had, how her body language might have changed, had she succeeded in making her husband love her, respect her or give her a flower, just one flower, once.

19

A FEW WEEKS LATER, ON HER MORNING WALK ALONG
the seafront, Marianne recited every word for "gray" that
she had so far learned. Sad, holes-in-the-laughter, plain, rooty:
the Bretons had hundreds of names for the gray shades of sky
and water. Their country made you want to keep on walking
until you'd forgotten what time it was and where your car was
parked, and you eventually forgot your old life and never went
back to it.

Marianne couldn't get enough of exploring Finistère's foot-
paths, hiking through its dense woods, along its beaches and
through wildflower meadows on the edge of pink cliffs. The
roads were narrow and winding and the granite houses old
and storm-beaten, their windows generally pointing inland.
As she passed the hamlet of Kerambail shortly before Kerdruc, she saw a menhir rearing up from a field of ripe golden
wheat, the stalks undulating around it like waves in the blus-
tery westerly wind. She remembered what Paul had told her
about these enchanted man-sized standing stones: at the first
stroke of the clock at midnight on Christmas Eve, the menhirs

would glide toward the coast to drink from the sea. In the dips they had deserted lay hidden treasures, and one had to remove them quickly to avoid being buried under the stone when the clock struck twelve.

Marianne heard a shot as she was approaching Kerdruc through the woods. It rang briefly in her ears before giving way to a deathly silence.

WHEN EMILE Goichon, Pascale's husband, heard the sharp crack in the kitchen, he knew that he had lost yet another housekeeper. He took the last match from the box, scraped it across the rough surface and raised it with a trembling hand to the Breton brandy. The library door slammed against the shelf containing Montesquieu's complete works. The match fizzled out.

"Outrageous! That woman tried to shoot me!" shouted the new housekeeper.

"That was my last match."

"And all I did, monsieur, was make plum pudding and say to her, 'Could you please pass me the cinnamon, Madame Pascale?' And what does she do? She tries to gun me down like a stray dog!"

"How am I supposed to drink this brandy?"

"How can you put up with all these tangle-haired, flea-ridden animals, monsieur, these three-legged mongrels and one-eyed cats. They eat off your best china plates. It's disgusting!"

"Do you have a match, Madame Roche?" he asked, staring at the source of these loud vociferations. A *young woman's beauty makes up for her lack of intelligence; an old woman's intelligence makes up for her lack of beauty.* But in Madame Roche, nothing made up for anything.

"This house is a den of iniquity! A den of iniquity, I say!"

"Piety is a sign that a person will do anything to be important in the world," Emile remarked, at which Madame Roche's mouth snapped shut like a mousetrap. Not a drop of warmth clouded her sharp brown eyes.

"I quit!" she blurted out.

"Bon courage, Madame! May God go with you. Greet him from us and tell him that he may stop by whenever he likes."

Emile waited until he heard the heavy oak front door click shut and the sound of the sharp, quick footsteps on the gravel die away. Then he pushed himself up from the old leather armchair and hobbled down the long corridor and past the fireplace in the living room. He spotted the shattered dish of cream on the sideboard, and next to it the sugar tin with a pistol handle poking out of it. He found the telephone in the bread bin, the bread in the laundry cupboard and a tidy pile of towels in the fridge, but he couldn't find any matches.

Pascale was sitting in the larder, rocking back and forth with her legs drawn up to her chest. Emile sat down awkwardly beside her on the cold stone floor. He had known Pascale for his whole life. He had seen her in her prime, during her golden age of strength and beauty, and had enjoyed every stage. He knew every woman she'd ever been.

He thought of the sharp knife in the kitchen. He wasn't going to cut the gas supply to the stove and he didn't lock the front door either. He wouldn't humiliate Pascale by protecting her from life and death.

Death was a strange thing. Emile had always hoped that he would one day be so fed up with life that the thought of Ankou—the end to which all paths led—would weigh less heavily upon him. But no, he wanted more than ever to live! He was irritated by signs of his decline: the biting drafts of the house in the woods, his diminishing strength, the Parkinson's. Such wicked twists of fate! No sooner has the mind reached maturity than the flesh begins to wither.

He kissed his wife behind the ear, the way she liked it. She giggled. He struggled to his feet and went off to look for a Maria Callas record. Her voice was one of the few things capable of getting through to Pascale when she withdrew so deep inside herself.

SHOCK HAD stopped Marianne dead in her tracks. A furious woman came striding along the path toward her, muttering sullenly and angrily to herself. She didn't deign to look at Marianne.

Now she heard strains of opera coming from the woods and walked hesitantly in its direction. After crossing a clearing, she reached a beautiful property surrounded by towering deciduous trees with a vine-covered flagstoned terrace and rounded windows. However, wherever she looked in the overgrown vegetable patch, the lettuces had run to seed and the rosebushes were choked with weeds.

Then she noticed hordes of cats climbing trees or lounging in the cool shade, and dogs sprawling in a corner of the gravel drive. She walked around the outside of the house as Maria Callas's voice spiraled into the heights.

"Hello? Anyone there?" she called over the aria.

A woman came toward her. She was carrying a tray with small plates on it.

"*Guten Tag,* I am your steward on this Lufthansa flight from Rome to Frankfurt," the stranger said to Marianne with a smile. "Please fasten your seat belt and keep it fastened throughout today's flight." She set down the plates of lobster tartar before the lounging cats, as if she were handing out drinks thirty thousand feet up in the sky.

The woman had spoken German! How long had it been since Marianne had last heard someone speak her language?

"How . . . how long is our flight?" she asked, also in German.

Pascale Goichon gave her a smile that immediately faded.

"I've no idea," she said unhappily. "I have to tell you that I've grown a little forgetful." Joy and grief tussled briefly on her face, with neither scoring a decisive victory. She turned away and began to reel off the names of the cats as she set down little plates in front of their noses. Petit Choux. Framboise. She leaned toward Marianne, as if about to confide in her. "They're the souls of the dead and of witches. Or of living people who felt lonely and sent out their cat soul to search for a home."

Marianne followed the woman into the kitchen, where she picked up the next tray. Marianne guessed that this was breakfast for the dogs she had seen. She took the heavy tray from the woman's hands and followed her outside.

Pascale stroked a greyhound. "Madame Pompadour. She founded a theater and a china factory, which is why her dinner is served on Sèvres porcelain. Do you understand?"

"Of course."

"Official mistresses," Pascale lectured as she fed the dogs, "were the rulers of kings. They decided more questions of state with their vaginas than historians would care to admit."

"Oh," said Marianne, feeling herself blush.

A strawberry-blond poodle with a cauliflower ear came strutting toward her. "Anne of Brittany. Our queen. She married the king of the Franks in order to protect her lands from him. She created the House of Princesses with nine courtesans and forty noble maidens. A state brothel."

Pascale gave the poodle's tummy a proud tickle, then introduced the other mistresses to Marianne: Madame du Barry; Julia and Vannozza, the mistresses of Pope Alexander VI; Lady Jane Stewart. Lastly, she pointed to a dachshund with perky ears and a jaunty tail. "Julie Récamier, who gave her name to the *récamière* chaise longue. It was her friend, Baroness de Staël-Holstein, who called Germany 'a land of poets and pinschers.'"

"Poets and *thinkers*," Marianne corrected her.

"Oh, same difference," answered Pascale. "And who might you be?"

"I'm Marianne Lanz."

"Aha, Madame Lance. My name is Pascale."

"What's going on in your garden, Pascale?"

"What do you mean?"

"I never had a garden like *this*."

"What *did* you have?"

"A lawn."

"A lawn? What kind of a flower is that?"

Marianne realized that this approach wouldn't get her very far. "Do you have anyone . . . living here with you?"

Pascale thought for a while. "I don't know," she said sadly. "All I know is that I don't tick properly anymore. But you know, Marianne . . . the worst thing is knowing and being unable to do anything about it. It just happens: one moment I'm here, and then everything's gone." She reached for Marianne's hand. "In America, people confiscate their stupid grandma's passport, cut the labels out of her clothes, drive her to the next state but one and leave her there. Granny-dumping, it's called. Not very kind, is it?"

Marianne shook her head. Although she knew Pascale was exaggerating, the thought made her shudder.

EMILE WATCHED from the terrace with crossed arms as the two women roamed through the garden. He had the feeling that the woman he recognized as Ar Mor's new cook would not be put off by his crazy wife. Who knows, maybe she was crazy too. Crazy people had it easy in Brittany: it was ordinary people who found it tough. Still, she wasn't from Brittany; she wasn't even French! And as with most older Frenchmen, he didn't take too fondly to Germans.

Emile hobbled into the house and returned with a jug of *chouchen*, a form of mead, and some glasses, along with a baguette, ham and cheese. Pascale was often oblivious to hunger and thirst, and Emile had to remind her to eat and drink— and then stop again.

Having devoured the baguette, Pascale fell asleep on the

lounger on the terrace with one of the cats warming her stomach. Emile covered his wife with a blanket and set a straw hat on her head to make sure that the sun wouldn't burn her face.

He didn't offer Marianne a glass of water or anything to eat. He didn't address a single word to her, even when Marianne took her leave with a quick *"Kenavo!"*

20

❦

OCÉANE AND LYSETTE'S BIRTHDAY PARTY LOOKED AT first as if it was going to be a disaster. A dozen five-year-old girls had swept through Ar Mor like a storm, stuffed themselves with cocktail sausages and continually demanded that Paul play with them. How was an old grandad like him meant to play with little sprites like these? That was until Marianne had somehow lured the screeching little princesses out onto the quayside to play blindman's buff and run egg-and-spoon and sack races. Paul burst out laughing when he recalled Jean-Rémy's kitchen fairy appearing with a bundle of flour sacks in one hand and a bouquet of spoons in the other. The girls had been enchanted, and Paul had been left alone to eat his plate of scallops with cider apples.

Now back at their mother's house, and with their birthday coming to an end, all that remained was to persuade the twins to go to bed.

"*Kement-man oa d'ann amzer,*" Paul began. "Back in the days when hens still had teeth, there was a brave little boy called Morvan. He lived very close to here and his fondest wish was to become a knight. When he was ten years old—"

"I don't want to hear that story about Morvan. It's so stupid," said Lysette.

Océane nodded. "Nor do I."

"Do you always want the same as your sister?" asked Paul.

Océane sounded as if she had a whole bag of marbles in her mouth as she said, "Of course I do, Nono!"

The three of them had made themselves comfortable on the old swing chair with the torn blue awning. Lysette was kneeling to his left, scrutinizing intently the hairs protruding from Paul's ears, while Océane was curled up to his right, resting her little head with its loose light-brown plaits against his upper arm, with her bent index finger, rather than her thumb, in her mouth.

"You don't want to hear the tale of Morvan Leiz-Breiz, who led our beloved Brittany to independence?"

"No, Nono," said Lysette and Océane in unison.

"All right then. How about the mischievous tricks of Bilz, the merry robber from Plouanet?"

"Stupid!" chanted Océane.

"Yeah!" said Lysette.

"Princess Goldilocks, Prince Cado and the Magic Ring?"

"Bor-ing."

"I can't believe you don't want to hear all our wonderful Breton stories again."

"We've had enough of them, Nono," said Lysette, tugging at Paul's ear hairs. The ex-legionnaire kept completely still as the five-year-old prodded his head.

"What *do* you want then?" he asked.

"The tale of Ys," Océane decided.

"The one about Dahut, princess of the sea."

"And the golden key."

"And how the underwater city was lost."

Dahut—the twins had fallen in love with her. Paul had told them the story of the sunken city of Kêr Is in Douarnenez Bay many times before, but had always tried to leave out the salacious details about the fairy Dahut—especially her habit of receiving a new lover every night.

He started all over again. "It was back in the days when the Romans began to build roads through Armorica. One of these Roman roads still leads from Carhaix to Douarnenez Bay. But there it disappears into the sea. It used to lead to the world's greatest, most beautiful city, called Ys, known to some as Atlantis."

"But maybe the Romans just wanted to collect fish directly from the beach?" whispered Océane quietly.

"And what if they didn't?" Paul whispered back even more quietly. Océane nodded breathlessly.

"The wise and powerful King Gradlon had built Kêr Is, the city in the deep, for his beloved daughter Dahut. Princess Dahut was the daughter of a fairy whom the king had once loved deeply. She ruled over water and fire. Dahut was not baptized, as she would have lost her fairy powers."

"Like us! We haven't been baptized either!" cried Lysette.

Oh dear, oh dear, thought Paul.

"The city was protected from the sea and the tides by a system of dykes and iron gates. King Gradlon alone had the golden key to the sluice gates and he wore it continually around his neck so that no one might open the gates by night and let in the tides. The city's cathedrals and golden houses, glittering silver towers and diamond-encrusted rooftops were visible from far inland. Every inhabitant lived like a king, and the children never had to go to school."

Paul gave a very free rendition of the rest of the story of Ys, but there was one part he simply could not leave out. One night Dahut stole the golden key from the chain around her father's neck to let her lover into the city, and it was this dullard who was responsible for the flood, having opened the doors at an unfortunate moment.

"King Gradlon leaped through the waves on his horse and was heaving Dahut onto the saddle behind him when the sea claimed its tribute by pulling her back beneath the surface."

"Aargh, that's so mean," said Lysette.

"Yeah!" added Océane.

"Are you going to make us a *krampouezh* now, Nono? With Nutella?"

"Name it and you may have it, my little sprites." These two were the only women to whom he would give anything. Anything, even pancakes until they were fit to burst.

"I hate it when you tell the children stories like that. You know you're not allowed to speak Breton to them!" said a voice from inside the house.

Paul closed his eyes.

Nolwenn signaled to the twins to go up and get ready for bed. She tossed Paul his car keys. "Make me happy: drive into a ditch!"

Lysette began to weep at the possibility that Nono might die, and Océane wept along in sisterly solidarity.

"Now look what you've gone and done!" Nolwenn hissed.

Paul's stepdaughter didn't like him. No, actually, she loathed him: a relatively major nuance. He didn't like her either, but loathing would have been too strong a word for his feelings. After all, she had given birth to the twins, who were the single best thing about her. Her mother, Rozenn, was a fabulous woman—a classy woman, a she-wolf. However, Paul had two unforgivable flaws in Nolwenn's eyes: his past as a foreign legionnaire, and the fact that he wasn't her biological father. There was nothing he could do about either of those matters, and therefore their relationship never changed.

Out of consideration for Nolwenn, Paul and Rozenn had never lived together, even though he had been with Rozenn for fourteen years and married for ten of those. *Had been.* Then that boy had come on the scene.

Rozenn's actions after their divorce, which Paul had made no attempt to block, were greatly to her credit: she had made sure that he saw the twins on a regular basis. Nolwenn had been quick to spot the practical benefits of this arrangement: Paul was a cheap babysitter. She had laid down clear rules. No Breton stories, songs, proverbs or sayings about the weather. The girls were French, and that was that. She would have loved to put up one of the signs that had graced school classrooms for generations: *No spitting on the floor or speaking Breton.* Anyone caught doing either of those things had a clog hung around their neck.

Once he had given the girls a parting hug and pulled the door shut behind him, he hissed furiously, *"Hep brezhoneg Breizh ebet!"* No Breton, no Brittany! And no Brittany, no homeland.

My God, he was thirsty!

He had trouble releasing the handbrake—it was going rusty again in the damp, salty air—but finally he managed.

On the drive back to Kerdruc, he spied Marianne walking along the opposite side of the road. She's very nice, he thought, winding down his window. "Trying to walk the length and breadth of Brittany, are we?"

She didn't immediately answer, because they were suddenly separated by a cycling race. Having fought their way up a rise, elderly gentlemen in neon Lycra shouted cheerful greetings as they freewheeled downhill.

For a fleeting instant Paul had caught the despondent expression on Marianne's face, but then she flashed him one of her bewitching smiles. She was like Brittany itself: hidden depths behind a beautiful facade. He wondered what she kept concealed inside her. She looked like she didn't want to be disturbed, so he gave a wave and stepped on the accelerator. In the rearview mirror he saw that strangely distant look settle on her girlish features again, as if she had lost something but didn't know what it was.

Paul needed some distraction. He rattled across Kerbuan farmyard, past Simon's rowing boat on its props, parked the car and then clumped through the kitchen garden to the back door. Simon was sitting smoking on one of the two steps that were the traditional way of preventing *korrigans*—dwarf-sized trolls—from climbing into the house.

"Hi. Say, you old goat, you wouldn't have something to drink?" said Paul.

"Young or old?"

"Something older than me."

"That's a tough ask."

They drank the first bottle, a Côtes du Rhône, in silence,

aside from Paul's mumbled thanks when Simon pushed a baguette, some salted butter and a slice of peppered pâté across the table to him. As always, Simon made a cross with his knife in the bottom of the loaf (out of superstition).

With the second bottle, a Crozes Hermitage, Paul found his tongue again. *"Evit reizhañ ar bleizi, Ez eo ret o dimeziñ,"* he said. I tamed the wolf by marrying it. "Why on earth did I choose Rozenn! If I hadn't taken her, I couldn't have lost her. What an idiot I am!"

"Well, *da heul ar bleiz ned a ket an oan,"* said Simon. The sheep doesn't run after the wolf. "Especially if the wolf has already found a fresh prey."

This didn't really dispel Paul's lovesickness for Rozenn, but there was nothing more to add.

Simon filled some *galettes* with goat's cheese, figs and butter, lit the gas and pushed them into the oven. Five minutes later, the men ate the piping-hot savory pancakes with their fingers.

"Am I too old?" asked Paul when they'd moved on to the third bottle, his consonants drifting away on the red waves in his repurposed mustard jar.

"For what? Drinking? You're never too old to drink, only too young. *Yar-mat,"* Simon said, and they clinked glasses.

"For women. Too old for women." Paul ran his hand over his thinning hair.

"N'eo ket blev melen ha koantiri, A laka ar pod da virviñ," Simon replied after a while. Blond hair and beauty don't bring the pot to a boil. He burped under his breath.

"True, it's personality . . . or something. I like all women—

the brunettes, the small ones, the fat ones, the ugly ones—but none of them wants me! Why? Have I got *too much* personality?"

"You're simply too good-looking, my boy," said Simon, and finally Paul broke out into a chuckle. He laughed away all his misery with Rozenn and Nolwenn, and Simon staggered to his feet. He returned with champagne.

"Much too young. Underage," he slurred, as he set down the bottle of Pol Roger in front of Paul. They poured the champagne into clean water glasses.

"No spitting on the floor or speaking Breton," Paul roared in a commanding voice.

"Yes, sir," cried Simon, and they looked over their shoulders and spat on the tiled floor.

When Paul had drained his glass in three long, vigorous swigs, he leaned toward Simon. "That Marianne . . ." he began.

"Hmm," mumbled Simon.

"There's something about her that makes you feel young again, as if everything you think and feel is okay. Know what I mean?"

"Nuh."

"I once stood next to her as she was ironing napkins in the sun on the terrace and told her everything about Rozenn," said Paul.

"What'd you tell her?"

"About Rozenn leaving."

"And then?"

"Then she did something." Paul got up and put his hand on Simon's lower arm.

"That's nuts."

"I can't do it as well as she can. Something was lifted from me. A shadow, I don't know. And then . . . it didn't hurt so much anymore. There's something in her touch."

Simon slowly nodded. "I told her about the sea. I don't know why. She listens with her heart. I bring my boat in and she waves to me from the window. No one has ever waved to me. Since she's been here, I don't feel I'm missing something on land anymore. Know what I mean? Marianne is like the sea, but on dry land."

Paul sat down again at the table next to Simon. "We've grown old, you rum goat," he whispered, as he groped for his champagne.

21

THE NEXT TIME MARIANNE MET PASCALE GOICHON, two weeks later, the old woman was cradling a dead crow in her hands.

"It's a present," she whispered, motioning with her chin to the skies. "She still loves me."

Marianne was curious. And concerned. This was what had driven her back to the Goichons' house. Jean-Rémy called Pascale *folle goat*, which almost earned him a slap from Madame Geneviève. "She isn't some madwoman in the woods! She's a *dagosoitis*! A white witch."

When Marianne had enquired why Pascale spoke German, Geneviève had explained that she had once worked as a stewardess on flights between Germany and France, and later all over the world. When she had her wits about her, she could speak six languages, including Russian and Japanese.

"Crows are messengers from the other world," said Pascale dreamily. "It fell directly at my feet." She glanced up at the bright blue sky again and sang quietly, "Moon, mother, wise old woman, heaven and earth, we greet you. You shine for all those who are wild and free." Then she walked off toward the back of the garden, singing as she went.

Next to the old stone hut in which many unused garden tools were stored stood some rosebushes in full bloom. Marianne noticed a closed screw-top jar beside one of the bushes. At first she thought it contained a tiny snake, but then she realized it was a pale umbilical cord.

Pascale pressed the bird into Marianne's hand; its feathers were as soft as silk. Then she kneeled down awkwardly and picked up a trowel. She dug a small hollow, slid the umbilical cord into it and shoveled the earth back on top. Then she did something that shook Marianne to the core: with one finger she drew three intertwining flames in the soil. It was almost identical to her birthmark!

By the time Pascale got back to her feet, the slightly dreamy look had vanished from her eyes; they were now alive with intelligence and alertness.

"You must think me a strange woman," she said.

"I think you're a special woman."

"Isn't 'special' another word for 'strange'?"

"Your German's good, but not that good," countered Marianne.

Pascale laughed. "I think you're a special woman too, Marianne. Come on, pass me that fowl."

"What did you just do?"

Pascale glanced down at the little heap of earth. "Oh, that. One of those old traditions. A woman from the village brought me her newborn granddaughter's umbilical cord. Ask a witch to bury your child's umbilical cord under a rosebush, and you can be sure that the child will have a fine voice."

"And that's true?" Marianne remembered helping her grandmother with home births. They would burn the umbilical cords in the stove so that the cat didn't get hold of them.

Pascale flashed her a mischievous grin. "It depends. There's nothing more real than your most fervent dreams. Am I right?"

Through the ivy-surrounded transom window Marianne could see Emile Goichon sitting reading at his huge desk. He looked up, but his impassive face showed no particular joy at seeing her there. He turned back to his book.

"I don't know," she said with a hint of sadness. "I've never hoped for much."

"You poor woman! Well, it's good that you've finally made it here then. We're always hoping for everything; it's in our blood."

Pascale laid the crow on the worn garden table and covered it with a napkin. "This land . . . You see, the Bretons are proud of their superstitions, which is why they sometimes feel superior to other people. Here, we are at the world's outer extremity, the *penn-ar-bed*. This is where the sun goes down, and everywhere we feel the breath of death, Ankou. It's the everyday half-shadow inside us all. We like mystery, the unusual. We long to discover a wonder behind every stone and every tree."

Pascale preceded Marianne into the kitchen, which looked as if it would have been the height of fashion sometime back in the thirties.

"Coffee?" she asked.

"I'll make it," Marianne said. She put the enamel kettle on to boil and tipped some coffee into the cafetière. Pascale was rummaging in the cupboards and drawers. "Where have they got to?" she asked impatiently, handing Marianne a packet of flour. "Is this what you drink coffee from?"

"No."

"How about this?" This time she was holding up a pot of jam.

"I'm afraid not."

"How odd one becomes. I cannot find *anything*. I don't even know what *that* is!" she said, pointing to the softly humming fridge.

Marianne thought back to the Post-it notes she had stuck on the equipment and appliances in Jean-Rémy's kitchen on her first working day. She found a sheet of jam stickers in the cool larder. While Pascale was sipping her coffee, Marianne wrote words on the stickers and attached them to the cupboards and shelves before attacking the larder. Pascale observed her and then studied what Marianne had written. She pointed to some jars. "Honey! Right?"

"Perfect."

"And that over there is sugar?"

"Exactly."

Marianne was caught off guard when Pascale impetuously hugged her. When the older woman released her, she caught sight of Emile standing sullenly in the kitchen, inspecting the notes on the cupboards, pots and machines. His dark eyes bored right into Marianne.

"What do you want here?" he asked in guttural Breton.

Marianne looked helplessly from him to Pascale, who translated for her. "He's very happy."

Marianne didn't believe a word of it. "I . . . I was trying to help."

Pascale translated again. Marianne didn't look away. If she did, she sensed that she would shrink in this tight-lipped man's estimation. Time seemed to expand to a bursting point. There was no movement on Emile's face; he was as inscrutable as the rock of the prehistoric cliffs.

"You're German," he said gruffly, and Pascale translated.

"You're unfriendly," replied Marianne in French.

It was the corners of his mouth that decided to twitch first, then Emile blinked, and finally the ghost of a smile spread across his face, lending it a magical glow for a couple of seconds.

"I'm Breton," he corrected her in a slightly milder tone before turning on his heel.

"I think he likes you," Pascale commented, adding with a sigh, "Don't hold it against him. For our generation the Germans aren't simply northern neighbors. They were occupiers; they bled our land dry."

Marianne didn't hold anything against him. He reminded her of her father, and yet her heart was pounding like that of a rabbit in a trap. She had been surprised by her own courage.

Pascale clapped her hands. "So what are we going to do now?"

"I . . . I must go back to Ar Mor. My shift's about to start. It's the summer holidays, and everyone's eating like mad."

Pascale's face crumpled. "Oh. I thought we might . . ." Her voice trailed off.

"Should I come again tomorrow?" Marianne enquired gently.

"Oh yes! Oh please do!" Pascale snuggled into Marianne's arms. "See you tomorrow, Marianne," she mumbled happily.

22

❧

A NEW LITTLE BELL SEEMED TO BE CHIMING OVER Marianne's head, and it had a courageous, impatient ring to it.

It was already the third afternoon she had spent with Pascale before her evening shift at Ar Mor—Emile had barely dignified her with more than two or three words—and she was attempting to put the overgrown garden in a semblance of order. As the two of them, dressed in dirty red overalls reminiscent of those worn by aircraft mechanics, pulled up weeds and chucked them into the wheelbarrow, Pascale told Marianne, in her lilting German, more about these people at the end of the world. A *lughnasad*, a Celtic harvest festival with a convention of druids, had taken place the previous night a few villages away.

"Druids? You still have druids here?"

"Brittany is teeming with them! There must be thirty thousand, all very Dionysian, and the convention was called to organize the *samhain*—the night from 31 October to 1 November when the living meet the dead. It needs planning." Pascale ran her fingers over her chin, and a few clumps of soil stuck to her skin.

"And how does one meet the dead?"

Pascale pensively stroked the blue flowers of a hydrangea, then appeared to pull herself together. Her voice was soft, as if she were revealing a secret for the very first time.

"On the night of *samhain*, when heaven and earth, life and death are aligned, the gates between the worlds stand open. The ancient gods and the new ones step out of the other world, bringing the dead with them, and we are permitted to visit their realm."

She made a vague gesture toward the garden. "From the sea, through wells or stone circles. There the fairies wait for us, the trolls and the giants. The veil between the worlds is gossamer-thin, like cobwebs. Yet some of us are able to push that veil aside on any day of the year."

"Why do the dead come to us during the *samhain*? Do they have . . . some advice to give us?" Marianne thought of her grandmother and her father. How she would love to see them again and confide in them.

Pascale looked grave. "Making contact with souls in the other world is not as easy as making a phone call! Some of us can hear them with our hearts; others need a druid or a witch to do so."

Emile shuffled out of the house, holding a tray with three glasses of cold *chouchen* on it. With labored steps he carried it over to the wrought-iron table under the apple tree bearing pinkish fruit, and nodded briefly to Marianne.

Pascale stood up, melded herself to her husband and closed her eyes. Marianne sensed how equal their love for each other was. Feelings of tenderness and affection welled up inside her.

Pascale continued to talk as she caressed her husband's expressionless face. "Whenever someone had a problem with this world or the other, they would call a druid. One person might have a problem with his wife, another with a demon, the next with his health. Druids were the guardians of all knowledge, religious, moral and practical. Even tribal chiefs sought their opinion, and the druids had an answer to everything."

"Were there female druids too?"

"Of course. Women could be priestesses as well. It was customary to send girls to priestesses for two seasons so that they could be trained as soothsayers, healers or druids. Yet they could do so on one condition only: they had to decide between a position as a high priestess and life at a man's side. Love and wisdom were mutually exclusive." She gave Emile another kiss, and he withdrew into the shade of the pergola without a word.

Pascale played with a buttercup. "Every woman is a priestess," she said abruptly. "Every single one." She turned to Marianne, her eyes as clear as water. "The major religions and their shepherds have assigned to women a position that isn't ours, making us second-class citizens. The goddess became God, priestesses whores, and any woman who put up resistance was branded a witch. And the special quality of each woman—her intelligence, her capacity for augury, healing and sensuality— was, and still is, debased." She brushed off the soil that was hardening on her trousers. "Every woman is a priestess if she loves life and can work magic on herself and those who are sacred to her. It's time for women to remind themselves of the powers they have inside. The goddess hates to see abilities go to waste, and women waste their abilities far too often."

Together they went into the cool kitchen. Marianne was pensive as she began to prepare tasty fillets of meat and fish for the dogs and cats on the delicate china plates. When they were ready, she walked outside, clapped her hands and called, "Ladies and mistresses, revered fruit and vegetables! Dinner is served!"

As soon as she placed the plates on the ground, the pack of dogs and cats fell upon them like a swarm of piranhas. Marianne smiled at the sight of her special orange-white cat, its coat shining like polished marble. "That little tiger doesn't have a name, does he?"

Pascale rested her head on Marianne's shoulder. "No, he's a traveler. But *this* wandering soul will give him a name," she whispered, looking at Marianne with unfathomable eyes. "Won't she?"

Marianne felt a shudder run through her. "Yes," she said. "When she has figured out where the journey leads."

"Thank you for not finding me repellent," murmured Pascale. Suddenly her face lit up with joy. "Yann!" she cried, all her melancholia streaming off her like water, and she went to meet the painter with outstretched arms. Yann gave her a big hug.

Marianne felt herself blushing for unaccountable reasons. She hid her dirty hands behind her back, and for one absurd moment she wished that she wasn't standing there in baggy overalls with a floppy hat on her head and grass stains on her face.

"Yann, this is Marianne, my new friend. Marianne, this is Yann, my oldest friend."

"*Bonjour*," Marianne managed to squeeze out. What was wrong with her all of a sudden?

"*Enchanté, Marianne,*" mumbled Yann.

They both fell silent and stood staring at each other. Marianne's brain had frozen: she couldn't think at all.

"What's up with you two? Have you turned to stone?"

He was taller than she was, and through his glasses she saw the sea in his eyes. His mouth was made up of two curling waves, one on top of the other. A dimpled chin. Countless deep wrinkles, radiating across his cheeks from his bright eyes like rays of light. Those eyes were beaming at her, drawing her into them.

"I think I ought to go now." Marianne had to control herself to avoid panicking and running inside. She felt a stupid, untenable smile trying to take over her face, so she swiftly covered it with her hand and walked indoors with her head bowed.

When she had finished changing her clothes, she was tempted to slip out of the house without so much as a "*kenavo.*" Then she remembered that her handbag was still on the terrace, so she walked stiffly out to say goodbye.

She didn't dare to look at Yann as she nervously picked up the bag. She was too hasty, though, and caught hold of only one handle. It flew open and her beloved Kerdruc tile slid out. Yann caught it nimbly and turned it to catch the light.

"Hold on, this is . . ." He looked at the inscription with bemusement.

"It's one of your very first Kerdruc tiles, Yann!" cried Pascale.

Yann passed the tile to Marianne, and their fingers touched as she reached for it. It was like a tiny electric shock, and as she looked into his eyes, she knew that he had felt it too.

23

⸙

THE NEXT DAY, MARIANNE DIDN'T DARE TO GO TO PAS-cale and Emile's as she had promised. She paced restlessly up and down in the Shell Room after her lunch shift. The orange-white cat sat by the window, observing her. Marianne took a quick look at herself in the curved mirror above the chest of drawers. She wasn't beautiful, she wasn't chic; she was merely an old woman among strangers. What on earth had happened there with . . . *Yann*. His name was Yann.

Something wobbled in her stomach when she thought of his face and the nice, full warmth of his hand. She'd never experienced this feeling—a sweet, nagging commotion, like bubbles bursting in her chest.

"What am I doing here?" she said to herself, letting the soft question hang there in the room.

Her original wish to die had turned into something different, something much more banal: she had run away, absconded. Wasn't it time to ring Lothar? *Hopefully Lothar thinks I'm dead.*

What should she say to him? I'm not coming back? I want

a divorce? And then? Was she going to spend her life as an assistant chef in a restaurant until she was too old to lift a cooking pot? With a friend who was a witch and forgot from one moment to the next who Marianne was? And yet it felt so good to hear and speak her own language.

Marianne longed to have a friend, one like Grete Köster had been. She deeply regretted the fact that she'd never shown as much trust in Grete as her friend had in her. But who knows: maybe friendship was the most patient form of love. Grete had never pried with Marianne; she'd accepted that Marianne never expressed how she really felt. She had appreciated Marianne as a listener, and had never attempted to talk her out of her marriage. "If someone suffers and won't change, then they *need* to suffer" had been her sole comment on the matter. That had hurt Marianne, and she'd told Grete that it wasn't so simple. She'd wanted to explain why she kept delaying the breakout from her self-inflicted misery from one year to the next. Soon, her explanations had begun to sound hollow even to herself.

She ran her fingers through her hair. It felt dry and wiry. She went over to the wardrobe and inspected its meager contents: a few T-shirts and cheap blouses from the local supermarket, two pairs of plain trousers and some no-nonsense underwear, a pair of linen shoes and two high-necked nightshirts.

She studied her face and the notches left by the years: the vertical line above the root of her nose; the crow's-feet around her eyes and the creases at the corners of her mouth; countless freckles, of which she hoped very few were liver spots. And her neck. My God, her neck.

There was nothing she could do about it: she was an old woman. But did that preclude her from longing for a little beauty?!

Within the hour, Marianne was sitting like an excited schoolgirl in Marie-Claude's hairdressing salon in Pont-Aven. She didn't consider for one second that it might have been the strange feelings and sweet commotion that had brought her here.

Marie-Claude slid her fingers searchingly through Marianne's graying long brown hair.

"If you could just give it a bit of shape," Marianne asked timidly.

"Hmm, it's more like reincarnation you need. *Mon Dieu*, you got here just in time," the hairdresser muttered as she beckoned to Yuma, her assistant, and gave her some quick instructions that Marianne didn't understand. Secretly Marianne hoped that she wouldn't end up with the same red locks as Marie-Claude. The hairdresser looked identical to her lapdog Lupin, who was enthroned in an elegant basket on a sort of podium next to the till.

Marianne closed her eyes.

WHEN SHE reopened them an hour later, Yuma was blowdrying her new hairstyle. Next to them Marie-Claude was busy picking nits out of the hair of one of the local farm lads. She was chatting to Colette, who was having her snow-white pageboy hairstyle trimmed in the next chair. The urbane gallery owner was wearing a salmon-pink suit, white python-leather gloves and white slingback pumps.

Colette raised her glass of Bellini to Marianne. "You look magical! Why did you hide it so well?" she called, then, turning to Marie-Claude, "she needs a drink."

Marianne's heart skipped a beat as she studied herself. Her mud-colored mop of hair was nowhere to be seen; in its place she sported a feathery bob that curved around to her chin and had taken on the color of young cognac. Yuma had arranged it to emphasize her heart-shaped face. Lisann had plucked her eyebrows too, although the unexpected pain of the tweaking had brought tears to her eyes, and the dyeing of her eyelashes had stung them.

Marie-Claude was now standing next to Yuma, examining Marianne critically through screwed-up eyes.

"Something's missing," she concluded, and motioned to Marianne to take a seat at the makeup station with Lisann. Marianne found this both ludicrous and wonderful. She took a long swig of the Bellini that Yuma had brought her; the champagne went straight to her head, and everything around her began to glow.

When Lisann had finished her work and passed her a mirror, Marianne realized that she liked her eyes. And her mouth. As for the rest . . . Well, she looked different from how she felt inside. Only a few weeks ago she'd felt half dead. Now she felt as if she were forty. Or thirty. Like someone else. And tipsy.

She questioned Lisann about possible remedies for wrinkles.

"Lipstick during the day, lipstick in the evening, and a lover at night," Lisann piped coquettishly. "Or the other way around: two lovers and one lipstick."

As Marianne was paying, Marie-Claude said, "Your admirer is going to be impressed."

"My what?"

"Or your husband." The hairdresser peered at Marianne's ring finger, but Marianne's hands were tanned from her daily outings and the white band had faded.

"*Je ne comprends pas*," Marianne said hastily.

"Don't you have a husband? Well, the way you look now, you could have a husband and a few lovers on the side. Probably not the youngest men, but there are enough gentlemen of an interesting age around here. Has anyone particularly caught your eye?"

"I don't understand," Marianne repeated, but she could feel the blood shooting into her cheeks. Marie-Claude noticed it too. Luckily she can't read my mind, thought Marianne, who could still see Yann Gamé before her and still feel that touch in Pascale's garden in her fingers.

"Colette, which lover could we recommend today?" Marie-Claude asked the gallery owner, whose presence made Marianne immediately feel dowdy once again.

Colette looked at Marianne with eyes like a cat's. Her face was a maze of wrinkles, but Marianne was still very impressed by her slenderness and perfect ballet posture.

"We should ask Madame what she has in mind," replied Colette. "Some men are good for life, but unsuitable as lovers. Others are good for sex, but are deaf to any difficulties or feelings."

"Yes, and then there are those who can't do either," Marie-Claude summed up. "That's the kind I've always had," she added, sighing.

MARIANNE AND Colette left the salon together and walked side by side down the steep lane. Marianne paused as they passed the fashion boutique.

"Please," she began, "would you help me? I need . . ." She pointed to her clothes. "I need style," she said simply.

"Fashion has nothing to do with style," said Colette in her husky voice. "It all depends on whether you want to conceal or reveal who you are."

She offered Marianne her arm. "Come on. Let's see what kind of a woman is hiding inside you. And when we've met her, we won't reproach her for having stayed out of sight all this time, *d'accord*?"

On the first floor of the boutique, Colette settled into an armchair with another Bellini and a cigarette, and shot instructions at Katell, the saleswoman. While Katell was away looking for the first items of clothing, from out of nowhere Colette suddenly related an anecdote about her former neighbor in Paris.

"Madame Loos was a woman who kept herself strenuously to herself," she began, sorting the heap of clothes that Katell had brought into two piles with a confident hand. "She had made it through life well enough—in her marriage, with her children, at work. Always in the right place at the right time. Always nice, polite and inconspicuously dressed. Then one night . . ." Colette leaned forward to stare at Marianne, who was peering uncertainly from all angles at a delightful dress the color of ripe Mirabelle plums, "one night something happened."

Marianne slipped into a soft, champagne-colored roll-neck sweater that showed her waist and her bust to advantage: she had never worn such a tight sweater before in her entire life. It further enhanced the glow of her new hair coloring. Then she pulled on a cool pair of dark jeans that Colette had laid out for her.

"Madame Loos banged on my door as if she'd gone mad. She needed my car, she said: her younger sister was at death's door in Dijon. I gave her the keys, of course. She sped away, but she crashed into another vehicle on the Place de la Concorde, and amid all the excitement she slapped a policeman, fled the scene with a guy from Rennes, told him the story of her life, had sex with him, borrowed his car and arrived too late: her sister was already dead. That looks good on you, by the way. Try on these pumps with it."

Colette got up and peered over Marianne's shoulder at the mirror. "Madame Loos returned the car, spent a second night with the man and came back to Paris a completely different woman—by bus."

She handed Marianne a fine-knit cardigan that draped itself lightly and softly around her body. When Marianne twisted to catch a glimpse in the mirror, she saw a woman who was perhaps no longer the youngest, but very chic and feminine. The only thing that didn't fit this new image was her timid, doe-eyed expression.

"Madame Loos managed to emerge from her hiding place, get rid of her husband and his mistresses and set up her own tearoom." Colette gently laid an amber necklace around Marianne's neck.

"What about the man from Rennes?"

"Completely incidental." She took off her sunglasses and placed them daintily on Marianne's nose. "One might have to be a little ruthless to seize back control of one's life, don't you think?"

Marianne gave an uneasy shrug. She regarded ruthlessness as the most socially acceptable form of gratuitous violence. But hadn't she herself acted ruthlessly by coming here? Her sense of guilt toward Lothar was growing ever more insistent. Did he not at the very least deserve some answers so as to know where he stood?

"How about something red? Red is *your* color," suggested Colette and called for Katell again.

24

THE WORLD HAD TAKEN ON A MORE INTENSIVE HUE AS Marianne stepped out of the boutique with Colette. Or was that the effect of the double cognac she had drunk after their shopping spree was over? She thought of the jeans—her first ever pair of jeans—that made her legs look longer than they really were; of the bottle-green leather jacket that contrasted beautifully with her new hair coloring, banishing the gray from her cheeks; of the red dress, the cream-colored sweater, the pumps in which she must first learn to walk, as the height of the heels almost took her breath away. She guessed that deep in the big shiny bags were other items of clothing bought as if in a frenzy with the aid of Colette's credit card.

Could clothes transform a woman? No, but they might help her to rediscover who she was. Marianne had found inside her something she thought she had never possessed: femininity. And now she was extraordinarily hungry, craving bread and cheese, and so the two women went into the bakery on Pont-Aven's market square.

"I bless you, oh bread, so that all witchcraft, shackles and slander by eye and mouth may be destroyed and dispelled," chanted the baker in Latin as he scored the sign of the cross in the bottom of the rye loaf. Only then did he allow Marianne to pack it away in her shopping basket.

Colette gave an inadvertent snort. "I've never got used to that trick with the bread," she said to Marianne. "During the Palm Sunday procession in Saintes, the women carry a hollowed-out loaf on the end of a stick; it looks like a phallus. The priest blesses the bread to protect it from the witches' gaze, and the women keep it for the whole year. They certainly don't eat it, so God knows what they do with it!"

Marianne giggled and dreamily caressed the silky fabric of the plum-colored wrap dress she was still wearing. It concealed her birthmark, but gave her cleavage she'd never known she had. Admittedly, Katell had sold her the requisite bra.

"No need to bless my loaf," said Colette loudly, interrupting Marianne's thoughts.

"If that's what you want, there's no problem, Madame," muttered the baker. "The bread is protected either way. You must know Pascale Goichon, the white witch in the woods. She consecrates fires and drives the ghosts from ships and rooms! She blessed this oven too," he said, pointing behind him.

Marianne's ears pricked up at the mention of Pascale's name.

"Lucky she isn't a black witch! Did you hear what happened in Saint-Connec four years ago?" He wiped his floury hands on his apron.

"Oh that old chestnut again." Colette was growing impatient.

"Madame Gallerne had been dozing in a near-death state for years. The livestock on the farm had been dying in mysterious ways, and nothing grew anymore. Fernand Gallerne was in despair, for an evil spell had been cast on his farm." The baker paused for dramatic effect. "And it could only be broken by . . ." He lowered his voice even more, until it was no more than a hoarse whisper: "Michel La Mer!"

"*Le magnétiseur?*" gasped the baker's young wife. He nodded. "He can do anything," she said rapturously, her cheeks turning a deep shade of pink. "They say he can drive out Satan and cure cancer, infertility, athlete's foot and mad cow disease. All with his hands!"

"Yes, yes," the baker interrupted rudely. "In any case, La Mer paid a visit to the Gallernes' farm and discovered that Fernand's neighbor Valérie Morice had cursed the land and was to blame for Madame Gallerne's illness. She'd always been so nice to them, but she was an unmarried woman with two children by an unknown man. She was the one who had cursed the poor wretches, purely—and literally—for the hell of it! La Mer lifted the curse for a hundred and fifty-two euros."

"A hundred and fifty-two euros!" Colette repeated in disbelief. "That's a lot of money for denouncing a woman!"

This earned her a glare from the baker. "Protection from the evil eye is priceless! La Mer charges a hundred and fifty-two euros for lifting evil spells from farms, a hundred and twenty-two euros for businesses and ninety-two euros for houses."

"And Madame Morice?" the baker's wife asked breathlessly.

"Ha! That woman! She immediately reported him to the police for defamation! She said that the whole village had embarked on a witch-hunt, and her children had been spat on at school! Then she cursed La Mer, and his powers have waned as a result. We ought to pray for his recovery."

"Well," stated Colette, "I don't believe in faith healers who run around the house with a wet cloth, as La Mer does, to banish the devil. I do believe that the baguettes need to come out of the oven, though. May I have one, Géraldine? Or don't you sell bread to normal people anymore?"

As Marianne and Colette emerged, giggling, from the bakery, Marianne bumped into a man who was gazing up into the sky, lost in thought. She apologized and pulled her sunglasses back down over her eyes.

"Yann!" cried the gallery owner happily. After the obligatory three kisses on the cheeks, Colette turned to Marianne. "May I introduce you to the most underrated painter in France, Madame? This is Yann Gamé."

Marianne felt the butterflies in her stomach. The way he looked at her!

Yann took her hand and pulled her toward him. The strength of his grip made her head spin.

"Hello again," he said earnestly.

Marianne involuntarily closed her eyes as Yann's lips brushed her cheek. He kissed her on the left, he kissed her on the right, and the third time his kiss was infinitely tender and very close to the corner of her mouth. Marianne hadn't kissed him; she was incapable of moving a muscle. She was scared that she would stand rooted to the spot like an oak sapling.

"Hi, Yann!" Her voice was like a splintering branch.

Good grief! He had no way of knowing that he was the first man to kiss her since Lothar. Everyone was constantly kissing

each other here, but for Marianne a kiss was as intimate as . . .
Sweet Jesus, her thoughts were hopping about like a sparrow.
She thought of Lothar, and she thought of what might happen
after kissing.

"Well, I hear the call of work. A few crazy English people
are coming and they want to decorate their entire house with
pictures. Who am I to stop them?" Colette glanced at her
watch. "I have to go. Yann, how about showing this fair lady
the Yellow Christ in the Chapelle de Trémalo, so she knows
why they call this 'Gauguin country'? All those biscuit tins
with pictures of chubby women on them can really get you
down. Yes? *Merci, mon ami. Au revoir!*" With that, she bade
them farewell, leaving Marianne and Yann alone in silence.

Marianne felt as if she were about to faint.

"Madame, would you do me the honor of accompanying
me on Thursday to an . . . *enterrement?*" Yann cursed his
words the moment he uttered them. Why hadn't anything
better come to his mind? He was out of practice at courting
women, but it was too late now.

Marianne hadn't really understood Yann's suggestion, but
she *had* registered that he wanted to see her again. The bubbles inside her chest burst from pure happiness. She felt a sudden surge of guilt, as if she were already being unfaithful and
cheating on Lothar.

They didn't talk as Yann drove her back to Kerdruc in his
decrepit Renault 4, merely glanced at each other again and
again, reading the budding love in each other's face with astonishment, as if they were only now learning its vocabulary.

25

MARIANNE HAD BEEN WAITING ON THE QUAYSIDE for twenty minutes by the time Yann picked her up. She simply hadn't been able to bear sitting in her room any longer, wondering whether she was dressed smartly enough. She could have spent many more hours changing her outfit. Jeans or red dress? Tight blouse or soft sweater? High-heeled pumps or flat-soled linen slippers? Good heavens, she simply had too little experience of what a woman should wear on her first date to make herself attractive but not too inviting. She had opted for the dark-blue jeans, pumps and a white blouse, which she buttoned up to the top.

She was incredibly excited, and had been for two days. She could barely eat, and above all she couldn't wipe this ridiculous grin from her face. Excitement didn't even come close to describing what she felt. Naked panic, more like. Foolish joy. One moment her complexion was pale white, the next bright red.

Eventually she had gone down to the kitchen to see Jean-Rémy and had let him pour her a shot of rum without any objection. It had calmed her down a little, but only until Jean-Rémy undid the top two buttons of her blouse, turned up the collar slightly and signaled to her to tousle her tidily arranged hair a bit. *"Très jolie, très rock'n'roll,"* he had said, and Marianne had gone shakily out onto the quayside to continué her wait.

Increasingly she felt like a boat at sea, drifting farther and farther from land until the coast was out of sight. The land of her past was fading in similar fashion. Sixty years appeared to have flashed past like a single day, and it was as if that day had occurred many centuries ago.

When Yann got out of his car and walked toward her, she was scared that she might either burst out laughing or dissolve into a never-ending fit of weeping. She was so nervous, her hands were sopping wet.

He gave her that look again. No man had ever looked at her so intently: Marianne could almost feel herself growing warm in the spotlight of Yann's eyes.

"Salut," he murmured as he bent forward to kiss her. This time all three touches of his lips were close to the corners of her mouth. He kissed her slowly and deliberately, and she inhaled his fragrance. He smelled of the outdoors, with a whiff of paint and nice tangy aftershave.

He guided her to his dilapidated car, opened the door and made sure that he also got to close it. She had no idea what to do with her hands and where to look.

Yann prayed ardently that he wasn't about to commit the most stupid mistake of his entire life. Over the past two days he had been continually tempted to come and withdraw his invitation. But a man didn't do such a thing. Invite someone to a funeral? What on earth had he been thinking?

Yann had often visited the fisherman Jozeb Pulenn in Penmarc'h to purchase ray and cod. The now late Jozeb had also been helpful in Yann's search for themes for his work. How often Yann had painted the Notre Dame de la Joie chapel, a Gothic church by the shore, and the Phare d'Eckmühl, France's tallest lighthouse, which dwarfed the adjacent village of Saint-Guénolé. He loved to remove his glasses and paint everything his senses could absorb, not only what his weak eyes were able to perceive.

Yet was that a good enough reason for imposing a funeral ceremony on Marianne? Yann hardly dared to look at her, yet when he did, he could feel her smile and a strange emotion welling up inside himself. That emotion was red and pulsing.

Marianne was shamefully conscious that she blushed every time she looked at Yann or tried to say something to him, so she restricted herself to gazing out of the window or observing the secure yet relaxed grip of Yann's hands on the steering wheel. Whenever they did catch each other's gaze, they simultaneously broke into a smile. It was the most wonderful silence Marianne had ever heard.

After half an hour's drive along the coast they reached the port of Saint-Guénolé and found a host of Jozeb's cousins, grandchildren, daughters and brothers-in-law waiting on the breakwater to greet them with proper ceremony. For the first time, Marianne felt slightly ill at ease, a feeling that was only exacerbated when everybody—the more elderly among them in traditional costume with white headdresses made of straw and lace, the younger ones wearing casual clothes and white scarves—gave them a welcome kiss. It took fifteen minutes to complete the greetings.

She eventually made it to an old lady standing next to a table on which an urn had been placed. Her face was as wizened as a piece of weathered wood, and she seemed to be leaning more on the urn for support than on her walking stick. It was only then that Marianne understood the purpose of this gathering.

Apple brandy was served, and two men carried the table onto the fishing trawler by the breakwater. The captain lowered the Breton flag to half-mast. As the engine started, Yann offered his hand to Marianne to help her across the short gangway.

When the trawler had puttered out onto the rolling open sea, leaving behind the foaming waves crashing against the cliffs and rocks, each of the funeral guests scattered a handful of the dead man's ashes onto the waters. The ashes had the texture of the finest sand, and Marianne hoped that she didn't happen to be crushing the deceased's heart, or even his eye, between her fingers. As she let the ashes drift out over the railing, she wished the unknown Jozeb happiness in the other world. If what Pascale had told her were true, then the sea was the widest gate into the realm of spirits and gods, where future, past and present were all irrelevant. The sea was like a church and an island, a final song steeped in darkness and tenderness.

A few of the mourners stood together at the ship's prow and struck up a *gwerz*, a Breton dirge. Marianne could understand only with her heart what these people were singing with such untrammeled emotion. It was a ballad of utter devotion, and she felt tears sting her eyes. Her heart was overflowing, and she groped for Yann's hand. He pressed it, then laid an arm around her shoulders and pulled her close. When a tear ran down her cheek and caught on her lip, he gently brushed away this salty sign of grief and touched his own lips to her warm temple. They stood beside each other and let themselves sway to the rocking of the boat.

Marianne felt momentarily as if destiny had determined this instant long ago. It was like waking in the middle of the night between two dreams, the moment when you grasp reality for what it truly is, not as it appears in the daytime. Blessed by fate.

Back on land, the group moved on to Jozeb Pulenn's house. Garlands of shells were draped from the apple trees. Yann talked to the fisherman's widow, and as they bade farewell, he spoke the sacred words: "Jozeb was always true to three things: himself, his family and Brittany." Then he took Marianne by the hand and they left the funeral, which now more resembled a garden party, with children playing catch and pulling cats' tails.

Back in the car, they exchanged a brief look.

"That was wonderful," Marianne said in a low voice. "Thank you."

Yann gave a sigh of relief as he turned the key in the ignition.

THEY DROVE on in his old Renault to Quimper, the county town, and visited the art museum. Yann didn't try to explain the pictures to Marianne: he wanted to see how the pictures explained themselves.

Lucien Simon's painting *Le Brûlage de Goémon*, which showed women burning seaweed in front of Penmarc'h's squat chapel while the sea foamed around them, the sky bent glowering over them and the wind billowed their headdresses and aprons, sent a shock wave through Marianne. It wasn't only that the Notre Dame de la Joie chapel still stood in Penmarc'h and looked exactly the same as it had in 1913 when the artist had painted it; it looked exactly as it had when it was built five hundred years ago. The simple, beautiful church would still exist when Marianne no longer did, when Yann, Colette, Lothar and everyone else had been wiped from the face of the earth. They would all die: only stones and art were immortal.

She suddenly felt an incredible fear of dying prematurely and not having had her fill when her final day came—her fill of life, up to the top and over the rim. She'd never felt such lust for life: the pain of having missed out on so much was threatening to blow her heart asunder. Never had the act she had considered committing struck her as more egregious: she had tried to put herself to death long before her time.

All this the picture told her.

Yann put his hand on Marianne's back, and her heart was pumping and beating, as if to say: it's far from over. Every second can mark a new beginning. Open your eyes and see: the world is out there and it wants you.

She turned and threw her arms around him. She had not exchanged more than four or five words with this man so far, and yet she felt as if he understood her better than anyone ever had.

26

MARIANNE ROAMED THROUGH THE GARDEN THAT she and Pascale had transformed over the past week by tirelessly planting bushes, saplings and seeds—columbine and godetia, poppies and hollyhocks, oleander and myrtle. They had fed the hydrangeas with lime and dug over the vegetable patch. The heavily laden fruit bushes were in magnificent shape, the hawthorn and anemones winked among them and the ground was covered with ranunculus, violets and tiny strawberries that had not yet ripened.

How she loved to burrow her bare hands into the soil! In fact, since she had been out at sea with Yann, she loved everything she did. She loved the enchantment of this part of the world, forged from granite and quartz, water and light. Magic was everywhere, even in butter cake, known as *gâteau breton* or *kouign-amann*. Mix flour, fresh eggs, salted butter and sugar in more or less equal parts, and don't knead for too long. Some said that it took a sprinkling of magic to make a *kouign* so good that it would enchant a person's heart forever, so they would never forget where they had eaten their first slice.

"White witches should be very skilled at baking," Pascale said as she showed her how to prepare the *gâteau breton*, but however hard she tried, Marianne's cakes never tasted as luscious and as enticing as Pascale's.

Marianne, who had never liked washing dishes, loved Ar Mor's scullery. She even loved the obdurate Jean-Rémy, whom she forced to write a love letter to Laurine every evening after work. He could never bring himself to send the letters, though, hiding them instead in an old lettuce crate in the cooler.

In the Goichons' stone shed Marianne found a scythe that was perfect for licking into shape the grass along the drive and between the holly bushes and apple trees, as the quails and orioles sang a song for her. She saw Emile peering out of the kitchen window as she set about mowing around the garage. She gave him a nod. She noticed that he was trembling a lot today, but she'd realized that he preferred her to pretend she hadn't seen anything.

Shortly afterward, the old Breton appeared at her side and motioned to her to follow him. They went over to the garage, whose door he opened with a squeal of hinges. In the half-light, Marianne could make out an old white Jaguar, and beside it, against the wall, a dusty Vespa, a bicycle, petrol canisters and some gas cartridges. He handed her a slip of paper and pulled some banknotes from his pocket.

Marianne stared at the list. Lightly salted butter, milk, goat's cheese, oranges . . .

Emile tossed the car key to her.

"Monsieur, I can't drive that *truc*."

Emile rolled his eyes and clicked his tongue in irritation.

He pointed to the car, opened the driver's door and gestured to the seat.

"I . . . I can't do it! I'm not allowed to! I'm never allow—" Once she was inside, Emile slammed the door shut. Marianne started to cry.

A QUARTER of an hour later, she was steering the British-built sedan along a narrow bumpy track through the woods.

"Open your eyes!" Emile ordered, as the car bounced through a tight gap between two beeches and the right-hand side mirror was knocked inward. She raised her eyelids.

She had sobbed so hard that Emile felt as if he'd behaved like a complete pig. Finally he had passed her his crumpled handkerchief and laid his left hand on hers on the gearshift. When he pushed down, she depressed the clutch, and he guided her hand and the stick into the next gear.

"Come on, accelerate!" The Jaguar leaped forward. She slammed on the brakes and took her foot off the clutch, and the engine stalled. "Not like that!" Emile clapped his hands angrily. "Again."

She started the engine and they jerked forward out of the woods and onto the street that ran through Kerdruc.

"Madame, there is a third gear," groaned Emile, "and a fourth. Put your foot down. *Allez!*"

They sped along the main road toward Névez. Marianne stared wide-eyed at the asphalt: it looked like a gray waterfall flowing under the wheels of the car. Little trickles of sweat had formed under her armpits.

She put the pedal to the floor, and Emile screwed up his

eyes. His speechless gestures ensured that they made it to the supermarket in Névez, where Marianne swung the car to a halt across two parking spaces. She peeled her trembling hands from the leather steering wheel. "Phew!" she gasped, her eyes glowing.

Emile was smiling as he got out of the car, but he turned his face away before Marianne could catch his expression. He wasn't finished with her yet. Once in the supermarket, he introduced her to Laurent, a jolly-looking man behind the well-stocked meat counter. Laurent had a perfectly spherical head, a waxed mustache, twinkling chestnut eyes and a thin wreath of hair.

"*Enchanté, Madame Marie-Anne,*" he said, winking as he stretched his hand across the counter. This done, Emile nodded to Marianne, gave her the money and the list again, and sat down in the small café between the car park and the petrol station to wait until Marianne had finished. He didn't intend to help her with the shopping. If this woman truly wanted to stand on her own two feet, then there was no way he was going to carry her!

WHEN THEY had driven back to Kerdruc and tidied away the shopping into the larder and the fridge, Marianne wound up for a thank-you speech, but Emile cut her off with a dismissive wave. "Thank you," she said anyway. "For that, and for the driving lesson."

"*E-keit ma vi en da sav, e kavi bazh d'en em harpañ,*" Emile whispered, as if reading her mind. As long as you can walk upright, you will find a walking stick. As long as you are brave, someone will help you.

She glanced at the gnarled old man. This was the first time he had wasted so much breath. Furthermore, he was smiling kindly at her.

Pascale came tottering out of the bedroom in Emile's pajamas and a pair of rubber boots. She bent forward to kiss Emile, sighing, her eyes half shut. He loved her so much.

"Do you still want to kill yourself, Marianne?" asked Emile, and Pascale raised a hand to her lips in shock, ready to stifle the cry that was trying to spill out of her throat.

Marianne turned pale. "How do you know about that?"

Emile tapped on his heart. "Why did you come here to die?" He asked it as calmly as if he were enquiring about her plans for dinner.

"I wanted to see the sea," answered Marianne.

"The sea," repeated Emile. His eyes were focused on Marianne's. "The sea contains both turmoil and profound silence. There are no ties between it and us, yet we still yearn for it to understand our thoughts and actions. And did the sea want you?"

"I would gladly have drowned in it," Marianne said quietly. "It would have buried everything. First it would have swept over my head and then it would have forgotten me. That's how it was supposed to be: I was on a quest for death."

"But then?" Pascale asked anxiously.

"Then life intervened."

MARIANNE MADE it back to the restaurant just in time for the evening shift, and found a white rose in front of her door. It had a delicate scent of raspberries. Next to it lay a postcard of Penmarc'h chapel, which had given her such a powerful reminder of her desire to live.

Yann.

27

MARIANNE WONDERED IF SHE DESERVED TO BE SO
happy. Since their excursion, she and Yann had seen
each other every day. He came for lunch to Ar Mor, waited
until her shift was over and then spent the afternoon with her
until it was time to go back to her pots and pans. On the days
she visited Pascale and Emile, either he would accompany her
and sit on the terrace to draw, or he would wait until late evening when Jean-Rémy let her leave work. Usually, though, he
came to see her twice a day, in the afternoon and the evening.

Marianne learned French from him more quickly than
from anyone else, which might have been due to the warm,
two-toned timbre of his voice. She loved driving around the
countryside with him in his Renault, visiting a fishing village
or one of the many castles and remote chapels. She also loved
watching him walk away from her, admiring the powerful
shoulders better suited to a carpenter than to a painter.

They were like two addicts, diving recklessly into each
other and drinking in the other's presence as if there would
soon be nothing more to drink.

She got used to the man with the marine eyes drawing her.

He never showed his pictures, but for now his gaze contained everything she needed to see: how he saw her.

He filled pad after pad with sketches of Marianne's face and hands as she went about whatever she happened to be doing at that moment: cooking or gardening, sitting still so as not to disturb the cat curled up on her lap, or singing gently as she peeled vegetables.

So far they had not shared a single kiss. Marianne was in no hurry: she knew it would mark the dawn of a new era. One kiss would become two, and two a flood. They would not want to linger for long on the other's mouth, and their kisses would move tentatively downward. And that scared her.

She quivered inside at the thought of Yann undressing her, seeing her naked, aging body: the skin, the folds and pleats, the bays and other offensive peculiarities the aging process held in store.

And yet . . . at the same time her yearning grew to feel Yann's hands not just on her cheek, arm and lips. But how horrible and terrible it would be if she did not please him! No, there was still a lot of time for kissing.

On a Monday, traditionally the quietest day at Ar Mor, Jean-Rémy gave her some time off. She and Yann drove east toward the magical forest of Brocéliande. As they traveled along the winding roads to Paimport, twenty-five miles west of Rennes, Yann broke the already familiar, cozy silence. He shut the road atlas on Marianne's lap.

"The grove of Brocéliande doesn't feature on any ordinary map: it is only to be found in our hopes and dreams. In our world it is known as 'the wood at the bridgehead,' but in the world of magic it is the enchanted forest of Merlin, a realm of fairies and the bridge into the underworld."

"The underworld? Is that the same as the other world?" asked Marianne.

Yann nodded. "The Holy Grail of Arthurian legend is buried in Brocéliande, and it is there that the spring of eternal youth rises. Anyone who drinks from it will live forever. It is said that through the fairy mirror—a completely smooth lake—lies the path to Avalon, where King Arthur waits for Brittany's call. Another legend says that at the bottom of the water-lily pond lives Viviane, the Lady of the Lake, in a crystal citadel."

Marianne listened and reflected on these words. The Lady of the Lake. She had never heard that name before, but as Yann spoke, she had the feeling that this lady had merely slipped her mind. "Who is she?" she asked in a low voice.

"She was the one who took away all Merlin's magic powers, offering him her eternal love in return. She pulled him down into the depths for a never-ending banquet that lasts to this day."

Marianne saw in her mind's eye a glass castle, surrounded by water and shifting shadows.

SILVERY SHREDS of mist greeted Marianne and Yann as they made their way under tall, ivy-clad trees, through the drooping foliage of oaks and birch thickets, into the enchanted forest. It was silent. An expectant silence. Another twenty minutes and they reached the Fontaines du Barenton.

"This is where Merlin and Viviane first met," whispered Yann, as if he feared disturbing the creatures of the forest. Marianne noticed bubbles rising gently through the crystal-clear waters from the gravelly bottom.

"The spring is laughing," said Yann. "It doesn't always, only when it sees two people like Merlin and Viviane who . . ." He didn't finish his sentence.

Who love each other.

Marianne looked down into the water. This was exactly how it felt in her chest: delicate bubbles sparkling up from the underground spring, then gently bursting. Inexplicable. Wonderful. Her heart laughed like this spring when she was with Yann.

Hand in hand they wandered through the silent woods, which seemed to Marianne to be exactly as they must have been a thousand years ago. Dense, bewitched, gloomy. Moorland, bogs and lush green grass. Paths that no forester ever leveled. The wind murmured in the mighty oaks, and the sun cast light-green shadows on the soft ground. Marianne felt as if their every step were dissolving time and space. Eventually they came to a circle of standing stones, surrounded by hawthorn trees. "Merlin's grave," whispered Yann. "His beloved banished him here."

He must have accepted this imprisonment joyfully, Marianne thought. An amazing man, who exchanged his powers for a woman's love. Merlin's grave was girded with megaliths, into whose many chiseled cracks rain-soaked slips of paper had been inserted. Marianne didn't dare pull one out.

"Wishes," Yann explained. "This is a *nemeton*—a place of

gods. Sometimes they look kindly on the secret wishes we put to them."

Marianne stared at the grave, then tore a strip of paper from the yellow notebook she used for vocabulary. She glanced at Yann more intensely than she had ever done before. Enquiringly, determinedly and yet so distant.

She jotted a few words on the slip, folded it carefully and pushed it into a crack alongside some others. Yann didn't ask what she had wished for from the gods, and in any case she would not have told him. Yet something inside him hoped that *he* might be able to make her wish come true.

They took a break beside the lily pond, not speaking, rapt with indescribable emotions. Marianne turned her face to the warm sun. Her features were relaxed as she sat there as if filled with a profound sense of peace, and Yann thought she looked like a dreamy sprite.

"When a fairy falls in love with a mortal man, she often worries that he will forget her the moment he leaves the magic realm," his mother had said when she told him fairy legends as a boy. "Fairies die if their beloved no longer remembers them. That's why a fairy always attempts to bind a man to herself. However, it is only if the fairy gives the man a dark, lethal kiss that she can keep him forever. In this world he dies, and he can therefore remain by his fairy's side in the other."

A sweet death awaits every Celtic hero in fact, thought Yann. It doesn't matter what he was before—a king, a hero or a simple painter. In the hands of a fairy, he is nothing but a man. A man who has given up everything he once held dear in life: fame, honor, money, power, recognition.

Yann observed Marianne again. Her face, the play of the light on her hair, her hands that were always warm. Yes, he decided, the smartest move for any man was to forget his foolish hankerings for power, put his fate in a woman's hands and let himself be absorbed by her.

Marianne held his gaze. More strongly than ever, Yann had the impression that he was facing a lady of the lake, and he was ready for her to confer immortality on him with a kiss. Now that he was an old man, he fully understood the legend of Viviane and Merlin. Women loved, and their love was so much greater and so much more lasting than power or manhood would ever be. He imagined how wonderful it would be to be loved by Marianne beyond his death.

Getting to her feet and covering the short distance between them in two strides, she felt as she stretched out her hand to Yann that he was offering his entire being to her as humbly as if she were a queen.

The two shadows on the banks of the pool merged into one.

28

⚜

A WEEK LATER, AS MARIANNE WAS PRACTICING HER French vocabulary with Pascale while preparing dinner, Emile brought in his accordion. A red accordion with ninety-six buttons. No one had played it for decades, and the pleats of the bellows had become porous. Emile claimed that his Parkinson's made it impossible for him to play, but maybe she could? When he opened the bellows, they wheezed and the keys refused to produce a single tuneful note.

Marianne lifted the accordion, passed the two leather straps over her shoulders, undid the buckles that pressed the bellows together, slid her left hand under the strap on the manual and pushed the air button, enabling her to pull the bellows apart without a sound. The instrument seemed to exhale.

She pushed the bellows together. An inhalation, a deep breath of heavy, nutritious air. Her ring finger felt for and came to rest on the only rough, raised button on the left manual—C. She flicked one of the five switches on the right keyboard manual.

Breathe in. Gently she pressed on C. Now she only had to pull the bellows to the left again and . . . She didn't dare.

"So," said Emile, "they say you only find out a woman's true personality when she makes music. One will read music like a picture, analytically and coldly; the next imbues every sound with emotion. And some are cruel, because music is their only lover, the only thing on which they bestow truth and passion, mastery and control. No one else comes as close to them as music and the instrument they use to rule their love. How do you play the accordion, when you eventually get around to playing it?"

"I don't. My husband finds it too loud and too obscene."

Emile gave a sharp cough. "Sorry? Your husband? You have a husband?" The gentle ticking of the kitchen's grandfather clock was the only sound.

"You ran away from your husband, didn't you?" Pascale finally asked.

"From myself, more like," said Marianne, her voice suddenly choked.

"Does Yann know that you—"

"That's none of our business," Emile interrupted his wife.

"Didn't you love him anymore?" Pascale ventured.

"I was tired," Marianne answered, unstrapping the accordion.

"Does he know you're here?" Emile enquired.

Marianne shook her head.

"And it's meant to stay that way, I guess," said the Breton.

She nodded. She was ashamed; she felt like a cheat, a fraud.

Emile Goichon rubbed his face with his rough, healthy hand. "Anyway, let's drop the subject." He beckoned to Marianne to come to the garage. There, the light blue Vespa looked

different. It had been cleaned, greased and filled up with petrol. Emile had put the scooter into working order.

"It's a 50cc, so you just need to accelerate and brake. The
accordion's too heavy to haul all the way through the woods.
I'll lend you this thing for as long as . . ." He paused. "For as
long as you want."

In the kitchen, Pascale was acting as if she'd truly forgotten
everything she'd just heard. Marianne agonized over how to
explain herself. In one fell swoop, everything she had worked
so hard to block out was back: Lothar, her bad conscience, her
sense of guilt about not confessing her reasons for leaving him
and their life together.

AFTER THE final guest had left Ar Mor, Marianne disappeared to her room without having her usual drink and daily
language practice session with Jean-Rémy. She lay staring at
the ceiling in the dark, observing the pools of moonlight, then
swung her legs over the side of the bed. She had a rising feeling in her stomach of the kind one gets in a lift that is falling
too fast.

She caressed the accordion. The bellows let out a sigh, a
short off-key chord. She listened. It wasn't possible: no accordion played itself. The moonlight shimmered on the instrument. Two thirty. Another three hours until sunrise. She
pulled on her jeans over her nightdress and draped the bottle-
green leather jacket around her shoulders. Then she picked
up the accordion and sneaked out onto the breakwater.

The cat lay curled up on the seat of the Vespa, but at

Marianne's approach it immediately got up, its eyes glinting in the murky darkness.

Marianne swung the instrument over her shoulders. It was heavy against her back. The cat stared at her. *It can't ask you any questions.* But it seemed to Marianne that *this* cat could.

She rode off into the night. She didn't pass a single car, no cyclists, not even a gull. She heard only the scooter's high-pitched buzz, tasted the dew on her lips and felt the nighttime chill creeping under her trousers and over her bare ankles. The weight of the accordion tugged her body backward, and the bellows seemed to open and close a few fractions of an inch at every bump in the road. There it was again: that sighing, the quiet chord.

When she stood on the edge of Tahiti Beach and gazed out over the blue-black waters of the Atlantic—above her only stars, beneath her only sand—she took the accordion from her shoulders, turned it around, strapped it to her chest and opened the bellows.

Breathe out. Breathe in.

She had always loved A minor. She moved her finger two buttons up from C.

Breathe out. Breathe in.

It was a lifetime since she had last played. Forty . . . no, a hundred years. She pressed down her ring and index fingers and eased the bellows apart. The melancholy chord rang out plaintively, nobly, majestically and boldly from inside the instrument, sending vibrations through her stomach and heart.

This was what she had loved so much—feeling the music in her stomach, her abdomen, her chest. In her heart. The sounds were transmitted to her body, and she pushed the bellows back together until the A minor chord transformed the night into music.

She released the buttons and let herself sink heavily onto the sand. It had taken the sea to wake the accordion from its stiff silence.

As with me.

Her thoughts had run away from Lothar so effortlessly, but now they swirled and roared around her all the louder.

Was he really such a bad husband? Am I not to blame in the end? Did I really try to change things? Did I perhaps not love him enough? Could we try to start over again? Hasn't he earned another chance? And if love is about taking someone for what he is, did I truly do that?

She had been away from home for so long—but not long enough. She had swum into an entirely new life, yet the forty-one years with Lothar were overpowering in scale; she couldn't shed them like an old nightie. They followed her wherever she went and with whomever she laughed. They were like this sea, gnawing away at the land, never leaving it in peace.

"*Merde,*" she whispered, hesitantly at first, then more vigorously, "*Merde!*" She screamed at the waves, "Shit, shit, shit!" and began to underscore every word with a chord. A *tango de la merde.* Her fingers didn't immediately hit the right buttons, for everything was mixed up on the accordion: the F was below the C; the D was under the A; the G above the C. She cursed, she squeezed, and the accordion produced entreating noises, screams of hatred, passion and longing. She tamed them, gave them space and strength, allowed them to expand in the darkness. She let the bellows breathe in the salty air, and when she was too exhausted to continue playing, she rested her head on the instrument.

She breathed in. She breathed out. She thought she heard a woman's laughter. Maybe it was Nimue, the lady of the sea? She looked up to find a crescent moon: a pale silver cradle, shrinking from the sun.

Her fingers started tentatively to move, trying to remember the most beautiful song she had ever heard played on an accordion—the song about the son of the moon. D minor, G minor, F, A7. "Hijo de la luna."

MARIANNE PRACTICED until her fingers could no longer defy the early-morning cold and damp. Her left arm ached from pulling and squeezing the bellows, and her back hurt from the instrument's weight. Dawn had uncloaked the night, and behind her there were the first signs of the rising sun in the east.

Exhausted, she released the instrument. She was on edge. She didn't know what was real and what was a dream. Slowly she played Piazzolla's *Libertango*.

Still no answers. Nowhere. Questions; only questions.

29

⚜

FOUR DAYS LATER, ON 14 JULY, AR MOR AND THE GUEST-house looked to Marianne as if someone had turned them upside down. Since early morning they had been transporting tables, chairs, half of the kitchen utensils and a makeshift bar from the restaurant out onto the breakwater. On all sides colorful lanterns were hanging from strings, there was a covered stage on the quayside, and French and Breton flags fluttered from the windows.

Pascale Goichon was still chasing evil spirits from the rooms and purifying them of negative energy. She was going to round off by blessing the hearths—the fireplace in the lobby and the one in the dining room—and casting a protective spell.

"Are we throwing a big party to mark the reopening of the guesthouse?" Marianne had asked with amazement.

"Yes and no," replied Geneviève. "We're actually celebrating the national holiday, but is there any better day to celebrate a renaissance than that of the *bal populaire*?"

The Bastille Day ball! That meant moving every activity

out into the street: eating, drinking, singing, music and dancing. That evening, waltzes and tango would ring out in Kerdruc, as well as gavottes and traditional folk music. Everybody would be celebrating in the open air. In every village in France, the whole day was given over to the ball.

Jean-Rémy and Marianne had been in the kitchen making preparations since five o'clock that morning. That evening there would be buckwheat pancakes and cider, *steak frites* and lamb cutlets, scampi and quiche, fish soup and lobster, cheese, lavender ice cream, mutton for the locals, and oysters, oysters and more oysters for the tourists.

Behind the open-air kitchen unit, a young man called Padrig was helping Jean-Rémy to serve. Laurine lined up bottles of apple cider, Calvados, pastis, champagne, rosé wine, Breton beer, Muscadet and large volumes of red wine.

Madame Geneviève was only partially satisfied with Padrig. The mason's son was overly jealous and protective of the alcohol stocks, tempted to drink them himself rather than leave enough for the guests. She hadn't been able to find any other temporary staff, though: Alain Poitier in Rozbras had already hired everyone she'd asked! What a sight it was over there. A bouncy castle in the form of a pirate ship, an ice sculpture of the revolutionary Marianne (scantily clad, with pert breasts) and a wooden dance floor with blue-white-and-red garlands. Geneviève cursed.

Marianne had been put in charge of tidying, washing up and providing regular food and drink for the musicians. She tried not to trip over the quintet's instruments as she carried sandwiches and bowls of *cotriade* to the men on the open-air stage. She pointed to the wind instrument. "It's a pommer,

Madame," said the smallest of the five men, who had bandy legs and a wrinkled face. He picked up the pipe and struck up a tune. The others set their soup bowls aside, took up accordion, violin and bass and began to play along. Marianne was catapulted back in time.

She was in Paris, in a dazzlingly lit hospital room, listening to music on the radio. Music you wanted to dance to. She saw old men dancing with young women; she saw a long, richly laid table, laughing children and apple trees, the sunlight on the sea at the horizon; she saw blue shutters on old thatched sandstone cottages.

When she opened her eyes, the vision had come true. She felt the warmth of the sunshine, and a wave of infinite gratitude swept through her. The men were in traditional costume— round black hats with silk ribbons, and cummerbunds—and they were playing a song just for her.

Without thinking, she shut her eyes, raised her arms and began to spin in time to the music. She danced and danced on her own, and let herself be carried away to a place where there were no lurking secrets, no questions, to a place where everything was fine.

She only stopped dancing when the musicians ceased their playing. She had been filled with a calm that blanketed every somber question.

"What's your name?" asked the violinist.

She called it out.

"Marianne!" cried the musician, turning to his colleagues. "Our first lady, our beloved, the heroine of our republic, our revolution, our freedom. Gentlemen, freedom just danced for us!"

"*Vive Marianne!*" they shouted in unison, bowing low to her.

Marianne went back into the kitchen with the feeling that she had just taken a great step forward in her true life.

The ball wasn't yet officially open, but the first Ar Mor regulars had already arrived: Marie-Claude, her highly pregnant daughter Claudine, Paul and the twins, who were watching them set up the buffet, Jean-Rémy nimbly, and Padrig with infuriating sloth.

Paul leaned forward to give Claudine's tummy a gentle tickle. "Don't you think Claudine looks fantastic? So . . . so pregnant."

"I don't want to look fantastic. I want to look slim," grumbled Marie-Claude's daughter.

"Why? You look great, especially your wobbly backside," Marie-Claude said, laughing.

"My backside keeps flirting with men while I'm looking the other way, and there's nothing I can do about it!"

WHEN NIGHT began to cozy up to the day, the whole of Kerdruc sang the "La Marseillaise." As the last note died away, the musicians launched straight into a tango, and the breakwater seemed to glow with a kaleidoscope of swaying dresses.

Paul was sitting with his arms crossed on Ar Mor's terrace. He was watching Rozenn, who was standing on the margins, observing the couples spinning past her.

The boy, as Paul called her new young boyfriend, hadn't danced with her once so far. She wouldn't be happy about that. Rozenn loved dancing, especially Argentine tango. She channeled all her romantic emotions into her body—reserve, lust, fear and pride.

Paul knew that refusing to dance with a woman was tantamount to ignoring an important aspect of her personality, a slight that she would never fully forget. That was because she had something to offer—her devotion—and she would never truly reveal her soul to a man who didn't dance with her. For Rozenn, Paul had taken secret dance lessons with Yann, who knew how a man should dance to make a woman fall for him.

Now Paul caught sight of the boy. Having just fetched two glasses of red wine from the bar, he had spied Paul at exactly the same time. He was coming toward him!

"Good evening, Paul," he said with exaggerated politeness.

"My wife looks delightful tonight, don't you think?" Paul cut him off.

"She isn't your wife anymore."

"Have you told her how beautiful she is?"

"I don't think that's any of your business." The young man turned to leave.

The musicians rounded off their up-tempo tango and struck up a plaintive *gwerz*. Couples who loved each other so achingly that only their bodies could express their emotion continued to dance; the others took refuge in their drinks or in their private thoughts.

"I knew you wouldn't be able to love my wife the way she needs to be loved," said Paul to the boy's back. The name he had managed so successfully to block out chose this moment to pop into his mind. *Serge*, the little milksop!

"She isn't your wife anymore!" said Serge again, angry now.

"She still feels as if she is, though. Want to bet?"

Serge turned away a second time.

"Want to bet?" Paul repeated more loudly.

Now Serge turned to face him, his arrogance deflated. "Our love is greater than anything you ever had with her," he hissed.

"In that case, you've no need to worry about the outcome of our bet. Or do you? Are you scared of an old man?"

Serge glared at him. Paul uncrossed his arms and smiled at the man who was sleeping with the love of his life, who woke up alongside her, argued with her and saw her laugh.

"What do you want?" snarled Serge.

"A dance. Just one."

"That's ridiculous."

"I know. Nothing to be scared of." Paul stood up, offered Serge his seat with a lavish gesture and then bent down to him one last time. "Watch and learn."

COLETTE SAW Paul call to the musicians. She spotted Simon walking toward her carrying something that looked like one of his peculiar presents, and noticed how he retreated when he saw her sitting so close to Sidonie. Yet she pushed everything she saw down into a part of her where it had no bearing. She and Sidonie were sitting on the renovated upper terrace of the guesthouse in silence.

Colette laid her hand in its short salmon-colored glove on the cover of the book lying in front of her, then pushed it across the table to her companion.

"For the anniversary of our friendship, 14 July," she said.

Her words rang stilted and hollow in her ears. Sidonie only reached for the book when Colette had withdrawn her hand.

"*The Language of Stones* by Roger Caillois," she read under her breath.

Colette saw Paul approach Rozenn and bow to her. She saw her turn away, Paul say something to her back and Rozenn spin around as if she'd been slapped.

"Caillois was a philosopher and sociologist. In the 1930s he was a member of the Surrealists, and later founded the Collège de Sociologie with Georges Bataille," Colette heard herself lecture in an unnaturally high-pitched voice.

"Oh," said Sidonie. "How nice."

"He sees stones as a counterweight to dynamics, for it is only through their immobility that man's quest becomes visible. You see, without stones we wouldn't notice that we're moving and . . ." Colette paused. What on earth was she babbling on about?

"Stones aren't immobile," said Sidonie after a while.

They were both completely focused on Paul and Rozenn. He was steering his ex-wife toward the middle of the breakwater; he was half pulling her and she was half pushing him, their expressions a mixture of truth and pain. Onstage the violinist gave a signal, and the first chords of a tango could be heard, led and carried out into the night by the accordion, then taken up by the violin.

"They do move, it's just that no one sees it. There's a place in America," Sidonie went on, "called Death Valley. Boulders roam across the sand. No one pulls them, but the tracks are visible. They're hundreds of yards long. Stones move."

"They move when we're not looking?" asked Colette. Are we really discussing stones? she thought.

"Yes," whispered Sidonie. "Nobody sees them moving."

"I thought we had a fixed position," said Colette.

"We?" asked Sidonie.

"We stones."

For the first time, Sidonie turned to look at Colette. "They say that standing stones in Brittany move on Christmas Eve when the clock is striking twelve, heading toward the sea to drink. But it's not enough for us stones to do what we want only once. We move because we're searching for the object of our desire," she said, and Colette didn't dare to blink for fear of missing a single moment of Sidonie looking at her.

"But what do stones desire?" she asked, staring straight at Sidonie, although she could already sense what it was. She sensed that she had always known what Sidonie was trying to express. Something inside her snapped in half. It burst apart like a rock, and she could taste powdered stone on her tongue.

MARIANNE CLEARED the tables, even rescuing several empty cider glasses from the flowerpots. She glanced over at Yann, who was sitting on a folding chair next to the stage, his pencil flying across the thick pages of a drawing pad. His eyes kept seeking Marianne amid the crowd, and every time they met hers across the intervening gap, time seemed to skip a beat. She felt something in her chest explode like a tear splashing on someone's hand. The next moment her view was again blocked by a dancing couple. Marianne loved the instants when she took a few steps to one side and watched Yann scanning the throng for her. *He's looking for me.*

She took a deep breath and then exhaled all the air from her lungs. Perfume, barbecue aromas, salt water, sea air. A night steeped in celebration and laughter.

He wants to find me.

She lifted her tray and spied some tartrate crystals in the glasses.

I'm in love.

She imagined what it would be like to sleep with Yann Gamé. Yet she soon forgot about it when she caught sight of Laurine, who was balancing two trays and was therefore unable to protect herself from the persistent groping of a drunken guest. Marianne strode toward the man and pushed him away. The stunned man spun around.

"Try that again," she announced, "and I'll chop your mitts off." The man turned pale and vanished into the swirling crowd.

PAUL SPUN Rozenn out of her rapid dance step to face him. It was just as it had always been: their bodies understood each other blindly; there was no need for their limbs to negotiate.

Initially, though, Rozenn had been completely defensive.

"One last dance, the last of our lives. I love you, Rozenn, but I'm going to let you go. Let this be my *kenavo*."

Only then had she stepped into his arms. Paul had asked the musicians to play her favorite song, discreetly slipping them a few banknotes to encourage them to do so immediately.

Rozenn was a cat, egotistical and devoted and yet wolf-like, brazen in her ingenuous passion and as elegant as a queen.

"Does he treat you well?" asked Paul, when she had completed a twist and two locksteps and was once more spinning within his ambit.

"He treats me like a lady."

"Oh, and how did I treat you? Like an Indian elephant?"

A surge of rage made her strut even more proudly and outrageously around Paul. She pushed him away; he pulled her to him.

"I felt like a heap of nothing after our divorce," he hissed into her hair as he steered her mercilessly backward through the other dancing couples.

"Then it served its purpose," growled Rozenn, slipping from his grip and scissoring her legs to the left and right of his thighs. He evaded them with a quick sideways movement and snapped her body backward until she lay in his arms with her head dangling.

"Is divorce forever?" he said, allowing himself to be sucked into the dark tunnels of her eyes. "Like marriage, until death saves you from one another?"

Rozenn flicked herself upright again, and Paul pulled her so tight that their lips were only a butterfly's wingbeat apart. He could smell her perfume, the soap she always laid in her underwear pile, and the cider that was the last thing she had drunk. Her fingernails impaled themselves into the flesh of his back. "You good-for-nothing bastard," she spat.

Their dance was a battle, in which passion deployed its full arsenal of weapons: humiliation and spite, yearning and torture, a faint echo of tenderness that caused equal offense.

Rozenn noticed Paul's manhood pressing against her hip. She gazed into his eyes, and he saw triumph, desire and deep despair in that look. They were like two magnets that switched poles as they clashed, and were forced apart before gathering for the charge, colliding again and again, recklessly, shamelessly, obsessively. It was lust. They wanted each other so badly.

Paul didn't need to look at Serge for confirmation that the younger man didn't like what he saw. Serge could see how Paul shook something deep inside Rozenn that he himself would never be able to touch. He was clasping his hands together so tightly that his knuckles went white. He couldn't stand up, even as Paul danced away from the breakwater with Rozenn and into the night; he just couldn't.

COLETTE COULDN'T tear her eyes from Sidonie's face. She felt like a pinball balancing on the quivering tip of the final flippers above the drain.

"What *is* it?" she had asked, and with those three words she had thrown everything into question, including her life. Especially her life. It could have all been so different.

"Do you still not know?" Sidonie said, waves breaking in her eyes. Tears.

"Is it too late?" said Colette.

Before Sidonie could answer, she was startled by the sound of glasses shattering on the asphalt, followed by shrieks and a furious man's voice. Serge had upended the table after watching Paul lead Rozenn off the dance floor and into the sheltering shadows.

Jean-Rémy, Simon and Laurent the butcher wrestled the raging man to the ground and locked him into the cooler with the cold-eyed mullets and half-baked baguettes.

The musicians onstage urged all the dancers to join in with a gavotte, the Breton circle dance, which only worked when everyone danced with everyone else: a grandfather with his niece, sporting copious piercings; the mayor with the village's scandalous widow; her lover with the vicar's wife, only joined by their little fingers. The men skipped on the spot as the women circled them with a mixture of flirtatiousness and diffidence.

Pascale found herself next to a boat mechanic from Raguenez, who asked her if she couldn't lend him the white witch she was obviously training, just this once for his garden. Pascale presumed that he must be talking about her rake, and accepted, although of course she would have to ask her husband first. From behind the bar, Padrig was handing out miniature bottles of *chouchen*, while Jean-Rémy watched Laurine bending down to talk to one of the Parisians who spent every July lounging in their expensive holiday homes in Port Manec'h. A civil servant in ironed jeans. The chef could hardly bear to watch her smiling and nodding while the eyes of the Parisian in his smart jacket bored into every part of her anatomy. He nudged Padrig. "Go and ask that ugly Parisian what he wants to drink."

"The only one I can see is very cute," murmured Padrig, as he minced away.

Jean-Rémy thought of all the flowers he had secretly bought for Laurine. They were lying in the cooler alongside the let-

ters he had written her and the compliments that had never
made it past his lips.

COLETTE LAID her hand on Sidonie's, and the latter's fingers
enclosed her old friend's. The sight of the two women, whose
faces expressed what their lips had never uttered, deterred
Simon from asking Colette for a dance. He carried the present he had wanted to offer her, along with his feelings, onto
the *Gwen II*, which was nearby. He now knew with desperate
certainty that Colette would never be his. His heart shattered
like an anchor chain snagged on the rocks.

THE BALL broke up soon after the midnight firework display.
The breakwater lay there like an exhausted lover who cannot
decide whether to pull the sheets over her repeatedly caressed
skin. Marianne scoured the bushes and the quayside for abandoned glasses. Yann had helped to put away the chairs and
was now sitting in the kitchen having a glass of Calvados with
Jean-Rémy.

She found the last glasses on the empty stage. She set down
the tray, then stepped out into the middle of the stage. The
song she had played to the sea rose inside her—the song about
the son of the moon. She began to hum the tune, and imagined that she was wearing a red dress, and that, at the end of
the song, flushed, laughing faces turned to her and applause
broke out. She opened her eyes, embarrassed: it was an unat-
tainable dream.

Yann stepped out of Ar Mor's doorway, from where he had been observing her, took her by the hand and helped her down from the stage. With the strength she found so delightful in him, he pulled her close. Very close. His body was radiating a warmth that worked its way under her skin. Then he gently took her face in his hands. His mouth moved nearer. She didn't want to evade it, and even if she had, he wouldn't have allowed it. He kissed her.

Marianne shut her eyes, opened them, closed them again and let him kiss her, kissing him back, drowning in desire. She immediately succumbed to this rapture. Only when it grew cold did they stop embracing and seeking each other's lips, again and again. It was good beyond compare, and when she searched Yann's eyes for something that might prove the contrary, she found only desire.

Yann carried her tray into the kitchen.

When Marianne looked in the mirror behind the counter, she caught a fleeting glimpse of the young girl she had once been. Her lips were red from kissing.

"I have to paint you," whispered Yann, stepping up behind her. Insistent yet apologetic, as if alarmed by his own urges. "I have to."

30

YANN AND MARIANNE DIDN'T SAY A WORD AS THEY made their way, closely entwined, up the stairs to the Shell Room.

The July day had left its warmth under the eaves. Yann lit the seven candles that Marianne had placed on the window-sill.

"I see you," he whispered.

"It's too dark for you to see me properly," replied Marianne. Her mind was empty. She wanted—oh how she wanted!—to sleep with this man, and yet she was scared.

Lothar's face appeared. She drove it away, locked it into an empty room and swallowed the key. Tonight would divorce her from everything associated with her former life.

"I see you with my heart," said Yann, and took off his glasses before picking up his drawing pad and a piece of charcoal. "Please."

She sat down on the floor by the window and leaned against the wall. Yann's charcoal chirruped on the paper. He didn't see her, and yet still he saw her. He drew her face. He moved closer. She closed her eyes, imagining that he would kiss her, his lips melding themselves to hers, and she would devour him.

Yann used up twenty sheets. Everything about her was unique, deep and authentic. He drew Marianne as he felt her.

She blew out the candles. Now she was on the island—her personal Avalon. Nothing mattered anymore: not time, not space, not place. She undid the top buttons of her blouse. Yann leaned forward to switch on the small art nouveau lamp on the bedside table. Marianne held her blouse together. Slowly he took her fingers in his and pushed them to one side. His hands were warm on her skin as they eased open her top. He breathed in, gazing steadfastly into her eyes. She was so scared.

"*Mon amour,*" he whispered, moving even closer, and his hungry fingers helped her to open the remaining buttons. As their hands met, a tempest struck her island, sweeping her fears away. She was gripped with uncontainable impatience.

"*Maintenant,*" she moaned. "Now!"

There was more tearing than undressing, more clumsiness than gradual exploration, and Marianne looked and kissed and touched as everything offered itself up for her to experience and savor at once. Looking at Yann, watching Yann, kissing Yann, pulling Yann to her, running her fingers through his hair, over his face, pressing his hands to her body, smelling him. It was clear that he wanted her naked. That he wanted her. As she lay on the bed before him, solemnity and serenity returned to her island.

"You're beautiful," he said, laying his hand on her birthmark. "That's your soul: fire, love and strength. You are a woman born of fire."

This time he traced her with his fingers and his mouth. He sculpted her body with his desire, and to her it seemed as if her body became more feminine, more beautiful, more erotic under his caresses.

Marianne bit the pillow with lust. She laughed and she moaned, she called Yann's name into the night, and still he didn't enter her. He touched her with great concentration, her passion and well-being his only concern.

She lost interest in herself, and felt as if she were jumping from a bridge a second time. She ran her hands over his skin, which was soft and supple, taut over firm muscles and less firm ones. She sensed that Yann too was fearful about showing himself to her. That reassured her.

They laughed and embraced, clinging to each other and kissing without end. They were filled with joyous abandon, affection and desire.

When, after a time, he entered her, infinitely slowly, Yann looked at her and whispered her name in that harmonious voice of his. Marianne. Marianne? Marianne!

And then he was so deep inside her, she panted, "At last!" Her cry delighted him.

At last. At last. At last.

She felt every emotion at once—rejoicing and stunned horror that she had gone without this for so long.

"*Je t'aime,*" whispered Yann.

Marianne had abandoned herself to him and didn't recognize her own body as it felt, moved, demanded, tempted and pressed against Yann. She wanted more, more, everything. Now, right now! She never wanted to forgo such pleasure again!

She loved his moans, his abandon, his movements. It was as if his every slow, pleasurable thrust were meant to convey to her how desperately he had waited for this moment, and how he never wanted to stop. They gazed into each other's eyes, and Yann smiled as he made love to her.

Without warning, Marianne experienced an orgasm that seemed to originate all over her—deep inside her, inside her mouth, underneath her belly button. She felt as though someone were sucking her into a deep well. She lay completely still and allowed the waves to break over her. She moaned. It was lust and grief, relief and torment. It was heavenly.

Yann stared unwaveringly at her and he didn't stop. He didn't stop.

When the waves ebbed away, she began to laugh, quietly at first, then with increasing freedom. Yann looked at her, reined back his movements, smiled and asked, "What?" She didn't know how to tell him in French that she realized this: that having orgasms gave a woman a sense of freedom and ease.

She laughed, stroked Yann's intelligent face and said in a voice she didn't recognize as her own, "*Encore.*" Again. *I want everything, Yann. Know my body. Know my soul. Start right away.*

MARIANNE GOT up and opened the window. The silky, cool night air felt freshly rinsed and it hit her flushed skin like a soft flurry of feathery snowflakes. She took a long, deep breath.

When Yann had come . . . *Mon Dieu*, she hadn't known that men could come like that. It was incredible. It was a drug to see him in the throes of passion, to feel him discharge his energy and try to bury himself deeper in her, to dissolve and melt within her, followed by the moment he arrived, sought peace and found it. The way he had looked at her and gasped her name.

"May I draw you again now?" he asked her from the bed.

"Before and after?" she said in German, then, imitating the tone of a shopping channel: "Do you too want a change of look?"

She handed him the tile whose depiction of Kerdruc harbor and a small red boat had brought her here. "That's why I came. It's as if your tile called me to your side."

He pulled her to him, enlacing her with his arms. "We take coincidences like that one very seriously here, very seriously indeed," he said deliberately. "They are life's signals to us."

"Those were precisely the kind of coincidences I was missing."

31

A MAN WHOM LOVE HAS IGNORED MUST DO SOME-
thing mindless until he is once more capable of lucid
thought, which was why Simon spent hours sanding his old
boat. Colette hadn't wanted him.

It was a steamy July day, the kind one wished would end
with a thunderstorm; the kind that brought new insights, cool-
ness and dreams, which it then poured into people's hearts.
Paul was sitting on a folding chair.

"There are many mazy paths to love. Probably more paths
than there are in the whole of Brittany."

Simon kept sanding.

"I mean, look at that chef. He thinks no one knows he's
in love with Laurine, but everyone knows—apart from her.
Maybe Laurine doesn't know herself whether she's in love
with him."

"So you're the great expert on women now, are you?"
grunted Simon.

"I divide women into three types—"

"You're always doing that."

"The first love being in love, the second love making people fall in love with them, and the third—"

"Are you back together with Rozenn?"

"Partly."

"I can imagine which part." Simon stretched with a grimace.

"I'm her lover."

"What? She's staying with Serge?"

"She likes him."

"And she sleeps with you."

"She likes that even more."

"Tell me, Paul, haven't you learned anything in your life? Women don't take seriously men who claim to be lovers. That's just the way it is: every woman wants a man who says to her, 'I want you entirely, or not at all.'"

"As if you'd know what you're talking about! Because you and Colette hit it off so—" Paul didn't manage to finish his sentence, because a motorbike cruised into the yard. It was Jean-Rémy.

"Now don't come on all uncle-like and offer him your accumulated wisdom about love, Paul."

The three men exchanged greetings, and Jean-Rémy took receipt of the honey that Simon had reserved for him and that he would need to make the honey sauces Parisians adored.

"A glass of cider?" asked Simon before Jean-Rémy could get back on his bike. The chef declined. "Would you want to be the lover of the woman you loved?" Simon asked sneakily.

Jean-Rémy glanced from Paul to Simon. "You must be

crazy. You can only be a lover if you don't love the woman. Otherwise, it'd be the death of you."

"That, my lad, is hearsay. Just wait until you're my age, then you'll realize that a man can do anything when he puts his mind to it."

"Aha. *Kenavo*," said Jean-Rémy, starting up his motorbike.

PAUL AND Simon arrived at Ar Mor just in time for the afternoon news. As there were no Monday guests, Madame Geneviève had allowed a television set to be carried out onto the terrace. Jean-Rémy wasn't back yet, and she guessed that he must still be scouring the markets.

"Can you all be quiet?" shouted Simon.

"It's time you bought your own television, mate," said Paul. "They've been around for sixty years—you can trust them."

"Hey, isn't that Marianne?" said Sidonie, the elegant sculptress, pointing to the screen. Simon reached for the remote control and turned up the volume. Madame Ecollier stopped polishing the glasses, and Laurine moved closer, clutching her broom. They all listened intently to what the newsreader was saying.

"There is a search on for Marianne Messmann from Germany. The sixty-year-old is mentally deranged and requires medical attention. Her husband, Lothar Messmann, last saw her in a Parisian hospital, from which she is assumed to have escaped after a suicide attempt."

Then Lothar Messmann appeared on screen, speaking in German. The newsreader continued: "Please report any information to your local police station or call this number—"

Madame Geneviève grabbed the remote control from Simon's hand and pushed hard on the off button.

"We don't need that number," she said decisively.

"She has a husband?" asked Sidonie.

"And an attractive one too!" mumbled Marie-Claude.

"She never struck me as being mad," said Simon. "A bit, but not mad-mad. Pretty normal, actually."

"There's no way we're handing her over to the police," Paul said firmly. "She must have her reasons."

"For changing her name as well? She introduced herself as Marianne Lance!" stated Marie-Claude.

"That's her maiden name," Colette said calmly. "She adopted it and walked out on her husband."

For a second there was silence, then everyone started to speak at once. "Remember when she first got here?"

"She had nothing with her except for her handbag."

"And no clothes."

"No money. Maybe he beat her?"

"And she was sad," Laurine interjected.

"What are we going to do?" asked Sidonie.

"The best thing would be to ring the TV station—"

"Have you forgotten that you're Bretons?" Geneviève Ecollier interrupted Marie-Claude. Paul and Simon immediately spat on the floor. "Well, that's that! No need to waste our breath on the police or telephone numbers."

Everyone nodded.

MARIANNE HAD stood stock-still in the bathroom doorway, as if numbed by the sound of Lothar's voice from her bedroom.

"I love you, Marianne. Please give me a sign. It doesn't matter what you've done; we'll find a solution. And if you don't hear this, my angel, please get some help. Please, my dear French friends, help me to find my beloved wife. She's confused, but she belongs to me, as I do to her." This was followed by the newsreader's French translation.

Mentally deranged. Medical attention. Oh God, the card! The card she'd sent to Grete! Had that given her away?

The speech Lothar had made sounded so sincere, but now Marianne knew how to distinguish a true sound from a false one. The Breton language had taught her this: she didn't always understand the words, but she could sense the emotion behind them.

With Lothar there had been nothing behind the words. *I love you.* He'd never said that before, and it sounded like a cheap imitation of a feeling, like a fake Dior handbag.

As she hurried back into the room, her hair still wet from the shower, she saw Yann sitting on the bed, his expression lifeless. "You have a husband."

Marianne didn't answer. She had to be quick now, very quick. The brittle brown suitcase she had found in the cupboard full of dresses closed with an easy click after she had stuffed her clothes, the tile and her other possessions inside.

"Does he love you?"

"I don't know. I don't know if I've ever really known." She hastily pulled on a pair of trousers and a sweater, and hid her damp hair under a beret.

"Where are you going? To him?"

Marianne didn't reply. She had no answers to these questions; she knew only that she had to leave. Leave Yann, from whom she'd kept secret her identity and her past, hiding the fact that she was only an old woman from Celle who'd lived a dull life. Not the kind of woman a man like him truly deserved. She had led him to believe that she was free, but she wasn't.

"Marianne. Please. *Mon amour—*"

She put her index finger on his lovely curving lips. The way he was looking at her, without his glasses in the bright afternoon light . . . My God, they had made love with ravenous desire the night before, gazing hungrily at each other, but it was clear in the hard light of day that neither of them was young anymore; they were aging. Yet their feelings were young, and old yearnings had waited to be woken inside them. Now, though, Marianne was overwhelmed with a wave of shame.

I've committed adultery.

And she'd enjoyed it. She would do it again if she could, but she couldn't. She had all these conflicting emotions inside her, but they couldn't be spoken.

She put on her jacket and slipped into her linen shoes, then reached for her suitcase.

"Marianne!" Yann got to his feet as he was, naked. He looked at her with eyes full of grief. "*Kenavo*, Marianne," he said quietly, pulling her into his embrace. She threw her arms around this man who was already more to her than Lothar had ever been. Her husband had never given the slightest hint that she was special or loved. This delighted and terrified her at the same time, and the terror drove her down the stairs and out of the guesthouse.

As she emerged into the afternoon sun, she drowned in a saturated blaze of light, air and intense color all around, in the trees and in the water. She cast a glance through the open kitchen door. Jean-Rémy. She had to tell Jean-Rémy that . . .

She heard a murmur of voices from the terrace, and the sound of a television set. She heard her name repeated in the general hubbub and she knew that everyone had seen her. Everyone now knew that she was a fraudster, a runaway and a crazy suicidal wife.

She didn't dare to face them. The little cat wound its way through her legs. She stepped around it without a glance, and the animal began to shriek. It didn't meow, it didn't hiss; it let out a shrill scream, as if it were straining its vocal cords to produce something other than a cat sound.

Marianne made no attempt to stem the flow of tears that blurred her vision as she strode up the narrow street that would lead her away from the harbor, away from Yann, away from the cat, away from everything and out of Kerdruc.

She walked and she didn't look back. The farther she walked, the greater her feeling of being sewn into a bag and drowned. She was finding it harder and harder to breathe. She felt as if she were about to die. Only now, that was no longer what she wanted.

32

ON HIS WAY BACK TO KERDRUC, JEAN-RÉMY HAD MADE an unplanned detour via Rospico and on to Kerascoet, a five-hundred-year-old weavers' village of renovated thatched cottages built of standing stones.

Madame Gilbert lived on the edge of the village. Jean-Rémy let his motorbike coast into her courtyard, which was surrounded by pine trees. As he removed his helmet, he heard the boom of the sea. He thought of the letters to Laurine that lay freezing in the cooler.

He found Madame Gilbert on one of the hidden terraces high above the coastal path. She was alone.

"Take off your sunglasses." Those were the first words they exchanged once he had pulled her from her chair and pushed her before him into her bedroom. She took off her glasses, laid them on the bedside table next to a picture of her husband and placed her hand, palm up, over her eyes to hide her wrinkles.

She had blocked out the heat of the scorching sun behind the blue shutters. When Jean-Rémy's eyes had got used to the half-darkness, and he had repeatedly moved himself against

Madame Gilbert, his thoughts turned to Laurine. Then he forgot her and thought of nothing, merely feeling, as Madame Gilbert occasionally moaned in amazement at his frenzy. Only when he felt from the tension in her body that she had come did he pull back.

Jean-Rémy didn't love Madame Gilbert, which was why he had become her lover. He hadn't been to see her for a long time, a very long time—almost as long as he knew he had been in love with Laurine. Since then he had not slept with any other woman to save himself for Laurine. It was stupid; then again, it wasn't.

Madame Gilbert didn't ask where he had been for the past two years. She was experienced and she knew that the pleasure of a man twenty years her junior wouldn't last forever.

She stroked the damp hair at the back of Jean-Rémy's neck with the tips of her immaculately manicured fingernails. In her arms, Jean-Rémy felt as if he were bidding farewell to an idea, an alternative life. After a time on the margins, he had now returned to his homeland, where affairs flourished but nothing lasted: everything could be carried off by the wind. Beyond the border had lain love, where things had deep roots that allowed them to withstand storms and fear. Sleeping with Madame Gilbert meant there would be no more room for love in his life.

She lit a cigarette and sat up. "There's going to be a storm later," she said.

"Will you welcome me again soon?" asked Jean-Rémy.

"You know the times, *mon cher*. Don't ring in advance, or else I start imagining what might happen when you're here."

"What do you imagine?"

Madame Gilbert pulled his head down until his ear touched her lips. Her lipstick was smudged from his kisses. She whispered what she imagined to him, and as she spoke, he closed his eyes. She kept speaking as he levered himself on top of her and into her again, and as she painted her arousal in words, he came for a second time.

Afterward, he gathered his clothes, the last of which—his helmet and scarf—he found out on the terrace next to the deck chair. The ice cubes in her glass had melted, turning the orange juice a milky hue.

When he bent over Madame Gilbert to kiss her, she said, "By the way, today is our anniversary. My husband thought it would be a good idea to celebrate our twenty-three years together at Ar Mor. So please reserve a table for us, will you, darling?" She peered at him through inscrutable eyes like bright marbles as cool as the sea.

RIDING BACK to Kerdruc, Jean-Rémy flicked up the visor of his helmet. When his eyes began to water, he could be sure that it was the wind. It was always the wind that extinguished things and drove them away, even tears.

HE ARRIVED at Ar Mor and walked past Laurine, who was laying the tables for dinner, without daring to look her in the eye.

She called quietly after him, "Jean-Rémy? Marianne's gone. She was on television. She has a husband who's looking for her, and she must be traveling to meet him now. Jean-Rémy, what's wrong? Are you crying?" She walked toward him, her eyes full of concern.

He shrank back from her. He still had the smell of sex about him, a mixture of perfume and the scent of Madame Gilbert on his mouth. He put the counter between himself and Laurine, washed his hands and face in the sink and then pretended to study the bookings.

"The Gilberts are coming for dinner," he said. "They've reserved for their anniversary. We should put some flowers on their table."

Laurine stared at him. "He just rang," she whispered.

"Yes, I was at the Gilberts' running some errands," Jean-Rémy hastened to add. "But Monsieur Gilbert said he would ring anyway."

"Monsieur Gilbert called from the airport in Paris. You're lying about seeing him." Her voice was as fragile as fine crystal.

After a long silence, he knew that she realized that he had spent the afternoon at Madame Gilbert's.

"I wish you were *really* crying," said the waitress.

Please, Jean-Rémy begged wordlessly. *Please don't let this be happening.*

It was only when she had walked away that he realized that he had lost two special women as he was moving between Madame Gilbert's thighs. Laurine. And Marianne.

He went into the cooler, double-locked the door behind him and cursed until he wept, spattering furious tears onto the letters he had written to Laurine but had never sent.

33

MARIANNE HAD STUMBLED THREE MILES ALONG the road before she realized that she wasn't fleeing toward the sea. She was standing at the crossroads that led right to Pont-Aven and left to Concarneau. She set down her suitcase, sat on it and rested her hands on the leather. She could hardly breathe for pain. Weakly she raised her thumb—the international signal of runaways and loners, of all those who can no longer bear to be stuck where they are.

No one stopped. The occasional car honked its horn. She continued to hold her thumb out into the empty air.

Eventually, a yellow Renault Kangoo drew up alongside her. A woman with a curly blond bob opened the door for her. Marianne scrutinized the woman's face to find out whether she had only stopped because she had recognized her.

The woman introduced herself as Adela Brelivet from Concarneau. "My name's . . ." Marianne began, then paused. There was a search on for Marianne Messmann, so that was the one person she wasn't. Also, the woman's smile irritated her: she showed her teeth, but her eyes remained cool. "My name's Maïwenn."

"Maïwenn? That's an interesting name. You know it's a combination of Marie and 'white,' don't you? White Maria?" Adela babbled. "Adela means something too. I'll let you in on a secret: it means love." She let out a shriek of laughter.

Adela talked for a full twenty minutes as the landscape flashed by. The small villages, the roundabouts, the red-and-white place names. Tears ran in a continuous stream down Marianne's cheeks. Yann. Yann! It hurt as much as if her heart had been cut out without anaesthetic. Adela prattled on, oblivious, as Marianne wept silently.

Concarneau, at last. When they pulled up at the traffic lights outside the covered market, Adela leaned across Marianne to open the door and wished her a pleasant journey. It sounded mocking. Marianne got out, pulling the suitcase after her, and the yellow Kangoo roared away.

Marianne turned this way and that. *Where to? Where do I go from here?* She watched a flock of crows heading inland from the Atlantic. Pascale Goichon, her dear friend and witch, had said that crows were a sign, so she followed them. She approached the market, her suitcase growing heavier and heavier. When she had reached the far end of the market square, still guided by the birds' flight, she came to the marine center, then the harbor wall, and suddenly she was gazing out over the wide, glittering gray-blue Atlantic. The clouds, hanging low over the land, did not venture out beyond the shore, acting as if they were an invisible wall that divided the sky into two—one part a deep, noble blue, the other a land sky, dotted with whitecaps. Two separate worlds.

The soft roar of the waves and the erratic, flighty beating of her heart overlapped inside Marianne's head. Fifty yards on, she happened upon an old, squat church whose thick sand-stone walls had been eaten away by salt water.

In front of the plain portal, a sign read: "Priest available." For spiritual emergencies, Marianne thought. Next to the church was a telephone booth. She stepped inside, took out a few coins, pushed them into the slot and dialed the number of a house at the end of a cul-de-sac in Celle. There was a whis-tling on the line, as if the wind were rushing through it, but then the sound changed and the phone rang. Once. Twice. After the third tone, Lothar picked up.

"Messmann!"

Marianne clapped her hand to her mouth. His voice was so close!

"Hello? This is Messmann!"

The digital display showing her credit blinked: a cent less every ten seconds. What should she say?

"Answer me. Now!"

Marianne's mind was empty.

"Marianne? Annie, is that you?" There was not a single word she wanted to say to her husband. "Marianne! Don't mess things up! Tell me where you are right now! I can see on the display . . . Is that France? Are you still in—"

She hurriedly hung up and left the telephone booth, wip-ing her hands on her coat as if she had to get rid of an invis-ible stain. She went into the church, and the cool air inside the sandstone building dried her sweat. Plain, bare wooden pews, a silver cross above the altar, a model ship in a corner. She made her way cautiously to the confessional box next to the sacristy; it looked like a worm-eaten wardrobe with three doors.

"Hello?" she whispered.

"*Allo*," replied a deep voice from inside the wardrobe.

She opened the left-hand door, saw a bench and a prayer stool with a purple velvet cushion on it, entered and closed the door behind her. She gave a sigh of relief. On the other side of the close-meshed iron grille the vague outline of a face hovered white and pale, its dark nostrils gigantic. The figure mumbled reassuringly.

She leaned back; she felt safe here. Safe from questions, safe from answers. Why had she run away from Yann? Where was she to go? Why was she still not dead?

"I wanted to kill myself," she began quietly.

There was no response from the other side of the grille.

"Damn! I've done everything wrong! I actually wanted . . ."

What did I want? I only wanted to live. Just live. Without fear. Without regrets. I want friends. I want love. I want to do something. I want to work. I want to laugh. I want to sing. I want . . .

"I want to live. I want to live!" she repeated out loud.

The whites of the priest's eyes gleamed fiercely on the other side of the grille.

"You see, I have a husband I can't bear to be with anymore. I had a life I can't stand anymore. But I no longer want to end it all," whispered Marianne. "That's . . . too easy."

Sixty. It definitely wasn't too late. It's never too late, she thought. Never, not even an hour before the void.

"I want to get drunk at last!" she said more loudly. "I want to wear red underwear! I want a family. I want to play the accordion. I want my own room and my own bed! I'm so fed up of hearing, 'You can't do that! What will people think? You can't have your cake and eat it. Dreams are all an illusion.' Mad—my husband thinks I'm mad, that's what he announced on television! I feel so ashamed, and I hate him for making me feel that way.

"And now I want to sleep with Yann again! Do you know how long it had been since my last orgasm before Yann? So long! I want a man who's interested in how I feel. I want desire and Yann and to eat lobster with my fingers." She got up, bumping her head. "And I don't want to leave Kerdruc. There you go!"

Oh no, I'm not going to leave Kerdruc of my own free will. They'll have to catch me and tie me up and carry me away.

She let herself fall back onto the bench before addressing the priest again. "Thank you, you've really helped me."

"You're welcome, madame," the man said in a low voice. In German.

Marianne jumped to her feet in shock and hurried out of the wardrobe at the same time as the priest. It wasn't a priest, but a man in a black roll-neck sweater with thick glasses, thinning blond hair and a notepad in his hand.

"I live out in Cabellou for half the year. I'm from Hamburg and I'm a writer. I'm sorry I didn't immediately . . . I was so surprised when you came in and sat down. And then you were in such full swing that . . . Good grief, no one could make up those things you said!"

Marianne stared at him. "Of course not," she said. "It's true."

"I wonder if my wife sometimes thinks I'm not really

interested in how she feels. Do you think that we men don't respect women enough as women?"

"Do you have a car?" she asked instead of answering.

The writer nodded.

"Could you drive me to Kerdruc?"

34

When she had got back from Concarneau, her room was exactly as she had left it: the bed messy, the wardrobe open, roses in the vase. The only thing missing was Yann. The imprint of his head on the pillow was still visible.

The view from her window to the sea over Kerdruc's breakwater, the old thatched cottages, the colorful boats and the swaying waters was just as it had been the first time she had seen it—so unsettlingly beautiful that it made the rest of the world difficult to bear.

She unpacked her bulky suitcase, went down to join Jean-Rémy in the kitchen, tied her apron around her waist and began to prepare batter for the pancakes, both sweet and savory, as if nothing had happened.

Jean-Rémy stared at her, his mouth gaping at first, then with a never-ending beaming smile. Geneviève Ecollier came into the kitchen and gave her a testing look. "Welcome back," she said. "You've walked a long way to reach us at the end of the world."

"And this is exactly where I want to stay," replied Marianne.

"Fantastic. Champagne?"

Marianne nodded, and as they clinked glasses she said, "You can waste half your life only ever looking at the man who has caused you the greatest pain."

"That's typical of us women," said Madame Ecollier after a while. "We think it's a mark of bravery."

"Thinking that someone else's life is more important than your own?"

"Yes, it's a reflex. Like the twelve-year-old girl who is placed at the exact position in the family where she disturbs everyone the least, punctually sets the table and clears away after her father, and waits patiently to be loved, as long as she behaves herself."

"I think that's stupid."

"But only recently, right? Before that, you were stupid too and you didn't even realize it. Everything was more sacred than yourself, and your own longings were the least sacred thing of all."

Marianne thought of Lothar and nodded.

"You've changed," said Madame Geneviève, her voice interrupting Marianne's train of thought.

"People never change!" Marianne retorted. "We forget ourselves, and when we rediscover ourselves, we merely imagine that we have changed. That's not true, though. You can't change dreams; you can only kill them—and some of us are very good murderers."

"Have you rekindled your dreams, Madame Lance?"

"I'm still looking for the rest of my dream," whispered Marianne. *And the part of me that dares to seize it. Oh Yann, forgive me. Please forgive me.*

"Where's Laurine got to?" she asked, trying to regain her composure.

"She has a job interview in Rozbras."

"What? Why?"

Geneviève pursed her lips and left the kitchen. Marianne found Jean-Rémy smoking a joint outside the back door. She stood up as straight and tall as she could. "What. Have. You. Done?" She grew angrier with every word.

Jean-Rémy blew a smoke ring into the air.

"Slept with another woman," he said with studied casualness. "It's better that way. I'm not made for one woman, and definitely not for one like Laurine."

Marianne pulled back her arm and dealt the young chef a resounding slap, which sent the joint spinning from his hand. His face twisted with suppressed anger, but he picked up the joint and hid his resentment behind an impassive expression. "Yann Gamé didn't exactly look overjoyed when I saw him earlier either."

Marianne slumped onto the stone step beside Jean-Rémy.

"Do you know what men do when they're suffering, Marianne? They drink. They sleep with other women if they're lucky enough to get it up despite their grief, and then they wait until things improve."

He passed her the joint, and she took a quick drag, then a longer one.

"*Merde,*" she said disconsolately.

"*Ya,*" agreed Jean-Rémy.

35

THE FLUSH ON LAURINE'S CHEEKS BORE WITNESS TO her exertions, her fury at Jean-Rémy and her aching heart. The waitress lowered her gaze as she gave Alain Poitier the outstanding reference letter that Genevière had handed to her with a stony face.

When Jean-Rémy had made his blunder, she'd felt as if something had sliced through her soul, and it wouldn't stop bleeding.

Alain studied her. "Mademoiselle, you've been working at Ar Mor for years."

"You know all there is to know, Monsieur Poitier," replied Laurine. "And I know that you own the restaurant in Rozbras and that you're Madame Ecollier's competitor. You make life difficult for her. But I wanted to leave, and so here I am."

Alain was confused by Laurine's straightforwardness and honesty. "Is that what she says? That I make life difficult for her?"

"She doesn't say anything about you, monsieur. Nothing bad and nothing good. Nothing at all."

ALAIN HADN'T expected Laurine's words to affect him so deeply. Genoveva . . . It was a long time ago, yet nothing had diluted his memories. He had fallen in love with Geneviève Ecollier at first sight. She had been twenty-five, he twenty-eight, and one heat-soaked summer day she had pierced him to the very core of his being with an intensity that put everything else he had ever desired in the shade. That was the day Geneviève Ecollier had celebrated her engagement to Alain's brother Robert.

Alain had come from Rennes to get a first glimpse of the woman Robert had told him about on the telephone and in his innocent, gushing letters. He had believed only a quarter of what his brother had said, and had braced himself to find a charmless farm girl. Yet Geneviève was nothing of the sort. She had a provocative sensuality and a lively manner, with cherry-red lips and dark eyes that bore into a man until he heard his heart snap in two.

Alain had spent the entire evening of the party in silence. He had been angry—with Robert for not lying to him about his bride, and with Geneviève simply because she was who she was, and was doing nothing to ensure that Alain did or didn't fall in love with her. He had observed how she behaved with Robert, full of gentle attentiveness, and with her parents and his parents. She managed to convince his austere mother, who distrusted any female that approached her sons, to treat her like a daughter who, on the contrary, needed protecting from men's nastiness. His father acted as if he were personally responsible for his son's success in attracting this wonderful woman, and displayed an almost dog-like devotion to Geneviève.

Later, Alain had mustered enough courage to ask Geneviève to dance. If he had merely been confused beforehand, he was hopelessly lost the moment Geneviève's body brushed against his in her red dress. They didn't speak, they simply gazed at each other, and their breathing intensified during the dance. He had felt her warm skin with his fingertips through the silky fabric; he had felt the heat that radiated from her eyes and her bosom. There was nothing to say that would not have belied the language of their glances and their hands. The longer they danced, unspeaking, the harder it became to find words. He knew, however, that they both felt something that their reason would not admit: I. Want. You.

Yes. Take. Me.

Their shared desire had tipped him over the edge.

Alain had always been the family hero: he had won everything, and his intentions had always been clear. He had never needed to cheat or lie to get what he wanted. With Geneviève, however, he lost his hero status. He lost everything, and now he would surrender his soul. All this was clear to Alain, not in words but in the depths of his conscience, as he and Geneviève twirled around the room to the music—in the very room in which there was to this day a painting that ran around the walls. In the old guesthouse.

Later, Geneviève had bought the hotel, as if she didn't want to relinquish to strangers what had occurred that evening.

WHEN YOU'RE young, and don't yet know anything about love and the world, it's natural to think and act stupidly. Not that Geneviève, his Genoveva, had ever been stupid. No, but Alain had. He had loved his brother's bride fervently and purely.

What about her? Geneviève was smart enough not to act upon it straightaway. She had been like July in Brittany, with its days that will not give in to the dark, bracing their bright streak against the darkness until midnight. Alain, with all the fieriness of youth, had refused to accept this. He had decided to stay in Kerdruc. He had pursued her with his lust, overwhelmed her with his love and seduced her with his longing. Passion was threatening to drown them both when Geneviève surrendered four weeks later.

ALAIN AND Geneviève had had three summers together, three autumns, two winters and two springs. They loved each other desperately, earnestly, deeply. But neither of them had had the heart to tell Robert the truth. He joined the navy and was away for months on end—wonderful months!

Then one day when a bitter, bullying south-westerly wind was blowing, Robert came home three days before they expected him, as the ship he served on as an officer had to go into dry dock early. He found his bride and his elder brother wedged together on the floor in Geneviève's kitchen in Trégunc. They didn't notice him, and he was able to watch them for long enough to realize that this wasn't the first time they had done this, and also that their sensations were unlike any that he had known or experienced with Geneviève, or ever would. He stepped over their tangled legs and opened the fridge to pour himself some cider. And that was when Alain messed everything up.

He had tried to let Robert have Geneviève, begging him, telling him that the wedding was in ten days. "And this," he had said, pointing to the kitchen floor, "this will stop."

Geneviève had said nothing, simply staring at Alain as he promised his younger brother that he could have Geneviève all to himself. She had got to her feet, still naked, and given Alain a slap, followed by a second one.

To Robert she had hissed, "The wedding's off," before grabbing her clothes, snatching her shoes and running out into the south-westerly wind. Only then had Alain understood that he had betrayed her love with his stupid wish to undo everything that had happened. When it came down to it, he had given in to guilt and fear. Not she, though: Geneviève had remained true to her love.

Twelve years after that last kiss on the kitchen floor, Alain had moved to Rozbras, and he had now been living on the other bank of the Aven river for twenty-three years. For thirty-five years Geneviève had refused to forgive him for his treachery.

ALAIN LOOKED at Laurine. She must be the same age now as Geneviève had been when they were so passionate, believing they had reinvented the meaning of love. He hoped that Laurine would never meet a man as stupid as he used to be.

"Are you in love?" he asked her.

"Not at the moment," she admitted after some hesitation. "Well, actually I am, but I don't want to be. Not anymore."

"I could do with a good waitress," said Alain.

"Can I start right away?"

36

AT FIRST IT WAS ONLY THE SCENT OF DUST AND ELEC-
tricity, but then gusts of wind tore around the eaves of
houses and through the gaps in door frames, lifting the tablecloths in Ar Mor and sending glasses smashing to the floor. It
was shortly after eleven o'clock at night.

Old Bretons battened down their shutters and drove their
animals into their sheds. The men went around the houses
looking for unattached objects that might be swept away.
They leaned into the wind as if they needed it for support.
Children and cats took fright, even if they couldn't remember the events of Boxing Day morning ten years previously, in
1999, when a hurricane had crashed through Brittany. It had
been the fiercest hurricane since records began. Its name was
Lothar.

The clouds hung low and black, and the first raindrops
were as thick and heavy as blood. Jean-Rémy, Geneviève
Ecollier, Madame Gilbert and her husband (both on their anniversary date) were with Padrig (the temporary kitchen help),
and Marianne at Ar Mor. Jean-Rémy didn't dare to look at
Madame Gilbert.

"You shouldn't drive in this," Madame Geneviève said to Madame and Monsieur Gilbert. She had to raise her voice to make herself heard over the rain pounding on the window-panes.

"Do you still have a suite available?" asked Monsieur Gilbert. He was an ethnopsychologist and extremely proud of the fact that he could put entire countries on the couch. He saw migrants setting fire to cars in Paris as an expression of their cultural depression. Madame Gilbert let the smoke curl from between her red-painted lips.

Geneviève smiled. "King-size bed, double bathtub and a mirror on the ceiling."

"That would be just the right thing for our special day, don't you think, *ma tigresse?*" Monsieur Gilbert suggested to his wife, and she nodded, smiled and hugged him, all the while looking Jean-Rémy in the eye over her husband's shoulder. Geneviève gave them their key.

There was a massive clap of thunder, followed by a hiss, a bang and a blinding flash that lit up the breakwater. The electric lamps flickered briefly, then went out. Now the only light came from the table candles. In the intimate darkness, Jean-Rémy saw Monsieur Gilbert's hand feel its way down to his wife's bum.

Suddenly the door flew open with a crash to reveal Laurine. She was completely soaked, her shirt transparent. Padrig stared at her, Monsieur Gilbert stared at her, and Jean-Rémy felt like murdering them all.

"Padrig!" he called angrily. "Give me a hand in the kitchen. I have to start the back-up generator for the cooler."

The rain was now beating against the windows with such

force that Geneviève had to shout. "Another Calvados to warm you all up." She poured six shots.

The sky was piled high with red-black towers of cloud. A streak of lightning split the blackness of the sky like a seam.

JEAN-RÉMY AND Padrig started the generator, and the lights flickered into life again. The dusky, sensual magic that had filled the room a moment earlier was banished by a cruel neon blaze.

"What's that?" asked Padrig, pointing to a half-hidden box of flowers and letters in the cooler. Without a word, Jean-Rémy held out the envelopes to him. Each bore Laurine's name and a date. Dozens of love letters.

"And you never gave them to her, you idiot?"

"I'll never be able to now. I've hurt her. None of these will mean anything to her now."

Padrig shook his head in exasperation.

LAURINE HAD put on her jacket and fetched the rest of her belongings from her locker in the staff toilets.

"Will you drive me home, Padrig?" she asked firmly, not deigning even to glance at Jean-Rémy. Madame Gilbert had her eyes trained on him, though, and Monsieur Gilbert was watching his wife and smiling, as if he knew everything and had come to terms with his wife's desires. He drained his glass.

The storm rumbled on; the rain was coming down almost horizontally, slicing through the air. Padrig and Laurine vanished into the wall of fog, and Madame Gilbert and her husband ducked underneath the awning with Geneviève and scurried up the stairs into the guesthouse. Jean-Rémy and Marianne stayed behind in the kitchen with a bottle of Calvados and a pile of unsent love letters.

"Was that the other woman?" asked Marianne after a while. Jean-Rémy nodded and propped his chin on his hand, then filled both their glasses to the brim.

Later, as she hauled herself up the stairs to the Shell Room, Marianne decided that she would commence the next morning by apologizing to everyone. She would apologize for coming, for leaving, and for not being honest with them. It was only when she was lying in bed with one leg on the floor so that the room didn't spin around her so much that she realized that she wanted to give a name to the cat. He should belong to her, and his nomadic soul would have reached its home.

"Good night, Max," whispered Marianne into the darkness. The cat purred.

37

WAS IT ONLY WHEN HEARTS BROKE THAT THEY RE-
vealed their true nature?

Sidonie, the sculptress, sensed a surge of something inside her that she hadn't experienced for many years: sadness. She caught a tear as it ran down her cheek, and examined her rough, chapped fingers. She failed to hear someone knocking on the garden door to her studio.

"Hello. Anyone there?"

As Marianne came in, Sidonie set down the two halves of the broken stone heart that she'd been sculpting on top of the laboratory report. It had just arrived from her doctor's office this morning.

Marianne's smile faded and was replaced by a look of concern. "What's wrong?" she asked, noticing Sidonie's tears.

"Nothing," said Sidonie. "Just . . . some dirt. And the sun."
And death and love.

Marianne crossed the studio in a few long strides and put down on the table the basket containing groceries for the Goichons and a bag of chocolates resembling small pebbles that she had brought for the sculptress. Then she embraced

Sidonie, who was too surprised to dodge her approach. To an unwitting observer it must have looked as if Marianne were forcing the other woman to dance with her. Sidonie's arms hung limply by her sides, her head resting on Marianne's shoulder, and together the two of them rocked back and forth, their feet moving in time.

As they performed this strange waltz, Sidonie sobbed, noiselessly at first, then more and more uncontrollably, until she had to cling to Marianne to prevent herself collapsing. Her sobs were interspersed with words of attempted explanation. She felt that Marianne's embrace was drawing something out of her—a torrent of fear, anguish, sorrow, and rage at the injustice of death.

Marianne felt Sidonie's emotions flooding toward her like a spring tide. She also felt pulsing inflamed areas as she let her fingers glide a few fractions of an inch, like sensors, across the sculptress's stout torso. Her fingers picked up what her eyes would never be capable of seeing. She wanted to heal her friend.

"Cancer" was the word that Sidonie kept repeating as she pointed to various parts of her body—her chest, her head, her kidneys and her abdomen. The cancer was everywhere. It had slumbered inside her for decades, then exploded in a matter of months.

Marianne's palms were burning. She had a taste of copper on her tongue, and she pulled Sidonie close to her again. Abruptly, the sculptress stopped weeping, as if her reservoir of tears had run dry. Now Marianne was rocking her and humming a melody until Sidonie stopped shivering. She guided her to an armchair in a corner of the studio, and slipped into the kitchen to make some tea. Catching sight of a bottle of cognac in the corner, though, she turned off the gas under the kettle and poured some of the vintage brandy into two cups. One she filled to the top, and handed it to Sidonie.

"Down the hatch," she urged.

Gradually she wheedled out of Sidonie how long she'd known (a long time), who knew (no one except her) and that she didn't intend to tell anyone, not even her children Camille and Jérôme: they ought not to feel obliged to uproot themselves for a few months from their normal environment and bear the burden of their mother's death. Not Colette either—under no circumstances!

"Why under no circumstances? I thought you were friends?"

"Yes, we're friends. Only friends . . ." The way Sidonie said *only* made Marianne prick up her ears.

"*Seulement la grenouille s'est trompée de conte*"—only the frog ended up in the wrong fairy tale—she said under her breath, quoting one of the countless phrases Pascale Goichon had taught her.

Sidonie stared at her. "I'm the frog," she said. "I'm never going to turn into a prince—not even into a princess's lapdog. I love Colette. She loves men. End of story."

"End of story?" said Marianne. "A terrible story."

Sidonie shrugged her shoulders.

"You must tell her."

"What?"

"Everything!"

"I'm not going to do anything."

"Do you just mean to lie down and . . . die?"

Sidonie shut her eyes. The fact that she knew she was soon going to die was one thing, but that someone else should say it out loud was quite another. Much worse. It made it true. "Exactly. I'm going to die. Just like that."

Marianne sighed deeply. "All right," she said, and stood up to pour them both another brandy.

Sidonie put on a record, and Maurice Chevalier's voice filled the studio. As she walked back to the table, the familiar pain seared through her, but this time it went deeper than usual. The devastation was beginning. She held onto a chair, which toppled over, banged against the table and swept the broken stone heart to the floor. She waited until the pain relented and took several deep, regular breaths. Marianne bent down to pick up the pieces of stone. There was something hidden in the core: a red streak with a shimmer of pale blue. She helped Sidonie to her bed.

"Anyway, why did you come here?" asked the sculptress.

"To apologize," said Marianne.

"But . . . for what?

"For lying to you all. For being married and for not being the person I pretended I was."

"Yes, but you're still yourself, aren't you?"

"Yes," said Marianne. "Yes, I am."

But I had forgotten myself.

WHEN MARIANNE had left Sidonie, she rode her scooter restlessly to Pont-Aven. She longed to escape into Yann's arms, and yet he was the one she had hurt the most. Could she really expect that he was going to make light of that? No, he would reject her, as every man of reason and honor would do. She headed for Colette's gallery and waited with feigned patience until she had finished advising a group of tourists from Hamburg. When they had left, Marianne turned the sign on the door round to *"Fermé."* Closed.

The first thing she did was to stammer her apologies, but Colette waved them away with a flick of her cigarette holder. Marianne's concerns were as inconsequential as the smoke that drifted out of the half-open window. "We like you," said the gallery owner. "Didn't that ever occur to you?"

Marianne smiled before pronouncing the hardest words she'd ever had to utter: she told Colette of her friend Sidonie's imminent death. Colette slumped back onto the chair behind her elegant bureau. It was only from the quaking of her shoulders that Marianne could tell she was weeping. She was weeping for all the years she had not lived with Sidonie, and she was weeping for the brief span of time that she had left to make up for what was gone forever.

The brandy's effects on Marianne had eased, and she was hit by a wave of sober shame for daring to meddle in other people's lives.

"Merci," Colette said in a tear-choked voice. *"Merci.* She would never have told me. That's how she is. She never wanted to make things hard for others, only for herself."

The sign would not be turned back to *"Ouvert"* again that day, nor in the weeks and months that followed.

38

THE MARK OF A MAGNANIMOUS SPIRIT WAS THAT THAT person never turned others' errors against them. Pascale Goichon walked toward Marianne with wide-open arms as she got off her Vespa.

"Oh dear!" she cried. "That man on television! Hopefully he'll stay in there and never come out." She enfolded Marianne in her arms. "Emile says he found him slimy," she whispered into her ear.

Her husband gave a curt nod as Marianne entered the library, then handed her the shopping list. When she opened her mouth to make her planned apology, Emile raised a hand in warning.

"You're not stupid, Marianne Lance, so stop acting as if you were. You didn't betray him; he betrayed you. He should have let you go and left you in peace, instead of exposing you before the entire nation. Would you get that into your head?"

I've never thought of it that way.

"A man in love will set off barefoot across the Congo to find his wife, but *he* just stands up in front of a camera like a silly cockerel and starts whingeing."

He was about to say that the man should grow a pair, but then he decided against it. He thought it wasn't proper to mention the family jewels in the presence of ladies, so he simply tossed her the list and the car keys instead.

MARIANNE DIDN'T notice anything in the supermarket at first. It was only when Laurent asked her confidentially whether he should start ordering her some specialities that Marianne paid more attention.

"Animal hearts, perhaps?" said the small, fat man with the black mustache, leaning in conspiratorially. "The heart of a deer, a bull or a dog, if you need one. Or a few chicken bones?"

She could sense his disappointment when she merely ordered fillet for the dogs and braising steak to cook the Goichons a German casserole.

As she was standing in the fruit section, sniffing the melons and rubbing the Greek asparagus stems together to see if they squeaked—a sign of freshness—a saleswoman came toward her.

"Are you buying those to enhance potency?" she asked. There was a mixture of awe, timidity and hope in her expression.

Shopping that day was like running the gauntlet, and Marianne had no idea why. Madame Camus at the cheese counter, Mademoiselle Bruno at the till and even the Moroccan cleaning lady Amélie hurled questions at her. "Will I find love this weekend? Is he the right one? Should I do everything my husband requests in the bedroom?"

Marianne decided to employ some of the often perplexing phrases she had picked up from Pascale. "A handful of love is better than an oven full of bread. If you squeeze your nose, milk comes out. You don't have to drink the sea dry." Every one of her responses was met with a nod and a grateful smile.

She chuckled as she told Pascale everything later, while the goulash was marinating in paprika, but Pascale didn't find it funny.

"I thought this would happen sooner or later, but not so soon. The people saw you on television, and something must have gone 'bang' in their heads."

"Bang? What do you mean, bang?"

"Laurent offered you hearts? That's so typical. Next thing you know he'd have asked you to bless his new car in return, or give his children a magic spell for school, or brew him a potion capable of bringing his wife to commit affronts against demure conventions."

"I don't understand."

"Nor do I, but it seems as if people here are hoping you're a white witch." Marianne noticed a new, more familiar tone in Pascale's voice. "They're going to start gazing after you at the market or trying to touch you quickly."

"What? But I haven't done anything!"

"Oh yes you have! You're from another country. You live alone. You were on television. Television is overpowering magic. To them you're a woman who has devoted her life to the goddesses of the sea and of love."

"Oh my word. And why do they think that?"

"Because we're friends. They think I'm teaching you to be

like me, and I have specialized in love. But we both know that your powers lie elsewhere, right?"

"Wrong."

"Your hands, Marianne. Didn't you know you're a healer? Why do you think you bear that birthmark? It means you're special."

Marianne studied her fingers, which were kneading pasta dough to make macaroni with fried onions and cheese. "I don't really know very much about myself," she explained sheepishly.

"Sometimes other people recognize us before we do." Pascale laid her fingers gently on Marianne's cheek. "Yann recognized you, as I did. Did you know that he can taste and hear colors? He's a synaesthete. He senses things that none of us can see or feel, and then he paints them. You saw that on his tile. You understood what he saw without knowing that you did. You both feel in the same way."

"I hurt him."

"I know, Marianne, I know. When will you go to him?"

When the details no longer make me so nervous, Marianne felt like saying, but she would then have had to explain everything else to Pascale. For example, why she couldn't say, *Yann, I love you.* It was not because it wasn't true. There was a simple answer to the question of whether she loved him: yes!

In love there was only yes or no. No I-don't-knows, no maybes; those were merely nos in disguise. But Marianne was incapable of saying "I love you." It sounded like a phrase associated with inevitable decisions: *Where do we go from here? Shall we move into yours or mine? Shall we buy a house? Let's go to Rome this winter. And where shall I put the saucers?*

It sounded like a variation on what Marianne had left behind when she had decided not to speak to Lothar in Concarneau. She liked the woman she thought she was on her way
to becoming, the one who was emerging from her shell, who
slept in her own room and decided when she wanted to do
what; someone who didn't immediately hang up Yann's wet
towels or pick up his shirts while he was absorbed in his art,
who didn't even put a teacup in the sink for once; someone
who didn't start thinking three days in advance about what
she was going to cook for dinner on Wednesday.

As long as neither of them said "I love you," neither had any
duties or a routine. You and me forever: now let's get down
to the details. Love-begotten obligations were the last thing
Marianne wanted. In every respect.

All those damn details! She knew them all too well, and
she suspected that she wouldn't be sufficiently careful and
would thus turn into such-and-such's wife, becoming part of a
"we" in which only the man decided. She couldn't stand that
part of herself.

But Yann isn't Lothar. No, Yann wasn't Lothar, but she was
still too much Marianne. She was afraid that she wouldn't last
for long when free.

WHEN SHE got back to the guesthouse three hours later,
she found a familiar and beloved face waiting for her: Grete
Köster. She was holding a glass of champagne, and was fan-
ning warm air toward herself with the postcard Marianne had
sent on the day of her planned suicide.

"It would have been a shame if it had ended with death and a drink in the afterlife," said Marianne's old neighbor, and the two women gave each other a warm hug.

Grete Köster held Marianne at arm's length. "Damn, you look good. What's his name?"

39

S HE RESUMED HER EARLY OUTINGS, BUT THIS TIME ON
the Vespa. Every morning she rode out to Tahiti Beach to
practice the accordion by the light of the rising sun. Yet she
still felt a lingering sense of unease and wariness. She looked
up at every unexpected engine noise, fearing that Lothar
might appear at any moment and force her to go back to Celle
with him.

The sun came up and set the sea sparkling. Marianne stood
there clutching her accordion, and gazed out over the sea and
its glittering reflections.

Never again. Never again will I go without this, she thought.

The sea's voice whispered inside her: *You're finally awak-
ening.*

The waves seemed hazy to her, as if some of Avalon's mists
had advanced over the swell. On their way back to the land,
they would tell the stories they had gleaned on their travels.

Do I love Yann in the same way as he seems to love me?

The sea answered her, but this time Marianne didn't understand its language. It was too mighty, and she felt small and
irrelevant.

Marianne loved Yann's hands and his boyish manner when he painted. She loved his eyes, in which, had she been a sea-farer, she could have read the briny depths, the eddies and currents, the swirls and tides. She loved the fact that he never clammed up when they didn't agree (a rare occurrence), and she loved him for the unwavering attention he paid her. As for the things they got up to when they were alone . . . He had a gift for making her feel beautiful, erotic and desirable with his gaze. His touch swept away all the comical aspects of age, the worries about not having perfectly smooth skin and having folds in which lurked the shadows of the years.

Marianne loved the feeling of being wanted. As Marianne. As a woman.

In my search for death I found life. How many deviations, side roads and senseless detours a woman can take before she finds her own path, and all because she falls into line too early, takes too early the paths of custom and convention, defended by doddering old men and their henchwomen—the mothers who only want the most dutiful outcome for their daughters. And then she wastes an immense amount of time ensuring that she fits the mold! How little time then remains to correct her fate.

Marianne was suddenly scared that she would lose the courage to continue to search for her own path.

And yet, life as an autonomous woman is not a song. It's a scream, a war; it's a daily struggle against the easy option of obeying. I could have obeyed, could have lived less dangerously, ventured nothing, failed at nothing.

As she took in the wide expanse of the Atlantic, she remem-bered how she had felt on that bridge in Paris when life seen from the Pont Neuf had resembled a trickle, its opportunities dried up, its possibilities blocked with silt.

That was wrong. It no longer held true. The longer a woman lived, the more she began to discover. If she could first set aside the conventional dreams of marriage, children, lifelong love and professional success, then a life would begin in which everything else was there to be conquered. There could only be meaning when every person found his or her proper place in the course of events. Life wasn't too short: it was too long to waste unduly on non-love, non-laughter and non-decisions. And it began when you first took a risk, failed and realized that you'd survived the failure. With that knowledge, you could risk anything.

Marianne unstrapped the accordion. She would ride to Yann's to face him and his love, even if, in his aggrieved state, he were to turn her away. For lying to him when he had asked about her past. For leaving him without answering whether she planned to go back to her husband. "Yann," she whispered to the sea, and turned to go. A single white rose was poking from the sand.

He must have left it there while Marianne was playing a song for the sea. He must have listened and watched as she played, wept and laughed, as she screamed at the sea and sought and found the right notes and words.

She pulled the rose from the sand and held it to her nose. He was sitting on a rock, very close by. The golden gleam of the sea dappled his face, and the waves were breaking in his eyes. He looked at her as Marianne felt no man had ever looked at her before. His eyes rested on her with great intensity, as if she were an island.

He was composed yet confused, as if he had known her the whole time he had searched for her. Marianne no longer found this strange. She too had found something, here at the end of the earth. In the mirror of the sea she had seen herself, and what she had once been intended for.

Never again. Never again will I go without this.

As she took a step across the heavy sand, he stood up and walked toward her. She let the accordion slide to the ground and flew into his arms.

"Yann!" she cried, then a second time, "Yann!"

"*Salut, Marianne,*" he whispered, and he embraced her with all his might and his love.

As HE had sat there watching his lover, Yann had renewed a long-forgotten promise to himself: nothing insignificant ever again. Everything was to be experienced at the highest pitch of passion and life. To expect something greater after life was to forget that life was the greatest thing of all. He had forgotten that, and now he wanted to live with all his strength and with no further dread. Love, paint, love: nothing that would tire his heart or offend his soul.

He wanted to tell Marianne that he understood. For a while her unexplained departure had almost killed him, but then he had understood. A few nights of love and caresses from him could not dissolve forty-one years of marriage. This woman had cast off her former life, but it still clung to her and would not yet let go of her. How could it?

She possessed greater courage than anyone he had ever met, for she had set out into a foreign world, armed with nothing but her determination. Yet beneath all that strength there was still the other Marianne, the vulnerable one. The warrior carried serious wounds, which could prove fatal if they were reopened, and that man—her husband—had cut her to the quick with his TV appearance, reminding her of all the scars she bore.

Yann had understood. Feeling her now, resting in his arms, was a second shock to his system. He stressed every word he whispered into her ear in a voice that brooked no contradiction and asked for no agreement: "Tonight I will not be without you, nor in any of the nights to come."

She looked up at him. "Why wait for the night?"

They drove to Raguenez, and made their way across to the island off the northern end of Tahiti Beach. There, they made love before the tide came in. They were on an island that no one else knew. When they looked out later over the rolling waves that hurled themselves against the cliffs, Yann asked, "Are you going to tell your husband at some point that you're alive? And that you're not coming back? That you want to be free, whether for me or for you?"

Marianne said nothing for a minute. "At some point, yes. Of course."

40

COLETTE HAD MOVED IN WITH SIDONIE TO LOVE HER and be loved in return. In view of the certain transience of her love, she felt whole for the first time in her life. It was all there. It had always been there, but she hadn't noticed: a love of women.

The second week after she had moved in, Sidonie asked her to take her to the stones she had always longed to touch. Stonehenge, the wandering stones of Death Valley, the magical palaces of Malta and the altar stones of Palestine. Her doctor forbade her to travel. Colette flew into a rage and implored him, but he stood firm, warning of a premature death from exhaustion, and she fell silent.

Everything had been in a state of flux recently, as if the steady maelstrom of the passing days had intensified its fateful blows in an attempt to catch up on something that could no longer be reeled in—the past.

Though summer was all around, bathing the August days in Finistère in dazzling light, and the numbers of tourists were growing from day to day, their lives settled into a new pattern.

When Marianne wasn't working at the guesthouse or for

the Goichons, she got up before dawn to play the accordion beside the sea and listen to the sound of the waves spilling their secrets to her—secrets that were older than the standing stones. On her days and evenings off she would meet up with Yann, and they would visit Sidonie and Colette as often as they could. The sculptress found peace in Marianne's embrace. Marianne told her what the sea, and its queen, Nimue, had whispered to her during their private conversations. It had said that death and life were like water. Nothing was lost. Their spirits would flow through the other world and find a new receptacle in another place and another time. A decanting of souls. She never knew she could hear the sea. But it turned out that all she had to do was listen.

Then, one afternoon, Colette and Sidonie were gone. A week later, Colette rang from Malta. "After all, it's life that carries the greatest risk of death, so wouldn't it better to do some living first?"

Having simply upped and left, they had spent a few days in Paris with Sidonie's children in the knowledge that they would never see each other again. Sidonie had insisted on this leave-taking: her children were not to watch her die. She wanted to tell them how much she loved them and how proud of them she was, and they threw a three-day party before setting out on their travels to see the world's most beautiful stones.

41

AFTER 20 AUGUST, THE FRENCH TOURISTS WOULD celebrate the end of their holidays in Brittany with one last *fest-noz* and head back to Paris, Provence, the cold cities and the French hinterland to dream of their Breton summer. "Crazy," they would say. "Remember eating all that wonderful fish? The costumes at the Filets Bleus, the festival of blue nets, in Concarneau? That organic Morgana beer from the Lancelot brewery? And the *pardon*, where everybody walked around in special hats and asked to be forgiven for all manner of things? It was all *so* authentic!"

Until then, it was possible to attend several parties each night. Every large village invited people to dance in the streets, which were covered with wooden decking for this very purpose. The gavotte dances excluded no one: the larger the circle, the more fun everyone had, and the quieter it was afterward in the woods and along the roads, where casual lovers strained not to make too much noise.

The *fest-noz* in Kerdruc had to compete with other dances on the same night in Raguenez, Trévignon and Cap Coz, which drew the many tourists who wished to listen to music and watch Breton bands and fireworks.

On the afternoon before the *fest-noz*, Geneviève Ecollier knocked on Marianne's door and beckoned to her with an excited smile. She led her downstairs and opened the door that gave into the room containing the dresses. "Find one you like," she said. "A musician must shine."

Marianne was going to play at the *fest-noz*. She would share with people the songs she had so far only shared with the sea, and Geneviève wanted to help her. She had come to this decision the previous night, as she, Marianne and Grete had sat chatting together. For the first time Marianne had spoken openly about how she had come to Kerdruc to kill herself, and how, day after day, she had put off her plans until nothing remained of her intentions other than a deep sense of shock that she might not have lived her life to the full. Then her untamed desire to seize her life with both hands had taken control.

Geneviève had stood up and bowed to her. She had great admiration for this woman who had mustered up the courage to rectify the mistaken path she had taken.

Unlike Geneviève herself. She was a woman who corrected nothing, hiding away the shadows of the past, in the form of dresses, like living corpses. She wished that a little of Marianne's talent for rewriting the book of fate might rub off on her when she opened the door to her past.

Marianne ran her hand over the dresses she had already touched once in secret. It was as if they were alive, disclosing their secrets in whispering voices and sighs, for in her fingers she felt an intermittent prickling that rose and then subsided.

One of them seemed to be on fire. The dress held a memory so powerful that it could not be washed out of the fibers. It glowed, sending heat up her arm and into her chest. She gripped it and heard a sharp intake of breath beside her. It was the red dress. Marianne took a step back and let Geneviève remove the dress from its hanger. She laid it over her arm, and her gaze turned inward to memories languishing in cages of lost happiness.

"I wore this dress to my engagement," she whispered, her hands gliding over the smooth, shimmering fabric. "The day everything began and nothing ended." Her expression softened. "I was wearing this dress when I fell in love with my fiancé's brother. Life was good to me, I was young and beautiful, and I loved the wrong man. Loving is different from being loved. Giving and seeing how a person flourishes and feeds off your love: the amount of power you possess, and the fact that that power makes someone the best they can be." She hung her head. "Alain didn't want my love, so what was I supposed to do with it?" Tears fell onto the dress.

Marianne let her weep. She realized that these tears were being shed for the very first time. Surrounded by the dresses in which she had lived for three summers, three autumns, two winters and two springs, Geneviève wept for the lost man and for the woman she had once been. There was nowhere her love was welcome, and through lack of use, its power had cooled and changed into hatred. It was easier to hate than to love when your love wasn't wanted.

Marianne ran a gentle hand over Geneviève's hair. How closely this woman had guarded her love, never allowing it to take wing again! Alain. *Of course*—the man who lived on the other side of the river. He couldn't be any nearer to the woman whose love he had batted away many years ago.

"Do you still love him?"

Geneviève exhaled, her mouth wide, and touched the dress again. "Every day. Every day I love him and hate myself for doing so." She grasped her tight plait, then stood up. "Let's make sure we get you into this thing, Marianne." She held out the red dress.

Marianne shook her head slowly. "You should wear it, Geneviève," she said softly, reaching for a different dress—a blue one that glittered like the sun-kissed sea.

42

⚜

ALAIN SAT DOWN NEXT TO LAURINE ON THE BRIGHT
stone parapet that ran along the river on the approach to
the *bar tabac*. The sturdy sandstone blocks had been installed
to prevent vehicles from taking an unplanned dip in the river,
as had happened all too often in the past.

Laurine gazed toward Kerdruc.

"Homesick?" Alain asked. She nodded. He followed her
gaze across the water to the far bank. It was a harbor that
Alain was condemned to see, but where he wasn't welcome.
Yet something was different over there today.

It was tempting him. It seemed to be quivering. In the blue-
tinged light of dusk, sparks were dancing—though in actual
fact they were merely the lights of a host of swaying red lanterns. Among them shadows shifted, gathering for the night's
festivities. Suddenly Alain caught sight of a red shadow. He
recognized that red. From his breast pocket he took a pair of
opera glasses, through which he had spent so many nights
peering desperately for a glimpse of Geneviève.

"Genoveva," he whispered. She was wearing her engagement dress, the dress in which they had fallen in love with each other.

Was that the sign he had been waiting for these thirty-five years? Or was it merely mockery. *Look, I've managed to forget you, Alain, and who I was when I loved you.*

Laurine observed her new boss. He was good to her, gentle and clever, but the view through those binoculars had brought out something in his face that only a woman in love could comprehend: Alain Poitier was no more at home on this side of the Aven than she was. She took his hand, but it wasn't clear who was clinging to whom—Alain to Laurine, or she to him. He belonged over there in Kerdruc, where two things were happening at that moment. Through his binoculars he could see that a van was rolling down the slope to the port and letting out four nuns and a priest; and from a taxi stepped a gray-suited man, who looked around with an expression of disbelief that he had washed up in this place at the end of the world.

"Is it normal to feel so sick?" asked Marianne, glancing from the gavotte players to Grete and back again with a pained expression.

"It's called stage fright, and it's completely normal. Everyone gets it." Grete burst out laughing. "Come on, Marianne. There's no water lily in your lungs, stealing your breath. Breathe out. All of us should breathe out more often anyway."

They were sitting in the guesthouse dining room. The bandleader beckoned to Marianne. Her knees felt like jelly as she listed the pieces she was intending to play. Right then, a flock of nuns came swarming through the door.

"Sister Clara!" Marianne cried happily. Behind her were Sister Dominique and Father Ballack. They walked toward Marianne, their robes swirling, and clustered around her. They had come to Kerdruc to thank her for rescuing Sister Dominique and had planned their trip to coincide with the *fest-noz* party.

"I'm so pleased," Sister Clara whispered as she hugged her. "So pleased that your journey has had a happy ending."

ALAIN DIDN'T know what to do. The vibes on the other side of the river appeared to have intensified. That was no ordinary Breton port hosting just another *fest-noz*: it looked like an enchanted forest.

Laurine was looking through the opera glasses. Alain had fetched his jacket and hung it around her shoulders. "That's Madame Geneviève. She's bringing out the racks to support the casks of wine. And that's Padrig helping her. And that's . . ." She paused and cleared her throat. "Monsieur Paul is dressed up to the nines. Claudine: dear me, she's *so* pregnant, she's going to burst soon! Ah, they're pointing to Marianne!" Laurine was ecstatic now. "She looks *so* beautiful!"

"Can you see Jean-Rémy as well?" asked Alain.

"I don't want to see him," said Laurine, passing Alain the glasses.

He scanned the far shore, and suddenly caught sight of Geneviève leading the man in the gray suit up the stairs to the guesthouse.

IT WAS when the man had written his name on the guest
form and passed it to Madame Geneviève that she started to
tremble. She read his name a second time. She hadn't recognized him in the lift, and even the creases stabbing down
sharply from the corners of his mouth to his chin bore little
resemblance to the man who had appeared on French television searching for his lost wife. It was Lothar Messmann.

"Where's my wife?" he asked in French, or what he believed to be French. For the first time in her life, Geneviève
Ecollier decided to adopt the default French attitude: never
understand anyone who wasn't French.

"*Pardon?*" she said in a blasé tone of voice.

*How I would love to chuck you in the river, you little gray
rabbit. You booked under your own name, of course, not Marianne's maiden name, and stupidly I only realized too late.*

"My wife, Marianne Messmann," he said, raising his voice.

Geneviève shrugged and walked around the reception desk
to guide him up to his room, giving the dining room a wide
berth.

These French people, thought Lothar. Such an arrogant
lot. Throughout his journey to the tip of Brittany, they had all
refused to understand him. He had been forced to eat things
he hadn't ordered. In the bus from Rennes to Quimper, two
toothless old men had spat on his German army sticker; and
in Quimper he had repeatedly been sent in the wrong direction as he searched for a taxi. He had several times passed a
crime bookshop, whose saleswoman had observed him dis-
trustfully.

He remembered the letter he had received ten days ago from a teacher called Adela Brelivet, who had informed him in turgid school German that she regarded it as her civic duty to respond to his TV appeal for information and notify him that she had picked up the aforementioned Marianne on a minor road outside Kerdruc and given her a lift to Concarneau. She had immediately realized that the woman had given her a false identity. Despite this, she was absolutely certain of her identity, and Monsieur Messmann should enquire at Ar Mor in Kerdruc, because she had heard that there was a foreign woman working in the kitchen there.

He wanted to find out how Marianne could prefer life without him. Why was she so unwilling to put up with him any longer? Oh, and how annoying it was that this women in the tantalizing red dress should refuse to tell him where Marianne was! She must be at the party, at which he would bet that they didn't even serve beer, only champagne and frogs' legs. Lothar hated this country. At least the room was all right, and he could look out of his window onto the lively quayside below.

Out of the corner of his eye, he had spotted a woman in a blue dress, with an amber bob, shielded by a group of nuns. No, that couldn't be Marianne. Marianne was smaller and not as . . . attractive.

He left his room and took some Breton lager that a gloomy-looking young man with black hair and a red bandanna passed him across the counter of the bar outside. The breakwater had filled with excited women, laughing men, teenagers, and children chasing each other underneath the tables around the dance floor.

Lothar began to push his way through the crowd, ignoring the looks that people shot at his formal suit with its six gold buttons. He was following the woman in the blue dress, which seemed to be constantly changing color and reflecting people's laughter and the stars overhead. As she turned slightly toward him, reacting to a call from an urbanely dressed woman with a cigarette holder in her black-gloved hand, he knew that the woman in the blue dress was indeed Marianne.

She looked taller. More beautiful. Inaccessible. He took a long swig of lager, and when he lowered his glass, he had lost sight of his wife, his view blocked by a phalanx of black backs. Those damn nuns again!

GENEVIÈVE ELEGANTLY climbed the steps onto the stage, lifting the hem of her red dress a touch. One of the gavotte musicians gallantly led Marianne by the hand to the stool on which she was to sit. Geneviève reached for the microphone and announced, "Let the *fest-noz* begin!"

"E flat," Marianne whispered to the musicians. She let her eyes wander over the crowd, and there, next to Jean-Rémy, she saw Yann with a sketchpad in his hand. Beside him was Grete, who gave her a double thumbs-up, and beside *her* was Simon, although his eyes were glued to his neighbor rather than to the stage.

Paul had stepped into the center of the dance floor with Rozenn, as if the musicians were playing for them alone. The nuns were looking kindly and affectionately at Marianne. Father Ballack's grin revealed his jagged teeth. Marianne felt herself relax under their benevolent gazes, and she saw the glow in Geneviève's eyes and the desire in Yann's. She saw Pascale and Emile, who was standing there with his hands folded, as if he were praying that his monstrous accordion might produce a decent sound; and she saw Colette hand in hand with Paul's granddaughters. She thanked the goddesses of time past for this instant when she could bathe in such warmth.

The drums struck up an urgent, intense beat, and Marianne shut her eyes, imagined she was by the sea and began to play the first chords of *Libertango*. The bass took up her notes, and she opened her eyes. The drums picked up the tempo, and Piazzolla's best-known tango grew in power and depth. Like waves surging higher and higher. Like fire leaping from one heart to another, kindling flames in each. Like an avalanche of singing stones.

The dance floor was already packed with spinning couples, and as the violin took up the melody, the waves of sound hit those who were sitting at the tables over mussels and wine. They swayed back and forth as the concertina captured the passionate accents and syncopation.

Paul and Rozenn crisscrossed the floor with heads held high and precise tango steps. Marianne's fingers flew accurately and easily over the keys, and the sea rocked before her. A sea of bodies—everyone was moving, and beneath the red lanterns it seemed as if imps and fairies were celebrating their departure for Avalon. Even Claudine was twisting her belly as if in a trance. Everyone was dancing, happy to be alive at the same time.

Everyone except for one man, whose silhouette seemed rooted to the ground.

43

⚜

"I HAVE TO GO OVER THERE," LAURINE SAID. SHE STEPPED toward the edge of the quayside, took a deep breath and swung her arms behind her. Alain, taking one great stride, was only just in time to stop her diving headlong into the water and swimming across the Aven.

He held the waitress back. "Laurine!" he whispered insistently. "He must come to you! Let him take the first step, and if he doesn't, there'll be no need to take any further ones together!" He held her tight until she had stopped struggling and had come to a complete rest in his arms.

"And that's from someone who stands still himself!" There was no longer any trace of hesitation in her voice.

Alain looked at her briefly, then let go of her and ran down the steep quay steps to the boats.

THE CLAPPING almost knocked Marianne off her feet, and there was an even greater swell of applause when the bandleader led her to the front of the stage to take a bow with the musicians. He took the microphone and said, "And that, my dear delighted ladies and gentlemen, was Marianne, the high priestess of tango, and a magnificent sea whisperer, who will continue to urge you tenderly to break all the rules."

He turned, and the drummer breathed in and struck up a new tango rhythm, accompanied by the bass player, who skipped every third beat. The bandleader played the first few chords of "Hijo de la Luna" on his concertina—D minor, G minor—and the crowd let out an enthusiastic roar. Marianne sensed when the moment had come to lay down a second strand of chords over the beat and add the tune. The violin joined in softly, sending the melody of the moon's song out into the night.

The full moon floated above their heads, couples twirled and Marianne glanced at the concertina player. They locked eyes, and with every nod of his head to emphasize the beat, the outlines around her blurred and she melted into the music. He led and she followed, until it was only their instruments flirting with each other, just as the sea hurled itself onto the land and then retreated, an alternating series of ecstatic passion and tender emotion. The air was filled with the crackling of women's silk stockings and the sound of men's breathing and steps on the wooden floor. No one spoke, everyone danced, and people's bodies obeyed their will and their passion.

Marianne's soul took flight and was free.

Those present that evening swore for many years afterward that they had seen a white aura around Marianne's body. The blue of her dress appeared to blaze with white-blue flames. A glow had formed around her, they said, and it was as if a priestess stood before them, calling to the moon with her song.

Everyone danced themselves into a trance like none anyone had ever experienced. They loved life more than ever before and knew that it would never end.

At the end of the piece, Marianne gave a bow. The applause continued on and on, and joy coursed through her veins, illuminating her eyes like two blue gas flames. She felt as if she were floating as she strode off the stage into the crowd. She searched for Yann, but instead she spied Geneviève on the edge of the breakwater, away from the light and the warmth, staring out to the cold and the silence and the blackness.

"How I love you," Geneviève whispered to the wind.

ALAIN UNTIED the mooring ropes with deft fingers and then paused. He had felt something close to his ear. Something warm. A voice? He looked up with irritation. Genoveva? There it was again . . . *Love* . . .

Laurine hung back beside the stone wall, her fair hair gleaming in the nighttime wind like a bright flame. "Why don't you swim?" she called down to him.

"Because I can't!" he yelled angrily. He turned back toward Kerdruc. The music was tugging at his nerves, tearing his heart from his chest. He longed to grow wings and fly to her, to Geneviève.

. . . *Love* . . .

At last the rope came loose, and Alain reached for the oars. He stood in the middle of the boat as it slid out into the stream, trying to ignore its violent rocking, and cupped his hands to form a megaphone. "Genoveva!" Then more loudly, "Genoveva!" Nothing moved, apart from the dress fluttering in the wind. "I! Love! You!"

He started to row, and with every stroke he roared, "Genoveva. I. Love. You!"

Love me. I want your love!

The red shadow faded into the swirling black and gray, and Alain was left alone on the current. He paused for breath in the middle of the river. Now he had become a smudge and he kept shouting the same words, hoarsely, desperately. "Genoveva, *je t'aime. Je t'aime*, Genoveva. Love me back!"

GENEVIÈVE DIDN'T move, staring wordlessly out over the river. She barely reacted when Marianne touched her on the arm. Her eyes were full of despair and fear.

Marianne turned to the priest from Auray, Father Ballack, who had joined her. "Father, can you row?"

He looked at her in disbelief. "Of course I can."

"Then please take Madame to her beloved. She has been waiting for thirty-five years to offer him her love again."

The priest tried to hide his shocked surprise. Marianne gently laid her left hand on Geneviève's shoulder. "It is time."

The older woman took the priest's hand, and he led her to a small red boat whose sails were ready to fill on command. Geneviève didn't move as the clergyman began to row them out into the middle of the river, where Alain was waiting. Her body was like a candle riding on the water.

Unnoticed by the dancing throng on the breakwater, the

two boats glided toward each other. Alain quickened his strokes. Geneviève didn't let him out of her sight as he drew closer with every pull of the oars. With a gentle jolt the two prows met, and Geneviève stretched out her hand to him.

Meanwhile, Yann had stepped up behind Marianne and put his arms around her. She pressed herself against him. "Look," she said softly, as Alain leaned forward and his fingers touched Geneviève's. But as they watched, a current pulled the boat from under him with a jerk and their hands separated.

Geneviève screamed, "Alain!"

Not now. Oh please, not now!

Before her very eyes, her beloved toppled to one side, into the deep.

Oh please, no! He couldn't swim! If he drowned, she knew she would follow him, and with the same certainty she knew that her hate would all have been in vain. She would have grown old without him. Her fingertips burned with the memory of her one and only lover. Alain!

She leaped into the water.

Marianne squirmed out of Yann's arms and ran along the quayside.

Geneviève's red dress billowed on the dark water, but she swam toward Alain until she had caught hold of him. Clinging tightly to each other, they spun in the current.

As Marianne turned to fetch help, she ran into a gray wall. Lothar?! She pushed past him to the harbormaster's office, ripped the life buoy from its holder on the wall and sprinted back along the breakwater until she had reached the end. Where were they? There! Two bright faces inches above the waves. It was low tide, and if they kept drifting downstream, the sea would suck them out of the estuary and carry them far from the shore.

Lothar grabbed the ring from her hands. "Let me do it," he said. "You won't be able to."

Their eyes met for a split second, then Marianne hissed, "You have no idea of all the things I can do," and seized back the life buoy. She hurled it far out into the Aven, along with her overwhelming ice-cold fury. It sailed almost ten yards through the air and landed right next to the shimmering patch of red. She had attached the rope tightly around her waist. She felt her strength waning as the river tugged at the life buoy and she staggered.

Lothar stepped in front of her and began to reel in the rope, inch by inch. She stood next to him, at a loss to explain why she was becoming stiffer and more numb with every minute she spent in his presence.

Geneviève and Alain clung to the buoy until Father Ballack had rowed up and helped them to clamber over the boat's low gunwale to safety. Only then did they toss the buoy back over the side, and Lothar pulled it to the bank.

"Thank you," Marianne said to her husband, brushing his arm with her fingers. It was an effort even to raise her hand.

Lothar replied with a terse nod—the light touch had sent an electric charge through him—and then smiled tenderly at her. "You played absolutely beautifully," he said.

His wife had a lover. She looked ravishing, and she was liked, even loved—that much he had seen in the faces that had turned toward her like flowers to the sun. She belonged to this land as if she had been born here, he thought, as if the people here had been waiting for her. Something began to crumble inside him. He raised his hand and ran his thumb over Marianne's lips. He bent forward and, leaving her no time to evade him, gave her a peck on the mouth.

Over his shoulder, Marianne glimpsed Yann, a mixture of pain and hope in his eyes. "Lothar," she said to her husband. "Can we talk later?"

"Whatever you want," said Lothar. "I've taken three days off work." He turned and looked with narrowed eyes at the man who had been embracing his wife so tenderly and familiarly on the breakwater a few minutes earlier.

He gazed after Marianne as she walked along the breakwater, and felt as if he were looking at a familiar stranger who had kept herself hidden from him jealously for many decades. Yann stepped up beside him.

"We should probably talk now," the painter began tentatively, "or would you prefer a duel?"

Lothar shook his head. No, he wanted his wife back. He couldn't figure out how Marianne had concealed her beauty from him.

Father Ballack walked toward them along the quayside on his own. "They wanted to be alone," he remarked apologetically. "A near-death experience usually arouses, um, the flesh." He grinned.

Marianne watched the rowing boat as it faded into the darkness downstream. It was as if Geneviève and Alain were looking for the source of the river that had given birth to their love. She had no doubt that between now and daybreak they would find it.

The red dot was swallowed up by the night.

MARIANNE WISHED that she too could become invisible. Whereas half an hour earlier she had felt sure about every aspect of her life—playing the accordion, staying in Kerdruc, loving Yann—now that had been reduced to a thick ash, blocking her nose and ears and mouth, and all in the space of those few seconds when Lothar had taken the life buoy from her hand. It was as if he had unmasked her, revealing what really lay beneath the dress, the makeup and this whole sham.

A hand in a leather glove gripped her upper arm. Colette! Their embrace was tight but tender. Marianne's eyes searched for someone behind the gallery owner.

"Sidonie isn't here anymore," said Colette quietly. "She knows she will find peace tonight. She sent me away, saying that I should celebrate life."

The world stood still inside Marianne, and her soul cowered.

"What should I do?" whispered Colette.

Marie-Claude's daughter Claudine forced her way between them without noticing that she was interrupting something. "Tell me if it's going to be a boy," she demanded from Marianne. "My mother says you can do that." She laid Marianne's hand firmly on her stomach, which curved up almost to her breasts.

"It's going to be a girl," said Marianne in a voice from the tomb.

44

M ARIANNE BRUSHED ASIDE THE HANDS THAT TRIED
to catch hold of her in the guesthouse, on the breakwater and on the way to the car. Yann's hands, Lothar's hands,
the nuns' hands. The hands of *fest-noz* guests wanting to
thank her, wondering why her wolf-like eyes seemed so dim,
and why she hurried off into the night without a word.

Colette tried to object during the quick journey, insisting
that they had to respect Sidonie's decision, as one should any
last wish.

Without looking at her, Marianne blurted out, "I've seen
four hundred and thirty-eight people die, and not a single one
wanted to be alone when the moment came."

They found Sidonie in her studio. Her hand was clutching
a pebble she had picked up in Malta, near temples that were
older than the Pyramids. Her breathing was visibly strained,
but she kept her eyes open for as long as she could, and stared
at Colette—at her eyes, her mouth, her soul.

"Thank you," she whispered. "Thank you for not listening
to me."

This woman's face was the sight that Sidonie had wanted to

see on this last of all days, and on every previous day. Always, ever since she had first laid eyes on the gallery owner. And Colette had come back after she had let her go.

"One's whole life is actually dying. From the first breath it goes in one direction, toward . . . death," Sidonie said in a voice that seemed to come from very far away.

Now Marianne held Sidonie's other hand. She was not scared by the cold current she felt in her arms and her neck and even in her heart. She recognized this chill: it was the icy stream of death.

Sidonie's eyelids fluttered and she sat up. "The stones," she whispered weakly to Colette. "They're singing."

Colette couldn't cope. She despaired, she wept and she groped for Sidonie's hand, but Sidonie tried to draw her fingers away to close them once more around the pebble. So Colette gripped her hand, the stone clenched between their two palms. Marianne reached for Colette's free hand, and together the three women went part of the way toward the frontier from where Sidonie would have to continue alone, as everyone before her had, and everyone after her would too.

They listened to Sidonie's shallow breathing. Suddenly, as if she could already see the mists of the other world, she whispered her late husband's name in surprise. "Hervé?" She smiled happily, as if she had caught a glimpse of eternity and what she had seen there held no fear.

The icy, prickling sensation under Marianne's hand where she was holding Sidonie's fingers broke off as suddenly. The pebble clattered to the floor.

Sidonie was gone.

It was long after four o'clock in the morning when Marianne left Colette alone with her friend's peaceful body, and set off back to Kerdruc on foot. She was cold in the sleeveless blue evening dress, and in her hand she held Sidonie's pebble.

She stumbled toward the black horizon. Streaks of lightning flickered in the sky, but without the usual thunderclaps that followed; only a distant rumbling came from the dark clouds. A ghostly calm hung over the land, and the silent lightning illuminated the noiseless meadows, the gray streets and the unlit houses. Only from Kerdruc harbor came a red glow.

You cannot tell love to come and stay forever. You can only welcome it when it comes, like the summer or the autumn, and when its time is up and it's gone, then it's gone.

The lightning flashed, striking out around her. The sky was ablaze.

Like life. It comes, and when its time is up, it goes. Like happiness. Everything has its own time.

Marianne had had what was due to her, and that would have to suffice. She tried to imagine in whose arms she might find peace, but discovered that she couldn't do it. Lothar? Yann?

Lothar had looked at her in the way she had been hoping for years that he might. He was her husband, after all!

Oh Yann, what should I do?

Just as she was reaching the outskirts of Kerdruc, a small shadow detached itself from a tree, jumped down onto the road and stared at her. It was Max, the cat—he had been waiting for her. He rubbed against her legs, but before she could pick him up, he slipped from her grasp and ran off. Glancing back, he stared at her again and then trotted away, as if to say, *Come along now! Quickly, or else we'll miss everything!*

The cat scampered toward the car park—the site of Marianne's first impression of Kerdruc, the place with the glass-recycling container. Under the trees was a raspberry-colored Renault, and Marianne spotted a lifeless figure on the reclined front seat—Marie-Claude's daughter Claudine!

The young woman's face was pale and bathed in sweat, and a damp patch had formed underneath her. She was holding a mobile phone, but the battery was dead. Marianne grabbed her hands and felt her racing pulse with her middle finger. It was beating like mad. She was having contractions!

With all her might, Marianne pushed back the seat and sat down between Claudine's spread legs. She reached for the cat and set it down on the passenger seat beside her, then started the car and drove off with a screech of tires.

"The baby . . ." Claudine groaned. "The baby's coming! Too early. Two weeks early!" She was hit by another wave of contractions. "Did you call it? When you put your hand on my tummy?" She gasped with pain again.

"Stop your nonsense," Marianne ordered. She kept her hand on the horn as she sped down the ramp to the harbor and raced across the dance floor, braking directly in front of the entrance to Ar Mor. Then she gave three short, three long and another three short blasts of the horn—the international SOS signal.

Three people hurried out of the restaurant: Yann, Jean-Rémy and Lothar. They were all a bit drunk.

Marianne instructed them to lift Claudine, who had almost passed out from the pain, out of the car. "Take her into the kitchen and lay her on the table!" she called, curling her fingers around Sidonie's pebble in a reflex. It felt warm, as if it had soaked up and preserved Sidonie's living heat. Marianne closed her eyes and sought to conjure up her memories of helping her grandmother Nane with home births. This time, though, she wouldn't be helping someone; she would have to do it all on her own. She hoped that her hands would recall the movements. She pushed the button that opened the car's trunk and found the first-aid kit.

The three men's faces turned to expressionless masks when they had laid the moaning Claudine on the cool stainless-steel table. Jean-Rémy rushed to the telephone and asked the operator for an ambulance. "We need to get her to the clinic in Concarneau," he whispered, waiting for Marianne to give the final command.

She turned over a large cooking pot and arranged bandages, scissors, compresses and the pebble on it. Then she held her hands under hot water to warm them up, and pulled on sterile latex gloves.

"Support her, Lothar," she said as she pushed her fingers into Claudine.

Claudine shrieked. "Oh my God! Bloody hell!"

"Her cervix is open, her perineum is bulging and she's cursing like a trooper!"

Jean-Rémy passed on this information to the emergency services. "They say we shouldn't drive her in that state."

The contractions came at ever shorter intervals, and Claudine screamed ever more loudly. "Bleeding son of a bitch!"

"Now they're saying that *they're* going to come to us." Jean-Rémy ran away.

"Men! They always want to be there at the beginning, but never for the outcome," mumbled Marianne. "She needs to breathe regularly," she instructed Yann, who was standing there watching her with inscrutable eyes. "Tell her everything's normal, everything's fine."

"Don't you need hot water?" the painter asked.

"The only reason midwives need hot water is for making coffee and keeping the men busy," growled Marianne. "Bring me a glass of brandy and some towels—clean tea towels. And the electric heater. Lothar, stop rubbing the woman. It'll drive her crazy, all that pushing and shoving. Move her nearer to the edge."

Yann bent over Claudine and urged her to breathe regularly.

"Fuck your mother, you bastard!"

WHEN YANN had gone out to fetch the towels, Lothar asked, "Why did you leave me?"

"Do you really want to talk about that now, Lothar?"

"I just want to understand!"

Yann came back into the room and directed the heater at Claudine.

"Jean-Rémy!" called Marianne. "Where's Grete?"

"She's in her room. With the fisherman. Simon."

"He can stay put, but fetch Grete. Are there any other women in the house?"

"A few *fest-noz* guests who've stayed on, and . . . Oh my

God!" The top of a little head had appeared between Claudine's legs. Jean-Rémy turned away and threw up into the sink.

"Shut up!" roared Claudine.

"Don't push anymore!" Marianne said loudly. "Pant! Jean-Rémy! Grete!"

She panted to demonstrate to Claudine what she wanted her to do, then sat down on a second pot, pushed a few towels under Claudine's thighs and gently laid her hand on the advancing head, applying pressure to guide it. Claudine braced her feet against Marianne's shoulders, leaving dirty marks on the skin. Jean-Rémy staggered out of the kitchen.

"What did I do wrong, Marianne?"

"Lothar! Everything. Nothing. You are who you are, I am who I am, and we don't go together—that's all there is to it."

"We don't go together? What are you talking about?"

Claudine screamed and pushed, but the baby didn't want to come out any farther. Marianne let her hands do what they needed to do, without thinking. She steered the little head downward using both hands until a shoulder appeared. The perineum seemed to tear, and she glanced up at Lothar, who shut his eyes in shock, and Yann, who was holding the brandy with a strangely enraptured expression. Then she looked back down to the tiny body as it forced its way entirely out of the womb.

She supported the child's chest so that its head didn't hang upside down. The remaining amniotic fluid splashed onto the floor.

"Take off your shirt, Yann," she said calmly.

"Victor!" cried Claudine, then again, "Vi-ic-tor!" She sank back onto the table and all her muscles slackened.

It was here. Marianne was holding the infant in her hands. She took a quick look at the clock: five past five. The baby was bloody, slippery and covered with yellow grease. She dabbed it with the sterile compresses, then took Yann's body-warmed shirt and wrapped the baby in it.

"It's a girl," she whispered into Claudine's ear, as the young woman slumped back heavily into Lothar's arms.

"It isn't crying," murmured Yann.

Marianne ran her hand along the little girl's spine and rubbed her feet. Nothing. Not a sound.

Come on. Cry! Breathe!

"What's wrong?" She asked the baby softly. "Don't you want to? You'll have a wonderful life. You'll love, be loved, laugh—"

"Am I too late?" asked Grete as she rushed into the kitchen in a negligee over which she had thrown on Simon's fisherman's shirt and jacket.

"The baby isn't crying, and I don't have a free hand to cut the umbilical cord."

"What's wrong with my baby? WHAT'S WRONG WITH MY BABY?" Claudine bit Lothar's hand, and he let go of her in surprise.

"What a couple of heroes we have here!" whispered Grete, gently pinching the baby's ear. The child didn't cry.

Claudine looked at Marianne, wild-eyed, and reared up. Grete held the umbilical cord higher and pressed down on Claudine's abdomen with the other hand. Marianne's gaze fell on Sidonie's pebble. She picked it up, prized open one of the newborn's tiny fists and gently pushed the stone between its fingers. Marianne felt a slight discharge from the small body similar to the lightning in the sky a little earlier. Silent, but mighty.

Sidonie? she asked wordlessly. *Is that you?*

The baby filled her lungs, her cheeks turned red and all of a sudden she let out a cry of affirmation. There was a huge clap of thunder outside. The men laughed with relief, and Marianne laid the child on Claudine's chest. The young mother gently embraced her daughter, her eyes full of astonishment, gratitude and shame.

Grete tore the straps off her nightdress and tied them around the umbilical cord in two places, while Marianne cut it with the sterile scissors. Tomorrow she would bury it under a rosebush, as sure as sure could be.

Claudine's face had regained some of its color, and Marianne got up to fetch her a glass of cold water, as Grete continued to staunch the bleeding from the umbilical cord. Marianne suddenly felt exhausted. The day's events could easily have filled a few years. The goddesses had demonstrated to her that life and death could take place within a single day, and sometimes it was impossible to distinguish between them.

A TEAM of paramedics came running into the kitchen. At last!

Marianne reached for the brandy, drank half of it and passed the glass to Grete, who drained the rest. She looked at Lothar, and from him to Yann. They were both standing there as if they expected something of her.

Yann was the first to move, pulling on his jacket over his vest, kissing Marianne softly on the forehead and whispering,

"*Je t'aime.*" Lothar took off his tie, unbuttoned his collar and asked, "Should I go too? And never come back?"

"As if that wasn't completely beside the point at this particular moment," Grete muttered almost inaudibly.

"Just go to bed, Lothar," Marianne said wearily.

"I don't know you anymore," he replied.

Nor do I, she thought.

"But I'd like to," he added softly, beseechingly. When Marianne said nothing, he delicately touched her cheek and left.

"I wonder who Victor is," said Marianne after a while. At this name, Claudine gave a start, and Marianne registered the silent request in her eyes.

Once the doctor had tended to Claudine, he came over to Marianne and shook her hand, saying "Nice work, Madame," before taking a sheet of paper on which he needed to fill out the relevant details: birthplace and time, people in attendance, father.

"Unknown," Marianne said to this last question.

The doctor turned to Claudine. "Is that correct?"

She nodded with wide-open eyes.

"Have you already chosen a name, Mademoiselle?"

"Anna-Marie," whispered Claudine, smiling at Marianne.

Sidonie's pebble was resting near the girl's face between Claudine's full breasts. It was the first thing Anna-Marie saw when she opened her eyes.

OVER IN Rozbras, a young woman was still standing beside the stone wall. Laurine felt alone, but not lonely. She realized that she would never be lonely as long as she was capable of taking even a single step. Yet she was saving this step until she found out toward whom she should take it. Life might often decide for her, but it would not completely rule her movements.

She was still gazing over at Kerdruc when Padrig brought the Peugeot to a halt beside her. He made her get in and drove her to a place filled with unbestowed flowers and unread letters.

45

༈

THE THUNDERSTORM HAD GIVEN BIRTH TO A RADI-
ant day. When Marianne walked over to her window
after only a few hours' sleep and opened it to let in the August
sun, she saw Geneviève, Alain, Jean-Rémy and the nuns covering a long table with white tablecloths outside. Geneviève
and Alain were teasing each other like playful children, and
touching continually, as if to convince themselves that the
other wasn't simply a figment of their dreams.

The *fest-noz* guests who had stayed the night emerged from
the guesthouse and sat down at the huge breakfast table. Birds
were singing amid the lush green foliage, a light breeze carried the scent of the sea, and the white boats rocked on the
glittering Aven. Father Ballack came out carrying an armful
of baguettes. Protected from the morning sun by the red awning on the terrace, Emile and Pascale Goichon sat hand in
hand, with Madame Pompadour and Merline sprawling at
their feet. Next to them Paul was dunking a croissant in a
glass of red wine and raising it to Rozenn's lips. As the *Gwen II*
drew closer from the Atlantic, heading for the quay, Marianne
recognized Simon, and beside him a woman wearing a cocky

sailor's hat and a striped T-shirt. It was Grete. Max was sunning himself on the seat of the Vespa.

No sign of Yann. *And no Sidonie, ever again.*

Marianne looked at the open window and clapped her hands to her eyes. The others didn't know yet. They didn't yet realize that there would never be another Monday pensioners' get-together in Kerdruc with Sidonie. When she lowered her hands, she saw Geneviève waving to her, her other arm curled around Alain, who was pressing his Genoveva tightly to his side. Geneviève pointed to an empty seat in the middle of the long table: everyone else had already sat down. The nuns, the Kerdruc pensioners, the pining chef. Grete. The summer guests, who thought they would never again spend their holidays without visiting this port. Only Yann, Marie-Claude the hairdresser, Colette and the most beautiful young woman in the village were missing. And Marianne. Geneviève pointed to the seat again.

That's my seat? She looked at all these wonderful people.

There was a knock. Lothar came in and stood behind her. "Marianne," he said. "I want to ask for your forgiveness. Give me a second chance. Or do you want to stay here?"

Marianne gazed down at the quayside. Whoever this seat among these extraordinary, loving people was for, it was not her. Not Marianne Messmann, née Lanz, from Celle, a woman who read magazines rescued from recycling containers and ate food past its sell-by date, who had done nothing except pretend. She had only imagined that she was something special, but she was no different than she'd been during the preceding sixty years.

Lothar was her life, and when he had arrived, he had

reminded her of who she really was, where she came from and what would always be inside her, no matter how much makeup she applied and how much she strutted around on-stage. There was a struggle inside her, but ultimately she felt that this, this here, was all a performance. She had had her share of happiness. She wasn't fated for more: not for this land, not for the man with the marine eyes, not for the seat among these amazing people, who were so much grander and more wonderful than she was.

"Come on, or else we won't ever start and we'll starve to death!" called Alain.

Marianne despondently combed her hair, put on a white dress, rinsed her mouth and pinched her cheeks instead of ap-plying rouge and lipstick as she had done with such joy in pre-vious weeks. The stranger who looked her in the eye from the mirror wasn't smiling. She was gray, and her eyes were empty.

"I am not you, and you are dead," said Marianne.

I only lived as long as you allowed me to, the unknown woman, whom she had taken for herself, seemed to say.

Lothar appeared behind her and spoke directly to her face in the mirror. "I love you. Marry me again."

As they approached the table, Jean-Rémy stood up with a glass of sparkling wine in his hand. "To Marianne. She can play the accordion, deliver children in kitchens and remove the salt from a soup."

"And make stupid people clever," called Geneviève to gen-eral amusement.

"And drive normal people mad," added Pascale, before asking her husband, "Or was it the other way around?"

The others rose to their feet with Jean-Rémy. Emile leaned on Pascale, and they all raised their glasses and cups of cider. "To Marianne," they announced as one.

Marianne didn't know where to look. It was unbearable to think that they liked and admired her. She squirmed with shame.

I'm a fraud. I'm not even a shadow of what they see in me. I lied to them. I'm a con artist.

It was as if she had used up all her courage the previous night, and she didn't dare to look a single one of them in the eye.

I've only pretended to them to be a special person, but none of it can be true. Nothing.

Lothar, who knew this nothingness so well, and had traveled here to find it, loved her nonetheless. He loved her. She knew that now. How could she simply discard that love?

"Why won't you sit down?" asked Geneviève. Marianne swallowed hard.

I love you. Marry me again.

"I'm going to go back to Germany with my husband," she said quietly.

Pascale knocked over her glass in shock.

"Please sit down right now," whispered Jean-Rémy. "Quickly."

Now everyone was staring at her with distrust, disappointment and astonishment.

"I'm not the right person for that seat," said Marianne a

little more loudly. "Please forgive me." She turned on her heel and walked away.

As MARIANNE was packing her suitcase, Grete pushed open the door. "Have you lost your mind? What was that all about down there?"

Marianne pressed her lips together and continued to pile up her clothes.

"Hello, wake up! If you're locked inside there somewhere, Marianne, send me a signal!" Marianne stopped.

"It's just the way it is!" she shouted at her neighbor in a voice that was cracking with emotion. "I'm just the way I am! Nothing more! Not that . . . musician. Not a sex bomb for Yann." It hurt her to utter his name. "Nor am I a healer or a sea-whisperer, and I don't make mad people normal! I haven't a clue about life. I'm nothing. Do you hear me? Nothing. Those people see a pure illusion." She collapsed onto the bed, weeping.

"Oh you poor little botched Betty!" Grete couldn't help saying.

"It's true," whispered Marianne, when her body was no longer shaken by sobs. "I can't cope with life here. I'm not made for it. And however hard I've tried, I can't manage to be the person I'd like to be, living freely, deciding what I want, not fearing death. That's simply not me. What am I supposed to do here? Keep playing the neighborhood German witch? I'm scared of this life, always being more than I actually am. I can't reinvent myself. Could you?"

Grete shrugged. If she'd been able to do that, she wouldn't

have spent twenty years with the faithfully unfaithful hair-dresser.

"You can do anything you want," she ventured.

"I want to go home," murmured Marianne.

THE TAXI was waiting with its engine running. Marianne shook the bystanders' hands, one after the other. Paul, Rozenn, Simon, Pascale, Emile, Alain, Jean-Rémy and Madame Geneviève.

"We never change," Geneviève said by way of farewell. "That's what you said, Marianne. We only forget who we are. Don't forget who you are, Madame Lanz." She gave Marianne an envelope containing her wages.

Marianne turned to Jean-Rémy and gave him a hug, whispering in his ear, "Laurine loves you, you daft man. And I know all about what you've got stacked in the cooler."

Jean-Rémy wouldn't let go of her. "I couldn't do it, just as you can't. We're both daft people."

Emile swung the accordion case into the trunk of the taxi without a glance. Marianne nodded to him and got into the car.

She didn't look back. Her breathing became more and more strained. When they reached the junction to Concarneau, where she had once hitchhiked, and turned right toward Pont-Aven, Lothar spoke for the first time. "I didn't think you'd come with me."

"This is what I want."

"Because you love me?"

"Did that ever matter to you?"

"Not enough, I presume, or you wouldn't have left."

She said nothing until they reached Pont-Aven, where she knocked on the door of Colette's flat above the gallery. When Colette realized why Marianne was there, her expression hardened. "So you're leaving the moment the going gets tough, eh?"

"I'm sorry . . ."

"No you're not. Not enough. You're obviously not sorry enough for yourself. You're still not." Colette slammed the door in her face.

Marianne stared at the wooden door. How was she supposed to take that?

The next moment, the door was flung open again. "Yann has his show in Paris on 1 September. At the Galerie Rohan, my old stomping ground. It was meant to be a surprise for you. That's because he's showing *you*. These are his first large paintings in thirty years. Now, though, he might as well hang them in a museum in the section called 'Twenty-First-Century Illusions.'" The door banged shut once more.

Marianne already had one foot on the step when Colette called out, "You're dead to me, Marianne!" Just further evidence that she had only imagined she'd found a home here.

"What did she say?" asked Lothar.

"She wished us a safe journey," Marianne replied.

As THEY stood outside Yann's studio, Lothar took her hand.

"Do you have to do this?"

"It's a matter of courtesy," said Marianne, pulling her hand from his.

The curious courtesy of telling a man, I love you but I'm not the person you think I am, and I want to go home. All of a sudden Marianne was seized by the wild hope that Yann would do anything he could to keep her from leaving.

Walking past the tall, wide windows of Yann's studio, it occurred to her that she had never seen the pictures he had painted of her. She took a deep breath. Was leaving the right choice?

As she entered the hallway that led to the bright, high-ceilinged room, Marianne heard sobbing. Neither Yann nor Marie-Claude noticed as she stepped into the studio. The aging hairdresser was weeping in Yann's arms in front of a painting of a naked woman. A magnificent naked woman.

Yet her weeping soon turned to laughter; she had in fact been laughing the whole time. She hugged Yann and covered his face with quick kisses.

They're laughing at you and your stupidity.

Marianne ran away. There was no need to answer the question of right or wrong now.

"So?" asked Lothar, when she was once more sitting beside him, holding back her tears. "How did he take it?"

"Like a man," gasped Marianne.

"Incredible," said Lothar. "Do you know, when you were away during that trouble with Simone, we had a chat. He raved about you so much that I found myself thinking, who's he talking about? He would never have let go of the woman he saw in you."

"It's not Simone, it's Sidonie, and there wasn't any trouble with her—she died. Sidonie's dead."

"Of course. I'm sorry." After a while he said, "Shall we stay in Paris for a few days?" adding with a little worried laugh, "But only if you don't run away this time."

A CAR engine started up outside, and Marie-Claude released herself from Yann's embrace. She had laughed as she told him that she hadn't recognized her reflection in a shop window, thinking, Who's that unfriendly-looking woman? until she had realized that it was her.

Claudine had only just told her mother about the dramatic delivery in Ar Mor, and that it was Victor who had got her pregnant. He was married, and Claudine had decided not to tell him about his baby. He should love her and choose her because he wanted her, not because he felt it was his duty.

Marie-Claude was a grandmother, and she had immediately run to see Yann to persuade him to come to Kerdruc with her so that she could thank Marianne.

"These are wonderful pictures. Has Marianne seen them yet?"

Yann shook his head.

46

MARIANNE FELT AS IF SHE HAD BEEN RETRACING her own footsteps since the train had pulled out of Brest, where she and Lothar had boarded it, left Quimper behind, and was now racing past Auray on its way to Paris.

She was someone else, and yet she was not. She was the same little Annie who had happened to have a great adventure. Her journey into a different world had at least convinced her of that: that her place was where it had always been. She had no right to a new life: that had been a misconception.

"That's Brocéliande over there," she started to say, pointing to a patch of forest on the horizon. "That's the forest of our dreams. It's where Merlin the magician is buried."

"He didn't exist," mumbled Lothar as he flicked through a copy of *Motor Sport* magazine.

"Who says so?"

"Common sense."

Marianne said nothing. She thought of the spring near Merlin's grave, and how she had stood alongside the stones that enclosed his prison of love. From the cracks in the stone poked countless slips of paper that people, having obviously lost all common sense, had left there to express their wishes. One of those people was Marianne, who had written, "Let me love and be loved."

"Do you actually want to hear what I got up to in Kerdruc?" she asked Lothar.

He shrugged.

"I drove a Jaguar and rode a Vespa, I cooked lobster, fed cats and dogs on Ming Dynasty plates, rescued a nun, posed as a model, and played the accordion on the beach."

Lothar looked at her in bewilderment. "How come you of all people can do all those things?"

"Don't you believe me?"

He stared at her, then looked down at his magazine again.

"Sure. Yes. Of course."

"Lothar."

"What?"

"Do you know what a clitoris is?"

His face turned a deep shade of red. "Please!"

"So you do?"

He nodded hastily and glanced around to see if anyone was listening.

"Well why have you never taken an interest in mine?"

"Your lover must have been better at it."

"Would this be the right time to bring up Sybille?"

"We've talked about Sybille. It's over."

"Our conversation lasted less than five minutes, and afterward you never wanted me to mention her again."

"Because it was over! I wanted no one but you!"

"We have to start talking to each other, Lothar. Properly."

"It's possible to overanalyze things! Time heals every wound—that's still the best solution."

"We don't have much time. Maybe twenty years if all goes well."

"You're always so dramatic!"

Marianne took several deep breaths. "Forget it. I'll tell you what I want. I want to go to work, I want my own room and I want to play the accordion."

"What's the problem? Do as you like!"

"All those things were always a problem for you."

"Oh come on. Only in your imagination."

Marianne faltered. Could that be true? Were her memories of her husband worse than he had actually been? Had she only dreamed it all up in order to hate him better? She looked out of the window, suddenly unsure. They had left Rennes behind an hour ago, and they would soon be arriving at Paris Montparnasse.

"Say something nice to me," she begged.

Reluctantly he slapped his magazine shut. "Marianne! I traveled to France to ask you to come home and marry me again! Isn't it nice enough that I want to live with you? What else am I supposed to do?"

Be romantic, loving, tender, interested and happy to see me! Look at me as if I were the most important person in the world for you. Desire me. Respect me. Be willing, just for once, to believe me. Be on my side. Stop reading your stupid magazine and talk to me!

"I love you," said Lothar. "Is that what you wanted to hear?"

Marianne had a dialogue in her head with herself.

Is that what you wanted to say?

That's why I said it!

Yes, but do you really mean it?

Marianne, I'm going to get off the train. If every woman did this, asking her husband what he meant, then—

But not all women do.

That's just as well! How would society survive? One has to consider the whole, not just oneself! It's called being grown up!

One always has to consider the individual. For every person is an individual, and everyone has individual, unique reasons. And every individual counts. That's what I call being grown up.

Marianne was sure that her memories of Lothar hadn't tricked her. But maybe she ought to start doing all the things for him that she wished for herself. Maybe she ought to be more feminine, more seductive, more self-assured, more interesting . . .

OH GOD, STOP IT. I FEEL SICK, roared the voice inside her head. It sounded like Colette.

"Yes, that's what I wanted to hear," replied Marianne after a while.

She felt Lothar's hand rest on hers. "We should buy new rings," he whispered, stroking her bare ring finger. "Otherwise, what would people think?"

She pulled her hand out from under his.

Paris, Montparnasse station. People were pressing between the shops as usual, and as Marianne passed a shoe stall, the salesman looked up and called, "*Ma chère Madame*, you look ravishing!"

"Thank you. Do you also sell shoes a woman can wear to the places where she belongs?"

"Of course!" He pulled out a pair of red pumps with white polka dots. "Do you want to find love there?" He winked at Lothar, who was watching the two of them suspiciously.

Yes, I do.

Marianne strode toward the nearest taxi.

"We can take the bus into the center. It's cheaper," Lothar suggested.

"And I'm sixty and I don't feel like taking the bus," answered Marianne, getting in. Lothar scrambled into the backseat on the other side. As the taxi pulled away, he reached for her hand.

"Forgive me," he whispered. He pressed her fingers, stiff with shock, to his meticulously shaven cheek, snuggled up to her and shut his eyes. Marianne didn't know what to do. Lothar kissed her palm. "Forgive me," he pleaded more ardently. "Forgive me, Marianne, for not having loved you as you needed to be loved." He ran Marianne's hand over his cheek, as if he were desperate for her finally to caress him of her own free will.

That was when it struck her that she hadn't hugged or kissed Lothar once since they had met again, nor had she wanted to.

"Couldn't we learn to love each other as we should?" he now implored her. He tried to pull her to him and stroke her hair, but she pushed him away.

"I lived your life, Lothar, not mine. For that I give you half the blame and myself the other half. I was too complacent, and so were you. That has nothing to do with love."

He bowed his head. "And if I . . . if from now on I live *your* life, as you want to live it?"

He hasn't understood. No one ought to live another person's life. Not me. Not him.

"With your own room. Your accordion. And things will be completely different as soon as I take early retirement. We can go on holiday to Kerdruc from time to time, if you wish."

Holiday in Kerdruc from time to time. Lothar in early retirement. Life in Celle.

The taxi braked. "There's been a crash up ahead," the driver said sullenly. Marianne noticed that they had come to a halt on the Pont Neuf, almost directly alongside the bulge in the stonework from which she had launched herself into the Seine with the aim of bringing her life to an end.

Had Lothar always smelled of damp? She unclicked her seat belt, opened the door and got out.

"Where are you going?" Lothar asked in panic. "Marianne!"

Marianne walked over to the spot where she had sought an end to it all but had found a new beginning. She would surely have passed the place without noticing if two drivers hadn't happened to slam their cars into each other.

Was life so accidental in its possibilities? Or did it all come down to seizing them? Now, with a clarity that pierced her heart and swept through her mind, she was certain: it only ever came down to the odd hour here or there—hours of one's own choices, hours of freedom. A great calm came over her.

Now she understood the rage that the gallery owner had hurled at her. For Colette, the Marianne who gave herself a chance had died, capitulated. She turned to where Lothar was sitting on the backseat of the taxi, peering out at her through the window.

I don't know why we women believe that sacrificing our desires makes us more attractive to men. What on earth are we thinking? That someone who goes without her wishes deserves to be loved more than she who follows her dreams?

"Marianne, we need to get going!"

It was then that Marianne realized what had happened to her.

It's exactly as I thought. The more I suffered, the happier I was. The longer I went without, the stronger was my hope that Lothar would give me what I needed. I believed that if I didn't ask for anything, made no reproaches, didn't demand my own room or my own money, didn't cause any arguments, the miracle would come to pass. That he would say, Oh, how much you have sacrificed! How my love for you has grown, because you sacrificed yourself for me!

The traffic was beginning to flow again.

How crazy that was. I was so proud of myself and my capacity for suffering: I wanted to be perfect at it. The more complete my uncomplaining acquiescence became, the greater his love would one day be. And my greatest abnegation—renouncing my own life—would have secured me his undying love.

She began to giggle. "Stupidly, though, there was never any deal that my suffering would be repaid with love," she said, and curious passers-by stared at her. "You're exactly the same!" she called after them.

Does love have to be earned through suffering?

Tears of laughter ran down her cheeks. She hoped intensely that the generations of women to come would manage better than she had, having been brought up by mothers who didn't equate love with abnegation.

"Marianne, let's go home!" Lothar had now got out of the car too.

She had never heard such insecurity in his voice before, such a beseeching tone, such willingness to debase himself. She wanted to call out, "Stop it! Debase yourself and you receive not love, but scorn!" No one is grateful if someone goes without for their sake: that is the cruel nature of the human race.

She walked back to the taxi, opened the trunk and lifted out her suitcase and the accordion.

"Where are you going?"

"I don't know," she said, slamming the trunk. The only thing she knew for sure was that she was desperate for more than she had ever wanted from Lothar.

He lunged for her arm. "Marianne, don't leave me. I beg you, don't go now. Marianne, I'm talking to you! If you walk out now, you don't ever need to come home!" His voice broke as Marianne shook his hand from her arm before turning to face him one last time.

"Lothar Messmann, you're not my home."

With that, she picked up her cases and set out in search of a home somewhere on this earth. She wept for the love she no longer felt for Lothar, and also for the love she had refused herself.

47

PARIS IN AUGUST. QUIET DAYS, THE QUIETEST OF THE year, when Parisians are in the south, and their cars with them. Empty are the streets, and the air is uncommonly pure. Paris had gone away, and the heat had gathered inside shuttered flats, kiosks and bakeries.

Marianne was sitting beside the Canal Saint-Martin, eating a brioche. The water nearby cooled the warm sheen on her skin. Four musicians were playing under the pedestrian bridge on the other side of the canal in the gentle light of approaching evening. The *Arletty*, a canal boat, puttered past.

It was four days since she had abandoned her husband on the Pont Neuf. She had had no idea of where she wanted to go, trusting her feet to carry her somewhere she could put down her suitcase and close a door behind her.

The envelope Geneviève had presented to her when she left had contained more than she was owed for her work at the guesthouse and Ar Mor. Madame Ecollier had paid her extra for her performance. Marianne's worldly possessions amounted to two thousand six hundred and sixty-two euros, a borrowed suitcase holding some simple clothes and a blue dress, a Chanel lipstick, a dictionary, a tile and an accordion. She was sixty years old, without a profession, savings or jewelry, and yet she felt richer than ever before. She planned to stay in Paris until she knew what she wanted to do next—wanted to do so desperately that she couldn't wait a single second longer.

Kerdruc did not feature in her plans.

She had come across the Pension Babette in the Marais area of town. Every one of its tiny yet bright and lovingly decorated rooms, furnished with a bed, a table, a chair and a chest of drawers, looked out onto a verdant backyard. She had watched people going about their lives in the buildings opposite, every brightly lit window showcasing a different dream: a man equipped with headphones and a baton who conducted inaudible symphonies; a woman who placed a heart in a tightly screwed jar on her bedside table and kissed it before she went to sleep; a couple who brandished potted plants as they argued, before she gave him a slap, he kissed her, and later they ate strawberries and dangled their legs out of the open window.

Next to the hotel was a small café, where the neighbors who hadn't gone on holiday greeted each other, drank pastis, ordered a *café crème* and read the newspaper. By the second morning, they had begun to say hello to Marianne as she ate her breakfast.

She had explored the city, first on foot and then by getting out of the Métro at random, until she had discovered one of the bicycle rental stations, which worked out cheaper than buying a day pass for the underground. Thus Marianne had ridden through Paris on a silver bike, through a Paris that was breathing again now that so many parking spaces were free. Saint-Germain, the Latin Quarter, past the Sorbonne and into the Marais, then westward to the Eiffel Tower and down the Champs-Élysées, tinkling her bell. Students were sunbathing in the parks and on the artificial beaches along the Seine, anglers were fishing in the canals, painters were dozing over sketches on their houseboats, and tourists were kissing against the setting sun on the Pont des Arts with its view of the Eiffel Tower.

Marianne was searching. Searching for the place that was meant for her; and if it were not to be found here, then she would have to travel farther afield. First, though, she wanted to be sure that that place wasn't Paris, the city that had given her an ending and a beginning. She was certain that it would send her a sign.

Again and again she had made her way to the park at the tip of the Île de la Cité in the hope that she might catch sight of the tramp who had fished her out of the Seine.

She brushed the crumbs from her fingers and stood up. The *Arletty* was gone, and the sound of a Vespa's engine echoed in one of the fjord-like nearby streets, covering the strains of *Libertango*. The melody suddenly brought everything crashing back, all the memories she had so successfully blocked from her mind, fleeing through the city streets with the sole aim of preventing her thoughts from flying out over the land, westward-bound to a port on a river and into a room in which a cat sniffed her pillow and mewed plaintively. Her heart was no longer prepared to ignore Kerdruc.

As the Vespa noise faded, an unstoppable tide of images rolled toward her. The sea. Yann above her. Jean-Rémy's feet dancing. Geneviève's eyes scanning Rozbras. White roses in a black vase. A horde of cats lapping at china plates, and the vertical needle of the Jaguar's speedometer. Sidonie's hand clutching the pebble. The flowering garden behind Emile's house in the woods. Geneviève's red dress.

Something stirred inside Marianne. Tomorrow was 1 September.

48

NOBODY WOULD DISTURB HIS PLANS. JEAN-RÉMY HAD declared at short notice on the last day of August that the kitchen would be closed, and indeed today, 1 September, no one had come. Not a single one of his regular guests: not Paul, not Simon, neither Marie-Claude nor Colette. Even Geneviève was away. It was their business what they did—he didn't give a damn! He was going to resolve the other half of his life.

He picked up something beside him, pulled one of his letters to Laurine from its envelope and read it.

My beloved, mon coeur, my sun, my light. Did you know that you are my very first love? That's the way it feels—exactly that way. I'm clueless—it's as if I were meeting myself for the first time. The longing that burns holes in my soul when you are not near me, the relief when you look at me and the desire to give you all of myself: my heart, my hopes, I would even give you my hands and my eyes. I want to entrust my future and my past to you, as if they only became valuable in your hands. Laurine, when I speak your name it means the same for me as love.

He folded the letter into the shape of a ship and placed it next to the paper boats he had already formed from other letters. Then he picked up the next one.

My flower, how exciting and elegant, how pure and how great you are. Simply having known you means I can die more serenely. Loving you means that my life will not have been meaningless and for naught, regardless of whether you love me or not. Yes, it is for you to decide whether to accept or reject my love, but it will not affect the fact that I will then smile in the face of death and say, So what? I knew Laurine. I saw her walk, I saw her laugh, I saw her dance and I heard her voice.

He folded this one with particular care. It was the last of his seventy-three love letters to Laurine. Seventy-three white boats and seventy-three flowers now lay beside him, and he tossed the very first of them—a white rose, which was on the verge of crumbling like parchment—into the river Aven.

As he let the first of the many love letters sail off after the rose, a flying shoe caught him square on the head.

"That's robbery!" cried Laurine. She was standing only a few yards from the breakwater with Padrig at her side. Jean-Rémy felt infinitely jealous. "Those are letters to me, aren't they? Padrig showed them to me, but you never handed them over!"

Now Laurine removed her other shoe and hurled it at Jean-Rémy. He ducked, and the shoe hit Max on the tip of his tail. The cat leaped into the air, spitting, and trotted a little way to one side, where it sat down indignantly and began to groom itself.

"They belong to me! Letters belong to their addressees!"

"Only when they've been sent," cried Jean-Rémy, "and I'm only sending them now."

"Ohhh, you . . . dweeb!" Laurine furiously stamped the ground.

But why were they shouting at each other, and why had Laurine taken her shoes off? Now she was also pulling her T-shirt over her head! Jean-Rémy felt short of breath: she was so unbelievably beautiful. Her skin. The curve of her waist. Her soft stomach. Her hips, as she peeled off her jeans.

"What are you doing?"

"I'm fetching my letter! I don't want to lose a single one of your words!" She discarded her bra and, lastly, tossed away her white knickers. The hair between her legs glowed golden, and she had a dancer's figure. She is the most beautiful girl in the world, thought Jean-Rémy, the bravest, the finest, the very best.

Laurine walked onto the quayside to rescue the first of the love letters. She had forgotten that she had decided to take a step toward Jean-Rémy, just the one. She was ready to take a giant leap. But Jean-Rémy got to his feet and ran toward her.

"No!" he shouted. "I know it by heart!"

By now the little paper boat had reached the middle of the river, spinning with increasing speed before it was swept away by the current.

There were tears in Laurine's eyes as she said, "But it was the first, Jean-Rémy. The first is always the most important one."

I'll write you as many as you want, he thought. Hundreds, thousands, year after year. You'll have a whole library of my words, and I'll ban salt from the kitchen, because I'll always be in love with you, even when we're already man and wife, and father and mother, and grandfather and grandmother. He didn't say this, though.

She wanted that letter? She would have that letter. Jean-Rémy pulled off his shoes and his shirt and jumped. As he swam, stroke after stroke, and the currents and eddies caught and wrestled with him, his mind was flooded with every sentence he had written in that first love letter to Laurine.

He swam, repeatedly craning his neck so as not to lose sight of the little boat. His arms burned, the water grew colder and colder, and he could hardly feel his toes, but he swam on as fast as he could, even if it meant following the boat out to sea and drowning there!

The river fairies seemed to be amused by this swimmer chasing after his own words. They made the paper boat dance, sent small waves skimming toward him, causing him to splutter, and drove the love letter hither and thither, as if they were tossing a ball to one another. Then they pushed it into a side channel of the Aven, and Jean-Rémy, who felt his waning strength begging him to give up and simply float on his back, pursued it with furious, powerless tears in his eyes.

Yet Nimue, the ruler of the sea, had an agreement with Jean-Rémy, and sent the letter sailing toward him. He had it! He turned to face Laurine, who was still standing on the quayside. He had swum a long way from the shore, and now he had to return against the current. When his breathing had calmed, he gripped the letter between his teeth and began to paddle back.

As he clambered up the ladder on Kerdruc harbor wall,

Laurine first took the letter from his mouth and then bent down to the breathless man. She took his head in her hands and pushed the wet black hair from his forehead, warming his body wherever she touched it with hers.

"Jean-Rémy," she whispered before kissing him, her lips lightly touching his. He was so stunned by his beloved's kiss, her closeness, her skin, her scent, her face and her smile, that he almost toppled backward into the water.

She stepped back and carefully unfolded the wet paper boat.

Laurine, you are everything to me. You are my morning, my smile. You are my fear and you are my courage. You are my dreams and my daylight. You are my night and my breath, you are my most important lesson. I beg to be allowed to love you, and I beg for no less than a lifetime by your side.

She read for a long time, savoring it, letting the lines echo in her soul. When she raised her eyes, there was great dignity in her expression.

"Yes," she said.

Yes. The most beautiful word in the world.

❦

L OVE? WHAT DO YOU MEAN, LOVE?"
      "An artist must love if he wants to be any good."
    "Rubbish. He's got to be free, or he's not an artist. Free of
love, free of hatred, free of every defined emotion."
    Arm in arm with Rozenn, Paul walked past the two men
and said quietly to her, "Our first brush with Parisian art
critics."
    "That's what it's like at previews," she whispered back.
    He let his hand slide down onto her backside. "Let's go and
find the cellar," he murmured.
    No one could really recall whose idea it had been to make
the trip to Yann Gamé's exhibition in Paris after Jean-Rémy
had abruptly gone on strike. Yann had wanted to cancel the
show. He had wanted to burn, destroy and rip up the pictures,
but Colette had stored them in a sealed container. She knew
that artists sometimes got this way shortly before their work
was due to be exhibited: they would become anxious that
someone might take away their paintings, and with them all
the emotions and ideas they had invested in them; they were
scared that their souls would be stolen.

Colette had chosen her date well. The first of September was the *rentrée*, when people returned to school and to work. Everyone was back in Paris and desperate to recover from being in the provinces by gorging on culture and novelty until they were in sync with the city's rhythm once more.

Pascale walked past the pictures like an astonished child. Emile had put one leg up and was sitting in an alcove beside a tall casement window that looked out onto Rue Lepic. Simon came over to him, clutching Grete's hand tightly. "It's odd seeing her when she isn't here herself," the fisherman said.

"She *is* here," mumbled Emile, turning to gesture with a generous sweep of his arm at Paul and Rozenn, Geneviève and Alain, Colette and Marie-Claude, who was being a little too loud and jolly to cover up her nervousness and the strange feeling of being a freshly minted grandmother. They were all filing slowly past the paintings of Marianne, as if they wanted to print every last detail on their memories. Many of them stopped in front of the picture that showed her as a shimmer of dazzling light onstage. It was called *The Moon Musician*.

"See, she's in their hearts and in their smiles, as they look at her and think of her. Particularly over there."

They both looked at Yann Gamé, who was gazing at a portrait of Marianne standing by the window of the Shell Room. Her birthmark, the glowing sky behind her, the line of surf in the background: it was a picture composed of countless shades of red, and the sea glittered in her eyes. Yann had named the painting *L'Amour de Marianne*.

"What *is* it about her?" asked Simon.

"She reminds you of your dreams, back when you still had some," Emile said slowly.

The fisherman nodded. "That's right. Look at them—they're all suddenly recalling their dreams."

Colette escorted guests over to the pictures, sticking the odd yellow dot on the card bearing the title of the painting to signal that it had been optioned and would be sold after the exhibition.

Simon, Grete and Emile observed the Parisians who were now appearing in growing numbers at the door of the gallery, some of them wishing to catch up with Colette. Colette looked very frail and pale, dressed entirely in black. Her love for Sidonie had softened her features, but her grief had hardened her movements and made them angular, as if without her companion she could no longer feel the boundaries of her body.

Now a man in a tweed suit, carrying an official-looking briefcase, approached Yann, stirring the painter from his brooding silence. They walked over to *L'Amour de Marianne*. The man pointed to the birthmark that had seared Yann to the quick like fire. Yann shrugged, and Emile got up and leaned on Simon so that the two of them might creep closer and eavesdrop on the conversation.

". . . genetic and genealogical research can use pigment disorders such as this striking example to conclude whether someone might be descended from Celtic druids . . ."

Yet Yann was no longer listening to the man, who was seeking to explain, in ever more excitable fashion what, in his view, the special pattern of Marianne's flame mark might mean, namely a trail back to the people who had produced so many magicians and knights, female druids and healers in King Arthur's day.

He glanced over at the woman in a red dress who had just entered Galerie Rohan and, slowly removing her chic dark glasses, was now looking around helplessly—at the twenty-seven oil paintings, eighteen ink drawings and thirty watercolors, all of them showing the same woman.

"Marianne!"

Marianne didn't hear Alain's call. She was seeing herself as she had never seen herself before. Her heart had been beating wildly and she had felt shy as she walked through the city to the art gallery in the red dress with its plunging neckline. It was knee-length, silk and a warm shade of red. She'd found it at a dressmaker's that did alterations, where it had ended up in the dusty shop window after its owner had forgotten to pick it up for two years. She had thanked the stranger for not being brave enough to face this dress, leaving it instead for her to discover.

Nicolas, the receptionist at Pension Babette, had not only dug up the Galerie Rohan's address, but had also gone out into the street to get a better view of Marianne in the light of the dying sun. "Breathtaking," he had said.

And now here she was, standing in front of these pictures that revealed to her a Marianne she would never have recognized in herself at first sight. Marianne holding her face to the setting sun. Marianne sleeping. One portrait of her just after a kiss, a smile on her lips, lost in reverie. A woman playing the accordion by the sea. A nude Marianne.

She saw herself through the eyes of a man who loved her, and she discovered that she was beautiful: she had the particular beauty of women who are loved. Her soul had been transformed. She saw that she had many faces: grief and indulgence, tenderness and pride, dreams and music. And there was one picture where she knew what she had been contemplating—a dead-end road. There was boundless desolation in her expression, her eyes lifeless, her mouth despondent, the lines on her face deep and coarse.

Without her noticing, the other visitors made room for her, and as she went from picture to picture, some of them gazed after her. "Isn't that . . . ?" "Looks just like . . ." "Do you think they're a couple?"

Finally she stood in front of *L'Amour de Marianne*. This face showed how she looked when she was in love. It told her all about her force and her strength, everything about her desires and her willpower: it was the essence of her being. There was a sense of freedom about it, a wild sensuality, an aura. Her love was like a blazing sea.

Yann stepped up behind her. She sensed his presence without needing to turn around. Neither did she need to ask whether he would have held her back: the power of the paintings had made this question superfluous.

"Is this how you see me?" she asked quietly.

"This is how you are," he said.

This is how you are. Your soul is a kaleidoscope of colors.

Marianne turned to face him.

"You have a new face. What should I call it?" he asked.

She looked at him, and she felt with fierce intensity that she could do a great deal with this man in the days she had left, and also that she would never again allow herself to be deprived of this feeling.

Of all the host of possibilities that were spread before her, choosing Yann was one of the easiest. Of course she could go out into the world and love other men—taller, smaller, with different laughter lines and different eyes that glittered like stars or mountain lakes or melted chocolate. She could travel to another end of the earth, with different friends, where there were different rivers and rooms in which she and her tile would sleep alone, and there would doubtless be a cat to visit them.

But that wasn't necessary. She chose the man standing before her. She could not do without him. They could deal with the details later.

"Marianne is alive," she answered. "That's the name of this face."

Happiness is loving what we need, and needing what we love—and obtaining it, thought Yann.

"Will you come back with us to Kerdruc?" he asked.

"Yes," said Marianne. Kerdruc had everything she expected from life.

Then, as if they could no longer bear to gaze at each other without feeling each other, they embraced with such force that their teeth collided as they kissed. They laughed, kissed a second time, more gently, but their laughter grew, and they stood there, intertwined, until it filled the entire room.

Epilogue

IT IS NOTHING BUT A LEGEND, THEY SAY. *LA NUIT DE samhain*: the end of summer, the beginning of the dark months. It is the night in which the ancestors and the living gather, in which time and space are superimposed and for twelve nameless hours the past, the present and the future become indistinguishable. The other world emerges from the mists to return our dead to us for one night. We bid them to question the gods, demons and fairies in the hereafter about our fates.

Yet when the human meets the elements, and the heroes the haters, each should stick to his own in the light, for very few souls survive the battle between the merging worlds. Anyone who loses his way on dark roads or by the watery gates to the other world will encounter spirits that only druids or priestesses can defeat. Anyone who ventures outside is sucked into the realm of the dead and must spend a year with them. If they do return, nobody will be able to see them anymore.

Marianne nevertheless walked through this night to the sea to meet her dead. She had left the feast in honor of the deceased on her own. It was not only the dead that were cel-

ebrated at this festival, for she and Geneviève had turned it
into a festival of women too, just as the forgotten Celtic and
Breton myths had once required: women's love dissolved all
borders, stretching beyond the reach of death and time.

The women of this world and the other were thanked with
an offering of burning sheaves of grain, which were covered
and extinguished after a minute's silence. This was the sign
that the summer was over, and a new cycle began when the
next sheaves were set alight. At each table there was an extra
place setting and a chair was left empty for those who were
bidden to come from the other world. All lights were put out
for a minute so that the dead could climb unseen into their
boats and set out for this world, guided by candles in the
windows.

It was the duty of every reveler to justify his or her forbidden
acts or forgive others theirs, and it behoved everyone to draw
up a list of the things they would like to have experienced by
samhain the following year. This life list was also Marianne's
idea.

The only person she had told that he didn't need to wait up
for her during this night of blurring worlds was Yann.

Yann. There had been nights with him and nights without him. There had been days filled with music and days of
mourning when they carried Sidonie's ashes to the stones and
buried them there. There had been hours of wonder when
Simon went on a tour of Normandy's Calvados distilleries
with Grete and they came back as a couple; and when Paul
and Rozenn said "I do" for a second time, and Marianne had
heard for the first time at the registry office that Paul's place
of birth was Frankfurt. He was a German, and yet could not

have been less of one. When he joined the Foreign Legion, he'd cast off everything he no longer wanted to be—the son of an SS officer. That was the secret that had overshadowed his entire life. Marianne continued not to speak a single word of German with him, for he willed it so, and her respect for someone's will had grown since she had possessed one of her own.

There had been minutes of joy when Jean-Rémy and Laurine made enquiries about baby names, and seconds of gratitude when Marianne looked out from her room at the peach-colored reflections of the sun and the sky in the Aven.

There were also those recurring Mondays at Kerdruc harbor when Marianne sat together with friends who loved her, chatting about God, goddesses, the world, and dreams both big and small.

NOW SHE was sitting by the sea on this night of all nights. She had set up a folding stool beside her in case one of the dead wanted to sit down.

With her eyes closed, she played a song for the dead, for women and for the sea. It had no title, and her fingers decided freely on the tune. "Sa-un," she whispered, pronouncing the Breton name for this timeless time. *Sa-un*, the waves whispered back. *Are you ready for your journey into the ephemeral?*

Marianne thought she heard steps and laughter. She thought she could feel gusts of wind as the dead ran over the sand, leaving footprints in it.

Are you happy? asked her father. He was sitting next to her with folded hands, gazing out at the black Atlantic.

"Yes."

My resilient girl.

"I love you," said Marianne. "I miss you."

He had your eyes, said her grandmother, moving over the waves toward her. *I loved your grandfather, and after him, no one else. It is a rare form of happiness when a man makes your life so rich that you need no one else after him.*

"Was he a magician?"

Any man who loves a woman as she deserves to be loved is a magician.

Marianne opened her eyes. Her fingers stopped playing. The beach was empty, no footprints in the sand, and yet they were all there: the dead, the night and the sea. The sea offered her a song of bravery and love. It came from a long way away, as if someone somewhere in the world had sung it many years ago, for those on the shore who didn't dare to take the plunge.

The Little French Bistro

A Conversation with Nina George   315

Reading Group Guide   320

Eleven Things You Should Know
    About Brittany   323

Selected Recipes   332

ESSAYS,
READER'S GUIDES,
AND MORE

A Conversation with
Nina George

**Your first book published in the United States,
The Little Paris Bookshop, was a bestseller in hardcover and paperback. What do you think reso-
nates with people in your writing? What do they
respond to?**

I am not afraid of feelings and not afraid to talk about
being lost in one's own life—and maybe the readers
feel that I want to console, to comfort their pain with
my stories. And, to be honest, one book lover knows
another, so *The Little Paris Bookshop* is a love letter
from a book addict to all book addicts. . . . When
readers write to me, most of them tell me that the
story opened up a door to themselves—to a hidden
inner personality that was locked in for some reason. After reading *The Little Paris Bookshop* they feel
somehow motivated: Let's go out and change something! So maybe we should put a warning on it: Be
careful—you may want to break free of your daily
routine.

How did you come up with the idea for *The Little French Bistro*?

On one of my first trips around Brittany, I sat at a tiny little *bar tabac* (these are places that combine a café and a bar with the opportunity to buy magazines or cigarettes). It's a common place to meet and chat in each village. There was a group of older gentlemen and ladies who were lifelong friends. And there it was, like a slap in the face, the idea to tell the story of a woman in her later years finding friends and a place where she can discover herself for the first time. Where she can be who she truly is.

The next day, we got lost at the "end of the world," because we couldn't locate our maps—and that was the moment I discovered the Port de Kerdruc. It was like coming home. And I knew I wanted to write about people and how they find themselves.

Tell us a little bit about Brittany and what makes it unique and different from the rest of France. What's your favorite thing about spending time there?

The Bretons are profoundly convinced that they are the cradle of European humanity. And they are right: The *Bretagne* is built on old stones and land where the former continent Armorica became Europe. The Bretons have Celtic roots, a different language (Breizh), and they feel a kinship with the Gaelic people of Scotland, Wales, and Ireland and their traditions. They are authentic in every way—no one tries to be something they're not. What I like most is their politeness. Politeness is everywhere: in traffic, in the bistros and boulangeries (please, never forget to say first bonjour when entering anyplace or asking anyone for help!), and in their interactions.

Bretons have another perception of time. If there is time to eat, eat. If there is time to chat, chat. If there is time to go shopping, do it. If there is loving or reading or dancing time, do it in full. Nothing in a hurry or a rush.

My husband, Jo, and I live in a little white house at the seashore, near the setting of *The Little French Bistro*. When I am in "Ty Lola" (as a Breton friend named our *cabane*), I start to listen to myself again. I watch the different sunsets, the rapid changing of the weather. I feel the intense peace and silence from this old country, where the land was born and rose up out of the wild sea. I remember the meaning of life. Okay, and I admit: I love to cook mussels and eat oysters directly out of the sea, and I enjoy the seasonal and regional food, the countless different cheeses, and, of course, Breton beer!

The last thing to mention is that the Bretons believe in many legends and are tolerant of all religions. They believe in Anna and Maria as well as in one of the 7,777 saints; they have witches and druids; they see God and Death (Ankou) everywhere in nature; and there is no concept for something like hell. The sea dictates everyday life, and the hidden places of magic stones (dolmens or menhirs) remind you that there might be more between sky and ground. . . .

There is such a strong sense of warmth and community in *The Little French Bistro*. How did you go about developing the different characters? Do you know people like them in real life?

Of course! When I do my "ensemble work," I pick up archetypes as well as certain character traits from people I know. When I imagined Marianne's inner life, I remembered all the ladies I had met when I worked in my parents' restaurants. These ladies of a certain age, sometimes married or widows, subdued themselves, suppressed their needs and crafts over their long lives. But in their eyes shimmered the silent and melancholic hope of finding their true lives. In the German vocabulary of *Philosophie,* you find the words *eigentlich* (true, real) and *uneigentlich,* the opposite of the true life you are meant for. There are many people living an *uneigentliches Leben* (inauthentic life). It is the hardest thing to step out of these self-constructed cages.

If you want to find these heartwarming people, just go to Brittany! Take some time, perhaps a year or two. Have patience, but if you ever have a Breton friend, you will never be alone again.

Both *The Little French Bistro* and *The Little Paris Bookshop* deal with the concept of love in different forms. Why do you think you're drawn to that subject?

The older I get, the more I know: it is all about love. How parents treat their kids, how women treat themselves, how nations treat other cultures. Love is a small word, and behind its four letters there is so much hiding: respect, patience, interest, empathy, passion, endurance, and confidence.

When you ask yourself what is the best thing in your life and what do you really need, I predict you will realize this: people. Everything else is just decoration.

What do you hope readers will take away from the book?
That it is never too late to start over. That it is not necessary to hide yourself, your yearnings, your skills. And, above all, to learn to take time. Maybe you should come to Brittany to slow down and to remember who you wanted to be.

(Translation © 2017 by Heidi Holzer)

Reading Group Guide

1. What elements of the story line affected you most personally? Was it Marianne's loneliness? The way she boldly set out on a journey through a foreign country without knowing a word of the language?

2. Which character(s) did you identify with the most and why? Were there any characters who left you feeling perplexed or annoyed? Why?

3. The landscape is as much a protagonist in the book as the human characters (and to some extent, the animal ones). Is there a place, a region, a season in which you feel especially at home? Why? What appealed to you most about the Breton landscape as described—the light, the sea, the rocks, the stillness, the wildness?

4. Food, music, and friendship: These are the essential ingredients that help Marianne reclaim her life. What things do you need in order to feel entirely, truly, and deeply alive?

5. Religion, superstition, and a woman's wisdom: Some scenes in the book touch on spiritual planes beyond the realm of established religions. What role do such planes have to play in today's world? How does belief in mythical forces, the invisible world beyond our physical one, change the characters in *The Little French Bistro*?

6. Most often, we cannot change our lives from one day to the next by making only a single decision. Instead, it takes many small steps to explore a new path. What steps did Marianne take in *The Little French Bistro* that surprised you? Were there other paths you would you have liked to see Marianne take?

READING GROUP GUIDE

321

7. Love between people who "have a few more years under their belts than others" is rarely the subject of a novel. Why do we sometimes find it difficult to believe that older people are capable of the same insane longings, hopes, relationship troubles, or desires as the young? Did you find the depiction of the lifestyles of these characters, most of whom are between sixty and seventy years old, relatable? Surprising?

8. Which of the characters in the book would you like to meet in real life? What would you like to ask them? Where and on what occasion?

9. It's said that books have the power to heal. They can change lives and cast the world in a new light.

Do you have the sense that *The Little French Bistro* has given you something that you could use in your life? Another perspective? A different understanding of culture? An idea that you have long wanted to try out in your life?

10. If you had the chance to ask the author a question, what would it be?

11. If the book were to be made into a movie, whom would you cast in the different roles?

Eleven Things You Should Know About Brittany

Nina George has been living at the "end of the world," in Finistère, for some years now. The bestselling author introduces us to the ten most fascinating places and unique attributes of her favorite region, along with a few insider tips.

(Text © 2017 by Nina George; translations © 2017 by Heidi Holzer)

1. Brittany is where the world begins.
Finis Terrae. The end of the world. This is what the Romans, in all their arrogance, called the western tip of Gaul. The angry sea. The wild coastline. The dour Veneti, who bound torches to their horses' tails at night to confuse the helmsmen of Roman battleships. Indeed, no Roman nobleman would be caught dead on this rock-strewn coast at the butt-end of the world.

This westernmost of Brittany's four *departements* still bears the name Finistère—although some Bretons prefer to call it the "beginning of the world." According to Celtic legend, this is where the first land rose up from the water and "grew" out of Brittany and around the globe, forming the continents.

The rocks and cliffs of Brittany display colors from winter gray and sky blue to delicate pink and brilliant gold, depending on the region. It is as though, in their presence, all the wondrous things in life were condensed into one landscape. Faces, animals, and forgotten creatures appear on enormous boulders in the play of light and shadow. Abbé Fouré, the two-faced priest, even had the gift of making these beings visible. His mythical figures, carved out of the cliffs, can be seen in Rothéneuf, 7.3 kilometers (4.5 miles) from Saint-Malo. And once you've discovered these creatures, you will see them again and again all over Brittany, this cradle of the world fashioned from stone, sea, and sky.

2. Just don't come here in August.

Brittany's weather in August is the worst anywhere in Europe. Really. Nineteen degrees Celsius (66 degrees Fahrenheit) in the drizzling rain. At the same time, the cost of a vacation rental triples, and the *crêperies* are packed with demanding Parisians, rude Dutch tourists, and noisy Americans. Some days, you can't even see the beaches for the algae. My advice: Come in January or February, in late June, or from September to October. The weather at these times is as smooth as silk. The sea displays its most intense colors. And you can take the occasional stroll along deserted beaches.

3. The most sensible items to bring along: a scarf, sunglasses, and a watch.

It's fall in the morning, summer at noon, and spring in the evening. Brittany's weather can sometimes change every fifteen minutes. The only constant is the wind. Everyone swears by the constancy of Breton wind: kite surfers off Saint-Malo and Quiberon, surfboarders at Pointe du Raz, stand-up paddleboarders in Ploumanac'h, and paragliders at Menez-Hom and in the Baie de Douarnenez. At the same time, the sea's bright reflection is so intense as to make sunglasses your second favorite accessory, unless you want to stumble blind across the dramatic landscape. This holds doubly true for hikers who circumnavigate Brittany along the stunningly beautiful coastal trail known as the GR 34. You can follow this ancient path, once patrolled by customs officers, all the way around Brittany for more than 1,800 kilometers (1,118 miles) right on the waterfront, from the mountain abbey of Mont Saint-Michel, rising above the tidewater, to Guérande, the source of the salt for the lightly salted butter known as *beurre demi-sel*. The sections I find the most beautiful pass along the coast of Iroise, between Pointe Saint-Mathieu and Trézien, and also in the more charming south, between Fouesnant and Port Manec'h.

The one thing you absolutely must take along, and not only on the hiking trail, is a watch. Because all life in public places vanishes on the dot from 12:15 to 2:30 p.m. Everything is closed: pharmacies, village supermarkets, banks. It is siesta time, and if the

Bretons hold one thing sacred, it's their "*la bouffe*."
Plan to stop for a picnic or lunch during these hours.

4. The national dish is *moules frites, galettes,* and, of course, oysters.

In every town you will find a restaurant that offers
a *formule*, a reasonably priced lunch menu that usually consists of meat or fish with a salad and dessert.
If you're not sure how to tell the difference between
a good restaurant and one of the (few) tourist traps,
look for one that is filled with workmen (and women)
at lunchtime—and also has a short menu! The local
working people appreciate a meal with generous por-
tions, fresh ingredients, and reasonable prices.

Have the waitstaff show you to a table and skip
the bottled water; order a carafe instead. It consists of
tap water with ice, and, as a gesture of goodwill from
the establishment, it's free of charge. This leaves you
room in your budget for the small, obligatory glass
of wine to accompany the main course. If you order
a *galette*—the region's hearty buckwheat pancake—
the *complète* is a good choice for beginners, the *gargantua* is for those with more experience. Pair this
with *cidre* (*demi sec*, and ice cold!), sipped from ce-
ramic cups. From September to April, the national
dish is *moules à la crème* (mussels with white wine
and crème fraîche) or *moules marinières* (onions,
parsley, wine) with a side of *frites* (French fries). If
you're in the mood for oysters, you will find the best
around Cancale and in Château de Bélon, near Riec-
sur-Bélon. Seated at a bare picnic table above the

Belon estuary, with a view of the Atlantic, you can enjoy a half dozen oysters, caliber three, for less than 20 euros ($23)—it doesn't get any better than this.

5. By the way, any type of wine you'll find at a Leclerc, Casino or Intermarché is better than anything you've ever sampled before.

If you are an avid cook, the supermarket culture in Brittany will bowl you over the first time you enter a store. There is an overabundance of meats, fish, fruits, and vegetables in the fresh food aisles, and the wines are of top quality—at a price that I can reveal only in a soft whisper: "far below six euros." If you are still a "wine novice," check out the winners of the Concours Général Agricole award. They have round, white labels with a gold, silver, or bronze oak leaf. Whatever your preference—white, rosé, or red—you will be very, very happy with these wines.

6. While we're on the subject of happiness, the Bretons love to socialize.

You don't need to speak French to get around here. All you need are three words: *bonjour* (hello), *merci* (thank you), and *au revoir* (goodbye). After all, courtesy is of paramount importance in Brittany. You encounter it everywhere: at the bakery, the hardware store, and even on the street! Take pleasure in the respect people show one another in traffic, where no one tailgates you. You see it in the longer waits at the boulangerie and the Intermarché, where the sales staff take their time chatting with their equally gregarious customers. And in the fact that the smaller and more remote the village or region, the more everyone will greet you.

7. Solitude is rare in the most scenic places.

When I discovered the most breathtakingly beautiful places for the first time, I had to concede that one is rarely alone there on weekends and during the summer vacation time. Not in my favorite places: the harbor of Kerdruc, with its sleepy charm; the lighthouse at Pointe Saint-Mathieu, including its ruined cathedral, whose stunning beauty and vast expanse liberate my soul; the Saint-Laurent Peninsula, with its wild Breton horses and enormous boulders; the D127, a devastatingly sublime stretch of road along the coast between Penfoul und Trémazan; or the peaceful, picture-perfect "Plage de Tahiti" beach between Rospico und Port Manec'h. Word of beautiful locations tends to spread, attracting everyone—from groups of hikers and speed cyclists to motorcycle cruisers—to the loveliest and wildest corners of the world, along with romantic couples in love, bands of families yakking away, or writers yearning for solitude. If you want to be alone, your best bet is to come in the winter or late fall, when you'll find mighty storm tides, often the best weather, and vast, empty beaches, which you will share only with the dinosaur-like seagulls and your own rambling thoughts.

8. Many beaches, no beach vacations.

Nevertheless, Brittany has a truly countless number of beaches. Coarse, fine, sandy, rocky, hidden, dozens of kilometers long. However, classic beach resorts with sunbaked tourists and bikini promenades are to be found only in places like La Baule and Saint-Malo. The remaining beaches belong to people who like to exercise—surfers with their paddleboards and kites; divers, swimmers, sailors, or canoers. . . . The Atlantic is not an ocean where you go to relax, it's a sportsman's sea. This is where the world's best sailors train—on a tidal ocean that rises and falls up to 4 meters (13 feet) per day, baring itself once a month. When the tidal coefficient is especially high and the tide retreats far out to sea, the ocean floor is laid bare at *marée basse* (low tide) and releases edible treasures such as palourde clams, spider crabs, and abalone. Get yourself a *pêche à pied* (fishing on foot) guide and follow the children out to the exposed ocean floor, where sirens and golden cities usually lie hidden. . . .

ELEVEN
THINGS YOU
SHOULD
KNOW ABOUT
BRITTANY

329

9. Where history weds the present.

From the legend of Dahut, the princess who invited her lovers into the golden city of Ys and caused the jealous tidal wave to open the gates, to the story of the "Bay of the Dead," the Baie des Trépassés on Cap Sizun, where the dead rise from the sea on All Hallows' Eve (the night of October 31), to take care of unfinished business, Brittany is a region that is deeply entwined in its own history. The sagas are layered with Celtic, Druid, Catholic, and fictional elements, and these stories are reflected just as colorfully in everyday life—small chapels are decorated with symbols from all religious faiths; high thresholds before doors prevent *korrigan* (trolls) from crossing them;

and the village festivals in early summer are often dedicated to the ancient customs of *pardons* (penitent processions). With 7,777 current religious and patron saints, Brittany is well protected, and yet the true ruler of this land is neither God nor Ankou (Death), who rides a water horse, but rather the sea. *La mer*'s tidal cycle shapes the Breton soul.

10. Present-day life can be strange sometimes.

I love my Brittany, even though its oddities drove me bat-shit crazy at first. Filling stations are to be found only on the highway or outside supermarkets. And the pumps at the latter only work with French ATM cards after 6:00 p.m. Not with a Visa, MC, or CB credit card. So make sure to always fill up your tank before 6:00 p.m. and plan ahead. Or the fact that sea salt encrusts the sensitive parts of your car. That's why you'll find Eléphant Bleu self-service car washes everywhere. I love one curiosity: salted butter caramels. Buy a tin of them for the folks back home—because this is what Brittany tastes like: sweet and salty at the same time.

11. Eccentrics have it easy in Brittany—it's the normal people who don't fit in.

As a German native, I am accustomed to having my everyday life regulated by signs that say "keep off the grass," "parents are liable for their children," and "stay on the path." But in Brittany, nothing is forbidden; *liberté* (freedom) is a basic right that encompasses all spheres of life. Suddenly, everyone is free to decide whether to leave the coastal trail in order to peer over the edge of the 50-meter (164-foot) bluff. Or sleep on the beach. Or touch an enchanted menhir that belongs to no one but itself. Everything here is "at your own risk." This amount of freedom drives many a person crazy—just not those who can tolerate freedom.

P.S. Only one thing is indeed forbidden. You are not allowed to take home any rock bigger than your fist. Because these rocks belong here, in the place where the world begins.

*ELEVEN
THINGS YOU
SHOULD
KNOW ABOUT
BRITTANY*

331

Selected Recipes

GLACE AU CARAMEL AU BEURRE SALÉ
(CARAMEL ICE CREAM WITH SALTED BUTTER)

Serves 6 to 8

1/4 cup heavy cream (*crème fleurette*)
1 cup fine granulated sugar
2 1/2 tablespoons salted butter at room temperature,
   cut into little pieces
1/8 teaspoon sea salt (best: fleur de sel)
2 cups whole milk
3 egg yolks
5/8 cup sugar
Tartine or warm apple pie (optional)

1. In a small pot, heat the cream on low for 2 to
   3 minutes, then remove from the heat and set
   aside.

2. In a medium saucepan, heat the sugar on
   medium-high heat, stirring until it becomes

amber-colored. Add ¹/₅ cup of the warm cream, and whisk it slowly in a continuous motion until smooth.

3. Add the salted butter to the caramel mixture and whisk until the butter melts, about 2 to 3 minutes.

4. Add the sea salt and stir.

5. Meanwhile, in a casserole dish, heat the milk on medium heat with the remaining warm cream until it's warm.

6. Add the milk to the caramel mixture, using a spoon to smooth any nubs. Over very low heat, stir the caramel until well combined.

7. In a separate medium bowl, use a hand mixer to beat the egg yolks with the sugar until a mélange forms with firm high peaks.

8. Fold the egg mélange into the milk-caramel and soften over low heat. Do not boil the mélange.

9. Put the cream in a medium bowl in the freezer overnight.

10. Remove the ice cream from the freezer, scoop into bowls or serve alongside a tartine or warm apple pie slice, if desired!

GALETTES

(SALTY AND THIN BUCKWHEAT PANCAKES OF BRITTANY)

Makes 12 thin galettes

For the dough

1½ cups buckwheat flour

⅛ teaspoon fleur de sel from Guérande

3 cups water (or a mix of 1½ cups cold water and 1½ cups cold milk)

1 egg (optional)

3¼ tablespoons lightly salted butter, plus more for brushing on the griddle

Special equipment: nonstick griddle pan or heating plate, wooden spatula

1. The night before, make the dough: In a large bowl, mix the flour with the salt. Add the water in small amounts and stir with a wooden spoon. The texture has to be fluid. Mix in the egg. Let the dough rest overnight in the fridge.

2. Remove the dough from the fridge a half hour before you start cooking. Preheat the oven to 200°F.

3. To make the galettes, melt the butter in a small pan over medium heat and mix it in with the dough.

4. Heat up the griddle to a low-medium heat and apply some more fresh butter with a brush. Place three-fourths of a ladle's worth of dough on the

griddle (about ¼ cup) for each galette. When the edges begin to lift up (1 to 2 minutes), flip the galette with a spatula and cook for another minute or so.

5. When the galette is cooked, transfer it to an oven-proof plate and keep warm in the oven. Repeat with the remaining batter.

6. Remove the warmed galettes from the oven, divide among plates, and serve.

Variation: Galettes Complètes

4 slices cooked ham
4 slices of cheese, such as Emmentaler, Gruyère, or Comté
8 fresh and sweet tomatoes, sliced thin
4 eggs, fried or sunny-side up
Sea salt and black pepper

1. Make four large galettes following the steps for the Galettes recipe.

2. Layer each galette with a slice of cooked ham, a slice of cheese, two or more tomato slices, and a fried egg. Season with salt and pepper.

3. Finish each galette by folding all four sides into the middle to serve. *Voilà, les galettes complètes!*

Variation: Galette Gargantua

Stewed onions
Fried mushrooms

1. Follow the steps on previous page for the Galettes Complètes recipe and add stewed onions and fried mushrooms to each galette.
2. Fold all four sides of each galette into the middle and serve.

KIR BRETON (COCKTAIL)

Serves 4

Fruit cordial or fruit liqueur, such as peach, black-
   berry, raspberry, or strawberry (typical Breton
   flavors are chestnut or black eye)
1 bottle of Breton cider (doux, demi-sec, or brut—
   sparkling Breton apple cider)

In four champagne flutes, pour the fruit liqueur and
top with the cider in a mix of 1:4, 5. For example,
pour 2/3 ounce cordial for 3 ounces cider. Sweet cider needs to be more chilled than a dry one. Enjoy
drinking this when meeting old and new friends!

BRETON CRUMBLE AVEC PALETS (CRUMBLE)

Serves 2

If you love crumble desserts, this is a very short and simple recipe. Instead of making a dough for the crumble, you can use original Breton butter cookies, such as palets or sablés!

2 big apples (like Bella de Boskoop)
2 sachets of vanilla-flavored sugar
Juice of 1 lemon
2 teaspoons cinnamon
A few drops of Chouchenn, Breton honey-liqueur, or Calvados (optional)
3 original palets Bretons or more

1. Preheat the oven to 350°F.
2. Peel, core, and cut the apples into 1/2-inch pieces.
3. Divide the apples evenly into two small oven-proof plates or glasses.
4. In a small bowl, mix the vanilla-sugar with the lemon juice and cinnamon. Spread the mixture on the apples. Add the Chouchenn, Breton honey-liqueur, or Calvados, if desired.
5. Crumble the palets, sprinkling them on the apples, and put the plates in the oven for 25 to 30 minutes. In the meantime, hug and kiss.
6. Remove the crumble from the oven and serve warm.

For additional Extra Libris content from your other
favorite authors and to enter great book giveaways, visit
ReadItForward.com/Extra-Libris.

ESSAYS, READER'S GUIDES, AND MORE

ABOUT THE AUTHOR

Nina George is the author of the bestselling international phenomenon *The Little Paris Bookshop*, as well as numerous other books that have been published around the world. She also works as a journalist, a writer, an advocate for authors' rights, and a speaker for women's rights. She lives with her husband in Berlin and Brittany, France.

Read on for an excerpt from Nina George's
New York Times bestselling novel

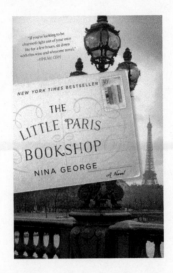

"If you're looking to be charmed right out of your own life for a few hours, sit down with this wise and winsome novel. . . . Everything happens just as you want it to . . . from poignant moments to crystalline insights in exactly the right measure."

—Oprah.com

"The settings are ideal for a summer-romance read. . . . Who can resist floating on a barge through France surrounded by books, wine, love, and great conversation?"

—*Christian Science Monitor*

"[A] bona fide international hit."

—*New York Times Book Review*

1

⸙

How on earth could I have let them talk me into it?

The two generals of number 27 Rue Montagnard—
Madame Bernard, the owner, and Madame Rosalette, the
concierge—had caught Monsieur in a pincer movement between their ground-floor flats.

"That Le P. has treated his wife shamelessly."

"Scandalously. Like a moth treats a wedding veil."

"You can hardly blame some people when you look at
their wives. Fridges in Chanel. But men? Monsters, all of
them."

"Ladies, I don't quite know what . . ."

"Not you of course, Monsieur Perdu. You are cashmere
compared with the normal yarn from which men are spun."

"Anyway, we're getting a new tenant. On the fourth floor.
Yours, Monsieur."

"But Madame has nothing left. Absolutely nothing, only
shattered illusions. She needs just about everything."

"And that's where you come in, Monsieur. Give whatever
you can. All donations welcome."

"Of course. Maybe a good book . . ."

"Actually, we were thinking of something more practical. A table, perhaps. You know, Madame has—"

"Nothing. I got that."

The bookseller could not imagine what might be more practical than a book, but he promised to give the new tenant a table. He still had one.

MONSIEUR PERDU pushed his tie between the top buttons of his white, vigorously ironed shirt and carefully rolled up his sleeves. Inward, one fold at a time, up to the elbow. He stared at the bookcase in the corridor. Behind the shelves lay a room he hadn't entered for almost twenty-one years.

Twenty-one years and summers and New Year's mornings.

But in that room was the table.

He exhaled, groped indiscriminately for a book and pulled Orwell's 1984 out of the bookcase. It didn't fall apart. Nor did it bite his hand like an affronted cat.

He took out the next novel, then two more. Now he reached into the shelf with both hands, grabbed whole parcels of books out of it and piled them up beside him.

The stacks grew into trees. Towers. Magic mountains. He looked at the last book in his hand. *When the Clock Struck Thirteen.* A tale of time travel.

If he'd believed in omens, this would have been a sign.

He banged the bottom of the shelves with his fists to loosen them from their fastenings. Then he stepped back.

There. Layer by layer, it appeared. Behind the wall of words. The door to the room where . . .

I could simply buy a table.

Monsieur Perdu ran his hand over his mouth. Yes. Dust down the books, put them away again, forget about the door. Buy a table and carry on as he had for the last two decades. In twenty years' time he'd be seventy, and from there he'd make it through the rest. Maybe he'd die prematurely.

Coward.

He tightened his trembling fist on the door handle.

Slowly the tall man opened the door. He pushed it softly inward, screwed up his eyes and . . .

Nothing but moonlight and dry air. He breathed it in through his nose, analyzing it, but found nothing.

——*'s smell has gone.*

Over the course of twenty-one summers, Monsieur Perdu had become as adept at avoiding thinking of —— as he was at stepping around open manholes.

He mainly thought of her as ——. As a pause amid the hum of his thoughts, as a blank in the pictures of the past, as a dark spot amid his feelings. He was capable of conjuring all kinds of gaps.

Monsieur Perdu looked around. How quiet the room seemed. And pale despite the lavender-blue wallpaper. The passing of the years behind the closed door had squeezed the color from the walls.

The light from the corridor met little that could cast a shadow. A bistro chair. The kitchen table. A vase with the lavender stolen two decades earlier from the Valensole plateau. And a fifty-year-old man who now sat down on the chair and wrapped his arms around himself.

There had once been curtains, and over there, pictures, flowers and books, a cat called Castor that slept on the sofa.

There were candlesticks and whispering, full wineglasses and music. Dancing shadows on the wall, one of them tall, the other strikingly beautiful. There had been love in this room.

Now there's only me.

He clenched his fists and pressed them against his burning eyes.

Monsieur Perdu swallowed and swallowed again to fight back the tears. His throat was too tight to breathe and his back seemed to glow with heat and pain.

When he could once more swallow without it hurting, Monsieur Perdu stood up and opened the casement window. Aromas came swirling in from the back courtyard.

The herbs from the Goldenbergs' little garden. Rosemary and thyme mixed with the massage oils used by Che, the blind chiropodist and "foot whisperer." Added to that, the smell of pancakes intermingled with Kofi's spicy and meaty African barbecued dishes. Over it all drifted the perfume of Paris in June, the fragrance of lime blossom and expectation.

But Monsieur Perdu wouldn't let these scents affect him. He resisted their charms. He'd become extremely good at ignoring anything that might in any way arouse feelings of yearning. Aromas. Melodies. The beauty of things.

He fetched soap and water from the storeroom next to the bare kitchen and began to clean the wooden table.

He fought off the blurry picture of himself sitting at this table, not alone but with ——.

He washed and scrubbed and ignored the piercing question of what he was meant to do now that he had opened the door to the room in which all his love, his dreams and his past had been buried.

Memories are like wolves. You can't lock them away and hope they leave you alone.

Monsieur Perdu carried the narrow table to the door and heaved it through the bookcase, past the magic mountains of paper onto the landing and over to the apartment across the hall.

As he was about to knock, a sad sound reached his ears.

Stifled sobbing, as if through a cushion.

Someone was crying behind the green door.

A woman. And she was crying as though she wanted nobody, absolutely nobody, to hear.

2

⁓⚬⁓

"SHE WAS married to You-Know-Who, Monsieur Le P."

He didn't know. Perdu didn't read the Paris gossip pages.

Madame Catherine Le P.-You-Know-Who had come home late one Thursday evening from her husband's art agency, where she took care of his PR. Her key no longer fit into the lock, and there was a suitcase on the stairs with divorce papers on top of it. Her husband had moved to an unknown address and taken the old furniture and a new woman with him.

Catherine, soon-to-be-ex-wife-of-Le-Dirty-Swine, possessed nothing but the clothes she had brought into their marriage—and the realization that it had been naïve of her to think that their erstwhile love would guarantee decent treatment after their separation, and to assume that she knew her husband so well that he could no longer surprise her.

"A common mistake," Madame Bernard, the lady of the house, had pontificated in between puffing out smoke signals from her pipe. "You only really get to know your husband when he walks out on you."

Monsieur Perdu had not yet seen the woman who'd been so coldheartedly ejected from her own life.

Now he listened to the lonely sobs she was desperately trying to muffle, perhaps with her hands or a tea towel. Should he announce his presence and embarrass her? He decided to fetch the vase and the chair first.

He tiptoed back and forth between his flat and hers. He knew how treacherous this proud old house could be, which floorboards squeaked, which walls were more recent and thinner additions and which concealed ducts that acted like megaphones.

When he pored over his eighteen-thousand-piece map of the world jigsaw in the otherwise empty living room, the sounds of the other residents' lives were transmitted to him through the fabric of the house.

The Goldenbergs' arguments (Him: "Can't you just for once . . . ? Why are you . . . ? Haven't I . . . ?" Her: "You always have to . . . You never do . . . I want you to . . .") He'd known the two of them as newlyweds. They'd laughed together a lot back then. Then came the children, and the parents drifted apart like continents.

He heard Clara Violette's electric wheelchair rolling over carpet edges, wooden floors and doorsills. He remembered the young pianist back when she was able to dance.

He heard Che and young Kofi cooking. Che was stirring the pots. The man had been blind since birth, but he said that he could see the world through the fragrant trails and traces that people's feelings and thoughts had left behind. Che could sense whether a room had been loved or lived or argued in.

Perdu also listened every Sunday to how Madame Bomme and the widows' club giggled like girls at the dirty books he slipped them behind their stuffy relatives' backs.

The snatches of life that could be overheard in the house at number 27 Rue Montagnard were like a sea lapping the shores of Perdu's silent isle.

He had been listening for more than twenty years. He knew his neighbors so well that he was sometimes amazed by how little they knew about him (not that he minded). They had no idea that he owned next to no furniture apart from a bed, a chair and a clothes rail—no knickknacks, no music, no pictures or photo albums or three-piece suite or crockery (other than for himself)—or that he had chosen such simplicity of his own free will. The two rooms he still occupied were so empty that they echoed when he coughed. The only thing in the living room was the giant jigsaw puzzle on the floor. His bedroom was furnished with a bed, the ironing board, a reading light and a garment rail on wheels containing three identical sets of clothing: gray trousers, white shirt, brown V-neck sweater. In the kitchen were a stove-top coffeepot, a tin of coffee and a shelf stacked with food. Arranged in alphabetical order. Maybe it was just as well that no one saw this.

And yet he harbored a strange affection for 27 Rue Montagnard's residents. He felt inexplicably better when he knew that they were well—and in his unassuming way he tried to make a contribution. Books were a means of helping. Otherwise he stayed in the background, a small figure in a painting, while life was played out in the foreground.

However, the new tenant on the third floor, Maximilian Jordan, wouldn't leave Monsieur Perdu in peace. Jordan wore specially made earplugs with earmuffs over them, plus a woolly hat on cold days. Ever since the young author's debut novel had made him famous amid great fanfare, he'd been on the run from fans who would have given their right arms to move in with him. Meanwhile, Jordan had developed a peculiar interest in Monsieur Perdu.

While Perdu was on the landing arranging the chair beside the kitchen table, and the vase on top, the crying stopped.

In its place he heard the squeak of a floorboard that someone was trying to walk across without making it creak.

He peered through the pane of frosted glass in the green door. Then he knocked twice, very gently.

A face moved closer. A blurred, bright oval.

"Yes?" the oval whispered.

"I've got a chair and a table for you."

The oval said nothing.

I have to speak softly to her. She's cried so much she's probably all dried out and she'll crumble if I'm too loud.

"And a vase. For flowers. Red flowers, for instance. They'd look really pretty on the white table."

He had his cheek almost pressed up against the glass.

He whispered, "But I can give you a book as well."

The light in the staircase went out.

"What kind of book?" the oval whispered.

"The consoling kind."

"I need to cry some more. I'll drown if I don't. Can you understand that?"

"Of course. Sometimes you're swimming in unwept tears and you'll go under if you store them up inside." *And I'm at the bottom of a sea of tears.* "I'll bring you a book for crying then."

"When?"

"Tomorrow. Promise me you'll have something to eat and drink before you carry on crying."

He didn't know why he was taking such liberties. It must be something to do with the door between them.

The glass misted up with her breath.

"Yes," she said. "Yes."

When the hall light flared on again, the oval shrank back.

Monsieur Perdu laid his hand briefly on the glass where her face had been a second before.

And if she needs anything else, a chest of drawers or a potato peeler, I'll buy it and claim I had it already.

He went into his empty flat and pushed the bolt across. The door leading into the room behind the bookcase was still open. The longer Monsieur Perdu looked in there, the more it seemed as though the summer of 1992 were rising up out of the floor. The cat jumped down from the sofa on soft, velvet paws and stretched. The sunlight caressed a bare back, the back turned and became ——. She smiled at Monsieur Perdu, rose from her reading position and walked toward him naked, with a book in her hand.

"Are you finally ready?" asked ——.

Monsieur Perdu slammed the door.

No.